Beautiful Rage

Beautiful Rage

Sandra Scoppettone

Five Star • Waterville, Maine

S

First Edition
First Printing: September 2004

Published in 2004 in conjunction with Tekno Books and Ed Gorman.

Set in 11 pt. Plantin by Ramona Watson.

Printed in the United States on permanent paper.

Library of Congress Cataloging-in-Publication Data

Scoppettone, Sandra.
   Beautiful rage / Sandra Scoppettone.—1st ed.
      p. cm.
      ISBN 1-4104-0201-0 (hc : alk. paper)
      1. Police spouses—Crimes against—Fiction.
   2. Teenage girls—Crimes against—Fiction.   3. Serial murders—Fiction.   4. Divorced women—Fiction.
   5. Policewomen—Fiction.   6. Sheriffs—Fiction.
   7. Virginia—Fiction.   I. Title.
   PS3569.C586B43 2004
   813′.54—dc22   2004053220

For Alison Heartwell, who led the way.
And Rubye Copus, constant friend, constant reader.

Acknowledgments

Many thanks to:

Linda Crawford, Ed Gorman, Bertha Harris,
Carolyn Kim, Annette Meyers, Charlotte Sheedy
and Elfrieda von Nardroff.

Prologue

On a glorious September day in Jefferson, Virginia it was still sunny at six o'clock, and on the top front step of the Boyer home was a half-drunk bottle of Sprite and Julie Boyer's notes from her high school history class. But Julie wasn't there.

The last time her sister, Marilyn, had seen her was at four-thirty when Julie told her that she was going to sit outside awhile. Marilyn wondered where she'd gone because it was Julie's turn to set the table. Besides, it was unusual for her older sister to wander off without telling someone where she was going. She went back inside and called her mother.

Mary Lee came out of the kitchen, the old-fashioned swinging door almost slapping her back. "What's up?"

"It's Julie. I don't know where she is."

"What's that supposed to mean?" Mary Lee wiped nonexistent dirt from her hands on the flowered apron.

"So what word don't you understand, Moth-er."

Mary Lee's normally pale skin reddened. "Don't you sass me, young lady." She took a step toward Marilyn.

Quickly, the girl said: "Her things are on the outside step, but she's not there and it's her turn to do the table."

"You looked in her room, called her?"

"No." Marilyn twisted her lips to the side.

"Don't make that face, it's purely ugly. Anyway, I don't see what the big uproar's about." Mary Lee walked to the bottom of the pine staircase.

"Julie," she shouted, her nasal sound diminished by the force of her voice.

There was no answer.

After three tries Mary Lee opened the front door. The Boyers lived in a development, their street a cul-de-sac. She looked both ways, saw Danny Pitts riding his blue bike and several other people working on their lawns. Then she called her daughter's name over and over. When there was no answer, Mary Lee picked up the things on the step and brought them in, where she put them on her grandmother's precious mahogany hall table.

Marilyn looked at her mother with her chubby cheeks even more puffed than usual into an "I told you so" expression.

"Take that look off your face, Missy," her mother snapped, and started up the stairs.

Cautiously, almost afraid of what she might find, Mary Lee turned the fake brass knob of Julie's room. Once inside she experienced mixed feelings: relief and fear.

Fear that Julie wasn't in the room. Relief that Julie wasn't in the room, sick. Mary Lee walked toward the single bed sheltered by a bright patchwork quilt and two lace-covered pillows. On the bed was Julie's red backpack, where she'd obviously dropped it when she'd gotten home.

Mary Lee reached out to unzip it, wavered a moment, considering the intrusion she would be making, then told herself that this was different, necessary.

Among other things, were Julie's make-up kit, house keys on a Simpson Family chain, and a brown, soft leather wallet. Inside were seven dollars—three spent from the ten Mary Lee had given her at the start of the week—and some change. Gingerly, as though the wallet might break, Mary Lee returned it to its home and zipped up the bag.

She stood next to the bed for moments, trying to discern what this meant, if anything. Julie never went anywhere without telling one of them. Still, it didn't mean Mary Lee should be alarmed. How far could her daughter have gone, after all? Her things were all here. And the way she'd left the drink and papers on the step indicated that she'd been called away for some profoundly important teenage reason, probably down the street to her friend Augusta's. Sure, that must be it.

She felt lighter and left Julie's room, almost bounded down the stairs, and went toward the phone in the family room.

"There?" Marilyn asked.

Mary Lee didn't answer her. She punched in Augusta Fleming's phone number. Augusta's mother, Sally, answered. Mary Lee asked if her daughter was there and was told no, she wasn't and hadn't been all afternoon.

Now Mary Lee began to feel a bit queasy. It wasn't that Julie didn't have other friends who she could have gone to see, but Augusta was the only one on the block. Surely, if her daughter had gone to any of her other friends' houses, she would've told one of them. She looked at her watch. Six-twenty. Another ten minutes before Emmitt would get home.

She began phoning other numbers.

At nine o'clock, after Mary Lee had called everyone she knew, and the girl's father had driven around the neighborhood with no results, and Julie had not returned, Emmitt Boyer phoned the sheriff's office.

Part One

"It was like she just vanished."
Mary Lee Boyer

— The Jefferson Standard

Chapter One

Sheriff Lucia Dove was at home when Detective Wayne
Steffey phoned.

"Hey, Sheriff, we got a missin' child out in Snowden."
He filled in the sparse details.

"Meet you there," Dove said. After hanging up the
phone she switched off an old Dane Clark movie, *Her Kind
of Man*. Dove had always had a sneaker for Clark . . . something about the guy. But she owned the video and had seen
this one dozens of times. Still, she was in her pajamas and
robe and, although it wouldn't take more than five minutes
to change, it was annoying. And she needed a cup of coffee
so she ran downstairs and clicked on the pot.

Going back up, she took the stairs double-time, wondering if she'd still be able to do this in another seven years
when she turned fifty. Hell, yes.

Dove's bedroom was totally feminine, but not fussy.
Pink and white were the dominant colors with touches of
lavender. Her brass bed was a family heirloom, one she'd
shared with her ex-husband, unfortunately. Sometimes
when she thought about him, she found that period of time
distasteful, but it had been so long ago that the year-and-a-
half marriage to Mike was almost a distant memory. After it
was over, she'd had her daughter. Oh, no, she couldn't go
there, think about Clare.

Dove threw her robe and pajama top on the bed. She
never wore her uniform except for formal occasions or when

absolutely necessary. She fastened her bra in place, slipped into a white blouse, and did up the buttons.

After pulling on light blue slacks, she sat on a plush, cream-colored chair to put on nylon knee-highs and slid on a pair of soft black leather, low-heeled shoes. In the bathroom she dabbed on a light pink lipstick and brushed blush on her cheeks. Hastily, she ran a comb through her curly, blond hair, cut even with her chin, took a last look, nodded with approval, and for once ignored her nose, which she thought was slightly small for her face, although no one else did.

Back downstairs she grabbed a travel mug, fixed the coffee the way she liked it, and went to the closet. She snatched her dark blue blazer from its wooden hanger. Her sheriff's gold badge was pinned over the pocket. On the shelf above was her hated black Stetson. She'd tried and failed to get permission not to wear it when she had to be in formal dress. After shutting the door, she dug out her cruiser keys from the wicker basket on the hall table and left the house.

Dove walked briskly to her black and white with *Sheriff* on the side, her own green Saturn snuggled safely in the garage. Inside the cruiser the engine turned over without a hitch and Dove backed out.

To run for the sheriff's race you had to live in the county where you worked, which was Snowden. But a year after she was elected, she had moved to the outskirts of Jefferson in Cumberland County because she knew she wasn't going to run again. To get to Snowden she had to go to Queens Highway, then take the Parkway across to 63. It was about a fifteen-minute drive this time of night.

She started to turn on the regular radio but stopped as thoughts flooded her mind. What if her family had never moved back here from Arizona when she was nine? What if, after going to Elizabeth Washington College, she'd moved? What if she'd never gone to E. W., left the state, attended another school? She'd been accepted at much bigger, more interesting places. But her father couldn't afford it and didn't want her to go so far away. Why hadn't she stood up for herself, applied for a scholarship? Her mother had tried to convince him of the value a bigger, out-of-state school would have on their daughter's life, but Roy Dove didn't want to hear any of it. He knew what was best for his children and there were two boys coming up behind Lucia. They were the ones who needed the best education he could afford. But even if the boys were favored where education was concerned, Dove was Daddy's girl.

She could still remember when she was about five or six how thrilled she was on Sunday mornings when he let her come in the bathroom and watch him shave. Then he'd take her out to breakfast at Johnson's for jelly doughnuts. He made her feel special then, all his attention on her.

Roy was in the fuel and heating business and saved every penny he made. Instead of giving his wife an automatic amount for food, Connie was forced to ask for it each week, then he yelled about how much she spent.

And that wasn't the only indignity Dove's mother suffered. She was an educated woman and enjoyed things in which her husband had no interest. One was the opera. Roy Dove thought it was a lot of screaming. So on Saturday afternoons, Connie would close herself in the bedroom and listen to the broadcast from New York on her little Philco. It was, of course, how Lucia had gotten her name. From the opera *Lucia di Lammermoor*.

All her life it had been mispronounced by schoolmates, teachers and colleagues. Although it was really *Lucheea*,

Lewsha and *Luseea* were how everyone except her family said it. The sheriff had asked her mother how she had gotten her father to accept the name, but Connie just blushed and said it was her secret.

Roy Dove had made fun of Connie's interest in anything cultural. Dove swore she'd never have a marriage like that and she didn't. She'd had something worse.

The sheriff passed the Elizabeth Washington athletic field, and as always a slight depression overcame her because that was where she'd met Mike McQuigg. Hell, what was she doing going down damned memory lane? It was never any good. For a moment she tried to make her mind a blank but it didn't work. Never did. Too much past life swirling around in there.

She switched to the present. So what was this going to be, this missing girl thing? A runaway? It was hard to believe Steffey wouldn't have sussed that out on his own. Something else must have made him get her out here. Then again, he knew missing children were special to Dove.

The thing about being Sheriff of Snowden County was that crime was the usual stuff: burglaries and robberies, drunk driving, domestic violence, and a few murders a year—drug-related or people who knew each other. There was never a mystery involved. She'd worked other places before this county, and she'd dealt with some heinous crimes, so she knew what it was like to solve a mysterious case. But that hadn't been true here and the job could get predictable. Basically, with a staff of thirty law enforcement officers she wasn't on the streets that much.

Sometimes she was sorry she'd run for the job, even though she'd broken the so-called glass ceiling and made it possible for other women to fill the post, at least in this part of Virginia. When she had been a deputy, a detective and finally a lieutenant, she was out there. Now it was basically a goddamn desk job and that was why she wasn't going for a second term. Dove wasn't certain what she'd do next. But that was a few years down the line.

She'd had missing children reports many times, and she was regularly called in on those, but here they always turned out to be false alarms, the worst being runaways, sometimes found, sometimes not. At least she'd never had an unfound runaway who hadn't left a note. That would've made her crazy. She knew she was obsessive and had that come her way, she would've stayed on it like a damn terrier.

She remembered a case five years earlier when she was a detective in another part of Virginia. They hadn't found the note for three weeks. So even though Steffey said none had been found, ruling one out at this stage would be a mistake.

Dove turned onto 63, which was also Old Parrish Road in this area. She was about three minutes away from her destination, Surrey Court. It was a middle-class neighborhood. There'd been a break-in about a year ago around there. She didn't know this area like the back of her hand, or anything, but she knew it some. Hard-working folks, decent values, family oriented. No trash. Jesus, she hated thinking like that. It was pure and simple Roy Dove thinking. And some of the people she worked with, of course. Now she was sounding like a snob to herself. Had to be something in between, didn't there?

When she turned into Surrey Court she could see that many of the houses were lit up and Steffey's brown unmarked car was sitting in front of what she presumed was number 124.

Her jacket hung up near the door, the sheriff sat on a well-used Barcalounger in the family room across from

Marilyn, Mary Lee, and Emmitt Boyer on a yellow slip-covered couch.

Dove noted that Mary Lee wore an apron although it was almost eleven p.m. Under it was a gray skirt and a blue denim shirt, sleeves rolled. On her feet were a pair of worn white sneakers and short, blue cotton socks. The woman's brown permed hair hadn't been combed for awhile and Dove could tell she'd been running her hands through it as the sides swirled out in a peculiar way.

Marilyn, who was a little overweight, was dressed like any fourteen-year-old: jeans, striped shirt, sandals. She was a pretty girl in an unformed way. Ordinary features, but no character yet. Her brown eyes were big like her mother's.

Emmitt Boyer wore his work clothes, his name stitched on one side of his dark green uniform, Mullen Motors on the other. Boyer was square-chinned with sad blue eyes, and his graying brown hair was closely cropped. His only distinguishing feature was a big nose, but it went with his large frame and bulky body.

Detective Wayne Steffey stood near the fireplace. He was a well-built man, ruddy complexion, black hair with a touch of gray. His eyebrows were slightly bushy over deep-set brown eyes. He wore tan slacks, white shirt open at the neck and a pale green summer jacket. He jingled change in his pants pocket until Dove gave him a look.

Mary Lee said, "Sure you don't want something, tea or coffee, Sheriff?"

Dove declined again and smiled, hoping to ease some of the terrible tension in the room. "I think we should get started." She had her notebook and a pencil at the ready.

The Boyers coughed, scrunched around in their seats as if they were at a show.

"What time did Julie get home from school?" the sheriff asked.

Marilyn answered. "Three-fifteen like always."

"She take the school bus?"

"Yes," Mary Lee said.

"Did you see her then?"

"No, I wasn't here. I worked 'til one-thirty, then I went grocery shopping."

"Where do you work?"

"Lee and Eackles. Realty. Closed on a house today," she said, smiling. Then, as though she suddenly remembered why the sheriff was there, her smile faded like a bulb dimming.

The sheriff nodded to give her credit no matter what the circumstances, made a note on her pad of the realty name. "So when was the last time you saw her this afternoon, Mrs. Boyer?"

"I . . . I didn't. When I got home she wasn't downstairs, and when I went up to change my clothes, I didn't go into her room. I like to give the girls privacy."

Marilyn muttered, "Yeah, right."

"Say what?" Boyer asked.

"Nothing."

Dove directed the next question to her. "Marilyn, what did Julie do when she got home?"

"Well, she took the portable phone to her bedroom so I guess she made a call. She was in there for a *looong* time. When she came out she gave me the phone and that's when she said she was going to sit outside."

"And that was when?"

"Four-thirty." She touched a pimple on her chin.

Steffey's cell phone rang, startling them all. He fumbled in his pocket, pulled it out. "Yeah?" After listening a moment he said, "For you, Sheriff."

Dove excused herself, took the phone. "Sheriff Dove."

"Hey, Arizona." It was Lieutenant Jack Fincham. He always called her that.

"What's up?" she asked.

"Heard there was some funny business going on there."

"Right."

"Can't talk, huh?"

"Right."

"Think I should come over?"

"No. Call you later." She clicked off, handed the phone back to Steffey. "Sorry," she said to the Boyers and looked down at her notes.

Mary Lee said, "It's like she just vanished."

"We'll find her," Dove said, hoping it was true. "By the way, you've looked everywhere for a note, is that right?"

"Yes, we have. Nothing."

"Would you mind if Detective Steffey looked?"

"Already have, Sheriff," he said.

"Everywhere?" she asked.

"Yep."

"Okay." Dove knew he might have overlooked it but had to believe he'd been thorough. "Mr. Boyer, when did you last see Julie?"

"Breakfast."

"How did she seem?"

"Seem?"

"Was there anything unusual about her behavior?"

"No."

"That when you saw her, too, Mrs. Boyer?"

"Yes. I made poached eggs. They're trouble but Julie loves them."

"Hate 'em," Marilyn said softly.

Boyer gave her a backhanded tap on the side of her thigh, and Marilyn wiggled downward, annoyance on her face.

"Marilyn, any idea who Julie might have talked to?"

"Probably Augusta, her best friend."

"Augusta who?"

"Fleming. Want her phone number?"

"Yes, thanks."

Marilyn gave it to her and Dove wrote it down.

"Course, it coulda' been her boyfriend."

Both parents looked at their daughter.

Emmitt said, "What boyfriend?"

"Well, guess he's not exactly a boyfriend, but maybe he is."

The sheriff pegged this kid for a troublemaker.

"What you talking about, Marilyn?" Boyer asked.

"Buster Clark. Julie hangs out with him sometimes."

"Never hearda' Buster Clark," Boyer said.

"You sure, honey?" Mary Lee asked.

"Sure I'm sure. Ask Augusta."

I will, thought Dove. "You know where Buster Clark lives, Marilyn?"

"No. But Augusta probably does. The thing is, Julie never went *out* with him, like on a date or anything."

"The children don't date," Mary Lee added. "They go out in groups, isn't that right, honey?"

"Yeah. I guess Buster was in their group."

The sheriff made another note to get one of her team to ask Augusta who was in the group. "Tell me about Julie, her habits."

"Well, if you mean would she just go off like that for no reason, the answer is no," Mary Lee said. "Julie's a very responsible child. She'd tell her sister or me. And she'd never

21

get in a stranger's car. That's one thing I instilled in them from babyhood almost: never get in a stranger's car."

"That's good. What I mean is, did she have things she did every day, any kind of routine? After-school activities?"

"Glee club," Marilyn said. "But that's during school."

"That's the idea though," Dove encouraged.

Mary Lee said, "Sometimes she babysits."

Dove got a sinking feeling. There were so many cases where the father of the baby came on to the sitter, worse even. "Did Julie drive to these jobs?"

"Oh, no. It's in the neighborhood."

"Don't let her drive," Boyer said.

"Well, she can," said Marilyn. "She took driver's ed."

"Don't let her though. Got enough to worry about and I don't want her crashing our car."

Dove thought it was strange that he'd be thinking about the car instead of his daughter.

"I take it then, Julie doesn't have her own car?"

"She's saving for one," Marilyn put in.

"Let's get back to her habits."

"I can't think of anything," Mary Lee said.

"Let me know if you remember any."

"For sure."

"Now please don't misunderstand," Dove said. "But I have to ask you this. Was there any trouble going on here at home?"

"What kind a trouble?" Boyer asked, jutting out his square chin.

"Any kind. Disagreements, Julie not abiding by your rules, that sort of thing."

"Nothing. Julie is a very good girl. Very responsible," Mary Lee repeated.

"Yes, I understand. Any reason she might run away?"

"No," the Boyers answered in unison.

"How about the rest of the family? Any problems between the two of you?" God, Dove hated asking this.

The Boyers looked at each other as if they didn't know. Then Emmitt answered. "No problems."

"One more thing. What was Julie wearing the last time you saw her, Marilyn?"

"Same thing she wore to school. Denim shorts, a yellow ribbed sweater and Nikes. Blue and white."

"Thanks." Dove stood up. "Do you have a picture of Julie?"

"Sure do," Mary Lee said. She rose and went to the sparsely filled bookcase, took a picture in a gold frame from the top and handed it to the sheriff.

"Pretty," Dove said. "I'd like to have it, if you don't mind. I'll have copies made and return it to you by tomorrow." She gave it back to the woman.

"Oh," said Mary Lee, as though giving away the picture was tantamount to giving up. Then, gently, she turned it over, slid down the backing, and removed the photo.

"Could you pencil in her statistics for me on the back. Height, weight, and any distinguishing marks."

"Distinguishing marks," Emmitt repeated. "What the hell's that mean?"

"Oh, Daddy," Marilyn said. "Like her fingernails, for example."

"Fingernails?" The sheriff asked.

"Yeah. Julie has green ones. Long."

Dove checked a smile. "Green fingernails. Anything else?"

"Nothing I can think of," Mary Lee said, as she wrote on the back of the picture, then handed it timidly to Dove, who received it in same manner to show respect.

"Well, I guess that's about it for now, folks. Try not to worry. Silly to say, I know." She thought of Clare, pushed it out of her mind. "But we'll be right on top of this and my guess is we'll have her back to you by tomorrow."

"Tomorrow when?" Emmitt asked.

Dove was momentarily startled by the question. "Tomorrow," she reiterated firmly and Boyer backed off.

At the front door, she retrieved her jacket. When she shook hands with the parents she mumbled more platitudes about not worrying too much, and she and Steffey left.

Steffey said, "What do you think, Sheriff?"

"Let's go down to the office."

"She's not a runaway, is she?"

Dove felt sick and said softly, "I didn't get that impression."

Chapter Two

When the sheriff pulled into the headquarters parking area, she couldn't help noticing that among the other cars was Jack Fincham's cruiser. She pulled into her designated slot. As Dove was getting out, Steffey parked next to her.

Inside, Pam Ashley, the dispatcher on the night watch, looked up from her desk. "Sheriff." She was twenty-two and Dove wondered how long she'd stay at the job. Pam was beautiful. Long dark wavy hair, piercing blue eyes, a cleft in her chin and dimples in both cheeks. If Steffey had his way he'd probably marry her. In any case, somebody would, and soon. Of course that didn't mean she'd stop working, but Pam was smart and Dove couldn't imagine that she wouldn't want a better job.

After Dove said hello to Pam and passed through part of the open office, nodding to a skeleton shift of one sergeant and four deputies, she went into her office where Fincham sat behind her desk, his feet up.

"Hey, Arizona," he said.

"Comfortable?"

"Sorry." Fincham grinned, lighting up his craggy face, and swung his legs off the desk to the floor making a clunking sound. He stood up, came around to the front of the desk where he parked himself against it.

"What're you doing here?" she asked, hanging her jacket on the wooden clothes pole.

"Thought you'd be coming in so I got myself ready."

Her back to him, she couldn't help smiling. Fincham was the best, even if he was sometimes annoying. She sat at her desk and he turned around to face her.

"Sit down," she said.

He pulled over a red leatherette chair. Fincham was a good-looking man in his late thirties. He had a full head of dirty blond hair worn slightly long (something she nagged him about) and green eyes, darker than her own, which were technically hazel.

One of the things she liked about Fincham's looks was his mouth. Most men had thin lips, almost non-existent, but he didn't. They were full but not fleshy. And she liked the way he dressed. Tonight he wore a crisp white shirt, the sleeves turned back once so the cuffs still showed, tan slacks, tan socks, and black loafers. No working man in Jefferson wore shoes like that. Maybe some that commuted into D.C., but not around here. Dove knew some people called him a dandy or worse behind his back, but she thought he looked "way cool" as the kids said.

Fincham started to put his feet up on the corner of her desk, then changed his mind.

"Why should tonight be different?" Dove asked, smiling. Fincham always did this.

"Didn't think you were in the mood."

She signaled with her chin that he could go ahead, which he did.

"What we got going on here?"

"Missing girl . . . maybe a runaway."

"You don't sound convinced."

"Not." She filled him in on what she knew, not needing to refer to her notes.

When she was finished, Fincham said, "So, you don't think she ran away?"

"No."

"What then?"

"Foul play," she said, and they both chuckled. It was a small joke they had between them, thinking the expression was ridiculous.

"What kind of *foul play?*"

"Wish I knew."

"Kidnap?"

"Unlikely. The Boyers don't have a pot to piss in, so to speak."

"What then? Worse."

"Sweet Jesus, Jack, don't even think it."

"You aren't leaving me with much else."

Dove played with a pencil. "Yeah, I know." She pushed down the lever on her intercom.

"Sheriff?" Pam's voice crackled.

"Send in Steffey."

"Right."

Fincham disliked Steffey, and Dove knew it.

"What's he got to add, Arizona?"

"Don't you call me that in front of him now."

"Do I ever?"

"Once. Once you did."

With his hand he batted away the accusation as if it were a fly. Fincham had started addressing her as Arizona a few days after she'd taken over the job. He said he couldn't stand the name Lucia and there were times when he was sure he wouldn't want to call her Sheriff. He knew from her campaign material that she'd spent the first nine years of her life in that state, so it seemed to suit.

Truth was, Dove liked it. But only when they were alone.

Steffey came in, nodded curtly to Fincham.

"I've told Lieutenant Fincham what I know. Anything to add?"

"Well, I, uh, don't know what you told him, do I?"

Dove could feel her face flush because, of course, he was right. Quickly, she said, "We have to look into the parents if the girl doesn't turn up by morning."

Fincham asked, "You think there might be something there?"

Steffey jumped in. "Ah, Sheriff, those parents don't know nothin'."

"You both know in a case like this the parents are the first place we look."

Fincham didn't like being lumped with Steffey and turned to him with an accusatory sound in his voice. "Sheriff says you looked for a note?"

"Course I did." Steffey wasn't crazy about Fincham either.

"Everywhere?"

"Hey, I even lifted up her computer, looked underneath."

"Computer?" Dove said, surprised.

"Picked it right up. Heavy mother."

"You turn it on?" Fincham asked.

"Turn it on?"

"Yeah."

Steffey looked from Fincham to Dove then back again. "Nah, you know I don't know about them things."

"Christ, Steffey," Dove said. "Why didn't you tell me there was a computer?"

He pressed his lips together, shrugged. "Just didn't think of it, Sheriff. What's the big deal, anyways?"

Dove said, "The big deal is there might be a note somewhere in the computer."

"Think this might be one of those Internet things?" Fincham said.

"What Internet things?" Steffey asked.

She ignored him. "Might be. Maybe she had some e-mail thing going with a guy, went off to meet him."

"Crazier notions than that," Fincham said. "We need to get into that computer."

She looked at her watch. "Can't do it until tomorrow. Too late now to even call them."

Steffey said, "They're probably still up, Sheriff. Worrying and such."

"And what if they're not?" Fincham asked, not looking at Steffey.

"I'm just sayin'."

"Still, if the Boyers go to work tomorrow, nobody will be home in the morning," she said.

"You think they will? Considering?"

"No, you're probably right, Lieutenant."

"I think I *will* call," Dove said. She flipped open her notebook for the number, punched it in.

Boyer picked it up halfway through the first ring.

"This is Sheriff Dove. Sorry to bother you, Mr. Boyer, but I just learned that Julie has a computer, is that right?"

"You find her?" he asked.

"No, I'm sorry." God. He hadn't even paid attention to what she'd said, so intent on finding his daughter. Understandable. She asked again about the computer.

"Yeah, she got one."

"I'd like to come over tomorrow and take a look," she said.

"It's one of them clones, nothing to see."

"I mean, I'd like to see what's in it."

"Oh. Yeah, sure. You wanna come back now? Nobody's sleeping here."

Sweet Jesus. No way did Dove want to go now, but she knew she had to. "You sure?"

"Yeah. You think there might be something on it help you, then you better do it."

"Okay. I'm sending over my Lieutenant, Jack Fincham."

Fincham raised his eyebrows and Dove winked at him.

"Well, I uh, don't know about that, Sheriff."

"I'm not sure I understand."

"Well, we don't know him. You, we know. Or that other detective."

Inwardly she groaned. "I see. We'll both come so you can get to meet him."

Fincham grinned.

After she hung up she said, "Guess we'll go now. Steffey, you can go home."

"Right," he said. "Call me if you need me, Sheriff."

"I will."

When he'd closed the door behind him, Fincham said, "How the hell did he get to be a detective? Doesn't even turn on the goddamn computer."

"Don't," she said. "Get your jacket."

"Yes, ma'am," he said and gave her a mock salute.

They rode over together. Fincham drove, put the blue flashing light on the roof of his car.

"These are nice people, Jack. Regular, hard working."

"Yeah. So?"

"So nothing. Filling you in, is all."

"Arizona, you're kind of off your feed tonight."

"What's that supposed to mean?"

"I dunno. Cranky or something."

"Tired," she said.

"Nah, it's more than that."

"Don't like cases that involve young girls."

"Right." Fincham knew about Clare. "Sorry."

She didn't say anything.

"What's your best guess?" he asked. "Something on the computer or not?"

"Not. Too easy."

"God forbid anything should make it easy for us, huh?"

"Yeah."

Fincham wished he could look at her full face, knew she was upset and worried, but not sure how much had to do with the case. Thing was, he was crazy about Arizona, and couldn't tolerate her being down.

He'd lived all his life in Jefferson, surrounding counties. Grew up in Stafford, then Spotsylvania, where he now lived with his wife and two kids. His wife. Bonnie Jo had changed in the eighteen years they'd been married. And not for the better.

Maybe they'd gotten married too young. Well, hell yes, there was no doubt about that. High school sweethearts, neither one of them with any education. But later Bonnie Jo had gone to hairdressing school and had that, while he'd flopped around from one thing to the other, unable to find what he wanted to do until he discovered law enforcement. The minute he started he knew he was home and did everything right, including night school, to get where he was now.

Bonnie Jo had her own place. *HAIR AND NOW*. Fincham thought it was a stupid name but he didn't tell her that. And he certainly didn't tell her that he and Arizona collected these type of names when they saw them on other salons or in a magazine or paper. They had a pretty fair list of them, too. It was one of the things they found funny.

Thing was, he and B.J. didn't find anything funny. He wondered if they ever had. Stale was the word for their marriage. Or maybe worse: over, dead. But he didn't plan to get out until the kids finished high school. Jack Jr. would be done at the end of this school year. Three more years for the youngest, Kim. Christ, could he hack it for three more years?

"Where are you?" Dove asked.

"Thinking about Bonnie Jo." He'd never gone into detail, but Arizona knew things weren't good.

"Want to talk about it?"

This was one of the things about her he liked so much. She was willing to talk about anything, actually had gotten him to open up more than he ever had in his life.

"Drinking like a fish," he said. There was no way in hell that he'd intended to say that, came out like some ventriloquist was operating him.

"All of a sudden?" she asked.

"No. Has been for a long time now."

"You never said anything, Jack."

"No."

"I'm sorry. Anything I can do?"

"Can't see what. She won't talk about it, of course. Doesn't think she's drinking any way unusual. See, she's got these two girlfriends and they . . ."

"Girlfriends, Jack?"

"Yeah."

"How old are they?"

"Oh, Christ." She was always pulling this feminist crap on him. "What am I supposed to say, she's got these two women friends?"

"Why not?"

32

He had no answer to that. "Anyway, they all drink the same, so Bonnie Jo thinks it's normal."

"And you don't think it is?"

"Hell, no. Lunchtime they go out, have martinis, you can believe that. Martinis, for Christ's sake. Who do you know drinks martinis?"

"Well, *I* do now and then."

"I never saw you drink one."

"Now and then, mostly then. Never mind about me, go on about Bonnie Jo."

"What's to say? They drink their lunch, then around four or five they go to Digger O'Dell's downtown, start again. By the time she gets home she's sloshed. Drinks while she's cooking dinner."

"You think she's an alcoholic?"

"Don't you?"

"I'm only listening to you, Jack. Not my place to judge, but if what you say is true, well, sounds like she's at least got some kind of problem."

"True? You think I'm making this up?"

"That's not what I meant and you know it."

Jack reached for his cigarettes in his shirt pocket, then stopped, remembering she didn't let him smoke in the car. Fucking rules all over the place. He could feel himself getting angry. This was stupid. It was talking about B.J., thinking about his lousy marriage.

"Let's change the subject," he said.

"Sure?"

"Yeah. Just riling me up. This the turn?" he asked.

"Yes."

All the houses on Surrey Court were dark except for the Boyers', which appeared to have on all the lights. Dove told him where to stop.

"Yeah, I figured," he said.

Emmitt Boyer was on the front step before they were out of the cruiser. As they approached, it was easy to see he wore a look of expectancy.

Dove said hello, introduced Fincham and they went inside. Boyer led them up to Julie's room.

The computer was on a hutch-type desk: monitor, keyboard and mouse on top, hard drive below. It was the usual putty color and bore the name *Mabbitt Computers*. She'd seen their ad in the Guide to Living paper but never seen the product before.

"Switch is down here," Boyer said, pointing to the tower component. He pushed the button and the computer made its rackety sounds as it slowly grumbled to life.

The monitor lit up, went from the *Windows* logo to a desktop picture of Leonardo DiCaprio over and over. Various icons dotted his face. They all stared at it as though it would reveal the rest of their lives. There were two icons that immediately interested the sheriff. One was for Julie's writing program *Word* and the other for *AOL*, which she knew stood for America On Line, her Internet and e-mail access. She clicked twice on that one and the program was launched. On a toolbar at the top was a file drawer with a green triangle next to it and underneath, the words, *My Files*. Dove put her hand over the mouse and clicked the triangle. A box flipped down with several lines of text. The one at the top said *Personal Filing Cabinet*. She clicked once on that and a much larger box came up, the words *Julieboy's Filing Cabinet* on the green border.

Within the box on the left side, it said: *Incoming/Saved Mail*. As she scrolled down, they saw there were hundreds and hundreds going back five months.

"Christ," Fincham said aloud.

"On a crutch," Dove replied.

Chapter Three

The second day into the case Dove, Fincham and Sergeant Dale Jenkins sat around her office, hashing over what they had, which was a lot of nothing. They hadn't found any kind of note indicating the girl was running away or planning to commit suicide. Dove and Fincham had spent several hours going through the e-mail Julie had received. They'd come up with a name, Lyle Taylor, and traced the messages both to and from. There was a definite cyberspace romance between them, but in the end there were no plans to meet. Taylor lived in Florida.

Still, they couldn't rule him out. His last e-mail had been written two days before Julie disappeared and she hadn't answered.

"Dale," the sheriff said, "I want you to get on this Taylor guy. Track him down, get a phone number. He could have sent that last message from anywhere."

"Right."

Jenkins was about ten years younger than the sheriff and was the only other female officer. Dove had made sure a woman was advanced to this spot and Jenkins was the best.

She was an attractive woman with brown hair cut short and brown eyes almost shuttered by heavy lashes. Her smile was simple, real.

"Lieutenant, you canvas the neighbors, especially the Flemings, then check Julie's computer and see if Taylor answered her last e-mail. I'm going to the high school to talk to teachers and find Buster Clark."

Fincham looked peeved.

"What?" she asked.

"Nothing." He took out one of his unfiltered Camels and held it between thumb and forefinger, no intention of lighting it.

Dove decided not to pursue Fincham's reaction because it really didn't matter if he didn't like his assignment, that was what he was going to do.

"You want me to re-question the parents while I'm there?" Fincham asked.

"Absolutely," she said. "Let's try to meet back here at two."

Jenkins left first.

"Hey, Arizona. I thought I'd be tracking Taylor."

"I need you talking to people, Fincham. We find Taylor, then you speak to him. You know, good as Jenkins is, she's a woman and one is enough for most suspects. Anyway she can't get them talking the way you can."

"Flattery will get you everywhere," he said, and left the office.

She *had* been trying to flatter him, but what she'd said was true. Fincham was as good as she was when it came to getting information out of folks.

It was hot outside so she didn't put on her outside jacket, just her blouse and skirt were enough. She wondered if they were going to have another mild winter. Funny what Northerners thought about this part of Virginia: hot all the time. But here in the Jefferson area, only an hour's drive from D.C., winters were winters like in the North.

The sheriff took 95 to get to Julie's school. There were three in Snowden County. Julie went to Lightfoot High.

The drive took eight minutes. The fact that Julie hadn't answered Taylor's e-mail bothered Dove. The correspondence between them, once it had gotten going, had a day at the most between responses. Why was the girl waiting to answer? Or was she never planning on answering? Had something happened that made Julie reluctant to continue this e-mail exchange?

Dove parked in a teacher's slot, as there was no other place. The building was red brick and three stories high. She walked around to the front entrance and pulled open a heavy wooden door. Right inside sat a monitor at a table. She hated the way things had changed in most areas, but the need for a monitor in high school bothered her a lot. And there certainly was a need. At least they didn't have metal detectors . . . yet.

"Yes, ma'am?" The monitor was a fuzzy-looking girl, as though she was out of focus.

Dove showed her shield. "Can you direct me to the principal's office?"

"Yes, ma'am."

The sheriff thanked her and walked down the silent hall, the heels and toes of her shoes making an eerie sound against the brown tile. When she came to the main office she went up to the counter, showed her badge again and asked to see the principal. She was told to wait a moment and the woman, whose hair was barbecue color, went to a phone and hit a button.

While Dove waited, her mind drifted back to her own high school days. She'd gone to another one, but it didn't look that different inside. She'd spent a fair amount of time in an office like this, sitting on a bench, waiting to see the Dean of Girls, Miss Henderson. Dove hadn't been a model student by any stretch of the imagination. She'd never done anything serious or dangerous, but she tended to start uproars in class by making faces or doing imitations of teachers and other harmless, but not tolerated, behavior.

"You're going to amount to nothing, Lucia Dove," Miss Henderson had said to her numerous times.

"Yes, ma'am," she replied, not believing this for one moment.

Too bad Henderson died before Dove became sheriff.

"He'll see you now," the barbecue-haired woman said. She pointed to a closed door.

Dove knocked and a deep voice told her to come in.

Behind a huge desk, Brian Stover, a man in his forties with a pencil-thin mustache and a prominent widow's peak, motioned her to sit down on the high-backed green Naugahyde chair opposite him.

Dove thought he looked like Zachary Scott. She'd seen him recently in *Mildred Pierce*, which she must have watched dozens of times. Joan Crawford was a favorite.

When the sheriff was settled, she said she was there about Julie Boyer.

"Julie Boyer?"

"Yes. And this is strictly confidential."

Stover looked pleased, as though he'd been picked for something special. Then the expression changed to a more serious one. "What's going on? Has something happened to Julie?"

Dove didn't want to tell him exactly and strove for something ambiguous. "Nothing has happened to her. She's part of an investigation, that's all."

"Julie Boyer, part of an investigation? That seems highly unlikely."

This wasn't going well. "All right Mr. Stover, but you must promise me you won't reveal what I tell you to anyone. Not even Mrs. Stover."

"I promise," he said, and like a child started to put his hand over his heart, then caught himself.

"Julie's missing. She disappeared yesterday between four-thirty and six."

He breathed a sigh of relief. "Then she'd already left school."

It was clear that what he cared about most was his own hide. "Yes. Now, what can you tell me about her?"

"Well, not much, frankly. I have over a thousand students here and only get to know the ones who are disciplinary problems. Julie Boyer, to my recollection, never set foot in here. I know her name because she's one of those students who excels. Her guidance counselor, Miss Bandy, would know more."

"And where would I find her?"

"Room 243 on the second floor. I'll buzz her before you leave this office."

"Thanks, Mr. Stover. How about Buster Clark?"

"Ah, now that's a different story. Clark's in here all the time. Can't reach the boy. Of course, considering his people, well, you know what I mean."

"No. I don't," she said, but feeling annoyed, actually knowing what he was getting at. For a moment she wondered if Clark was black.

Stover passed a thin hand over his well-groomed hair and whispered, "Trailer park," as though he was saying *heroin den*. Dove knew the third word after "trailer park" was "trash." Though implied, Stover couldn't say that.

"Father's been gone since, who knows when, and the mother gets welfare."

Oh, such a dirty word, Dove thought. "Any siblings?"

"I think there's a much younger sister in elementary school.

Different father. Why do you want to know about Buster?"

"I've been told that he and the Boyer girl hung around together."

"Really?" He raised his eyebrows in surprise and disdain.

Dove knew, even if Stover didn't, that "nice" girls often liked to be with "bad" boys. She'd done it herself and checked a smile when she recalled Tom Foley. God, her parents had been crazed when they'd found out she was seeing Tom. He'd worn a leather jacket even in the summer and ridden a Harley and that was enough for them. She thought it was neat that he had a motorcycle and long sideburns, which her parents couldn't abide either.

"Yes, apparently they may have even been . . . what? A couple, I guess."

"Oh, I find that very hard to believe, Sheriff."

"Because?"

"I thought I made it clear what kind of boy Clark is. Julie Boyer . . . well, they're night and day."

"Nevertheless, it's been reported that they were at least in the same crowd. So, can I see him?"

"If you can find him."

"Excuse me?"

"He was expelled about a week ago. I'll give you his home address, but from what I understand, he doesn't spend a lot of time there."

Dove felt a little jolt to her heart. Clark was out and about on the day Julie disappeared. Even though it was after school hours, a boy who has been expelled might be at loose ends.

"What was he expelled for?"

Stover took in a deep breath as though getting ready for a long recitation. "Stealing."

"Stealing what?"

"Supplies: paper, ink, clips, that sort of thing."

"To sell," she offered.

"Exactly."

Dove rose, and thanked the principal, then asked him for Clark's address and if he would buzz Miss Bandy without telling her what she wanted.

He did both.

Miss Bandy had such a little office, the sheriff wondered if it had at one time been a supply closet. There was room for one small desk and two chairs.

Bandy was a gray-looking woman with sharp red hair piled on top of her head and clipped there with a purple barrette. Dove thought they clashed. Her makeup was vivid, and she wore a dark eyeliner under brown eyes.

Her unadorned, freckled hands drummed the top of the desk in a slow rhythm while Dove explained the situation and asked for her silence on the matter.

"I understand. Discretion is my middle name." Bandy smiled obsequiously.

"Good," Dove said, and knew she loathed this woman, but ignored it. "Is Julie a good student or above average?"

"I'd say she is an excellent student. I am extremely gratified that she wants to go to college, even if it isn't out of state. She could get in almost anywhere she'd like to go. It's my policy to encourage girls to branch out, see the world, so to speak." She flung out an arm to underline her policy.

"And where does Julie want to go?"

"Elizabeth Washington. There's nothing wrong with the school, mind you. It's just fine. But it's here in Jefferson."

"Perhaps her parents can't afford anything else," she said, thinking of her own past situation.

She nodded sagely. "Yes, I know that's the problem. She'll continue to live at home."

If she's not dead, Dove found herself thinking. "Was Julie open with you, Miss Bandy? I mean, did she confide?"

Bandy smiled. "Almost all the girls confide." She replaced an imaginary loose end of hair, the way people do when they know they've been tooting their own horn.

"Is there anything you can tell me that might help?"

"A confidence is a confidence," she said.

"Surely, the circumstances make this a little different, don't they?"

Bandy thought this over, as though contemplating the meaning of relativity. Finally she answered. "Is she officially missing?"

"Officially? Do you mean do we have an APB out on her?"

"APB?"

Oh, please, thought Dove. Surely everyone knew what the letters stood for by now, considering all the police shows on television. Bandy was probably one of those snobs who said she didn't watch TV. "All Points Bulletin. You know," she said to be ornery, "like on the TV cop shows."

"I don't watch television," Bandy sniffed.

Dove checked herself before she laughed out loud. "Well, it means exactly what it says. And yes, she's officially missing." Both were a lie. They couldn't do an APB until twenty-four hours had passed and they could declare her officially missing.

"I see. Then why must I keep this quiet? If it's an . . . what was it again?"

"An APB," Dove said through her teeth.

"Yes, an APB. If it's that, then surely everyone knows."

And they would, but how could Bandy know that? Dove

gambled that it was a guess and lied again. "It's a special broadcasting system only for police. No civilian could know." Dove pictured all those snoops out there listening to their police band radios.

"Oh, I see." Bandy bought it. "At any rate, there's hope you'll find her?"

"Of course."

"Then, when you do, I'll have broken a confidence."

"Miss Bandy, we need all the help we can get to find her."

"I don't see how breaking a confidence would help."

Dove was becoming exasperated. How could she word this so Bandy wouldn't feel she was betraying Julie? "Do you know anyone by the name of Buster Clark?"

"I'm the guidance counselor for girls, Sheriff."

"I wasn't suggesting that you were his counselor," she said sweetly. "I want to know if you've ever heard the name?"

"Yes. I have."

"And would that be through some of the girls you talk to?"

Bandy bit the inside of her top lip. "Yes. It would."

"Did Julie Boyer ever mention Clark's name?"

She shook her head. "I can't answer that."

"You can," Dove said, losing it.

"I beg your pardon, Sheriff," she said.

"Look, Miss Bandy. This is important. I have to know certain things so I can look for the Boyer girl."

"So you said. However, just as you have your duties and responsibilities, I have mine."

"How about the name Lyle Taylor?"

"I have the same answer, Sheriff."

Clearly, this wasn't going to work. "Is there someone

else I can talk to who might be *more* helpful."

Bandy was not unaware of the emphasis on *more*. "Perhaps her homeroom teacher, Mrs. Lawson."

Dove stood up. "And where would I find her?"

Bandy looked at her watch. "I believe she's teaching an English class now."

"And?"

"And?"

She tried not to sound pleasant. "And where would that be? The room number."

"I'm not privy to where teachers teach every class, Sheriff."

No, but you know what she's teaching at this very moment. Still, maybe that was all Lawson taught.

Bandy directed her back to the main office. Dove thanked her very politely because if Boyer was found dead, then she'd have to come back and Bandy would have to talk to her. At least she thought the damn woman would. But she wasn't going to worry about that now.

Amelia Lawson was, as Bandy had said, teaching a class. Dove stood to one side, and studied the woman through the glass pane in the door. She was striking. And incredibly young-looking. Dove thought it was point of view again. As she grew older, others looked so much younger than they actually were.

Lawson had long sand-colored hair, pulled back in a single braid. This was a look Dove didn't usually like, but on her it was attractive. From this distance she couldn't tell exactly what color her eyes were, but they appeared to be dark. She wore subtle make-up. The shade on her full lips was pink. Lawson was wearing a summer suit, probably seersucker, with a pale blue blouse.

The bell rang and Dove was startled. Doors to the hall opened and kids poured out like swarming insects, including the ones from Lawson's room. The sheriff stood back as they passed, not noticing her, so intent on themselves. But that's the way teenagers were. She remembered the self-absorption of her own teen years. What else could possibly matter but what *you* wanted to do right then? She had to keep this in mind as she focused on Julie.

When all the children had left Lawson's room, Dove went in, walked over to the teacher, introduced herself, told her who she wanted to talk about and easily extracted a promise of silence. Up close Dove saw that the woman's eyes were brown and that she was obviously in her thirties.

There were no other chairs so Dove took a student seat attached to a desk, placed her hands on top as though waiting for an assignment.

"I don't believe Julie ran away," Lawson said suddenly.

"Why not?"

"She's just not that kind of girl." She swung her head so her braid, resting on her shoulder, would flip backward. "Julie loved school, her family, friends, everything. So there wouldn't be a reason."

"How about a boyfriend?"

"You mean would she run off with a boy?"

Dove nodded.

"I . . . I can't imagine it."

"You hesitated."

"Well, only because I was thinking of a boy I've seen her with."

"Who's that?"

"His name is Buster Clark. I think he's her boyfriend, but I still can't imagine them running off together. Of course, I wouldn't have thought Julie would be interested in Buster to begin with."

"Why not?"

"I wouldn't have thought he was her type. Buster is a troubled boy."

"And Julie would find that, what? Distasteful? Unacceptable?"

"Well, no. Not because he's troubled necessarily, but more because they don't seem a likely couple. Buster's been expelled, is right now, caught stealing, been picked up on a DUI, has a nasty home life. They just didn't fit."

"I remember when I was Julie's age, I was very attracted to a 'bad' boy. Lots of girls were. Never happened to you?"

Dove noticed a flush start on Lawson's neck.

She looked away, out the window. "Ronnie Davis," she said almost in a whisper. Then quickly, "But only for a week."

Dove laughed. "Mine lasted longer, until my folks found out."

"Same here," Lawson smiled. "But you know, it's different with kids today. They don't date in the same way, so the parents don't actually know. They travel in groups."

"Then why did you think Julie and Buster were an item?"

"I'd see them alone on the grounds."

"You ever talk to Julie about Buster?"

"No. If she'd come to me I would have, but that would more likely be her guidance counselor, Miss Bandy."

"Miss Bandy is keeping her counsel," Dove said.

"Ah. Well, I guess she must."

Dove didn't reply to this. "How about the name Lyle Taylor. You ever hear it?"

"No, I don't think I have."

Dove inched her way out of the seat, stood and offered her hand, which the teacher took.

"Thanks, Mrs. Lawson."

"I know you'll find her."

"If you think she didn't run away, any ideas what might have happened to her?"

They looked each other in the eyes. Dove could tell Lawson didn't want to speculate, didn't want to even think about what else could have occurred.

She took her off the hook. "You've been very helpful."

Actually, she hadn't, except to confirm that Julie wouldn't have run away.

Now it was time to find Buster Clark.

Chapter Four

Lieutenant Jack Fincham had interviewed people in five of the ten houses on Surrey Court, and as easily predicted, no one saw anything, no one had a thing to say about Julie Boyer except that she was: "terrific," "fabulous," "a nice, quiet girl."

He'd also interviewed Mary Lee Boyer again. Emmitt had gone to work and Marilyn to school. While he was at the Boyer house, Emmitt had called three times. Mary Lee confided that her husband never called, not even when he was going to be late. At first Fincham wondered how Boyer could go to work under the circumstances, then realized he probably would've done the same to keep from going crazy. The girl's mother's story remained the same and she basically added nothing to what he already knew. He'd have to go back that night to interview Emmitt.

There was no one at home in the other four houses so he sat in his cruiser and smoked. God, it tasted good. Arizona made it hard for him to indulge, so there was something to be said for being on his own today. On the other hand, it was a damn good thing she was so anti-smoking because, as Bonnie Jo was always telling him, he was killing himself, for sure. Course he didn't give a rat's ass what *she* thought except it was probably true, in this case. He'd been smoking since ten, same brand, unfiltered Camels. Working with Arizona he'd had some time-outs and noticed he'd slipped back to two packs a day from three.

Arizona. Lucia Dove. Jesus. Fincham knew he was in love with her, but he couldn't bring himself to do anything about it. First, she was five years older than he was, and although that wasn't much, it intimidated him a bit. He had no idea how she felt about something like that. Hell, it wasn't only the age difference, he was fucking married and the father of two.

So what? He hadn't been in love with Bonnie Jo for more than seven, eight years, if he'd ever been. He tried to remember why he'd married her. She was a looker, no doubt about it, and they'd been high school sweethearts, which meant it was expected that they marry. And he'd been too dumb and green to understand that because he'd slept with her, it didn't mean he had to marry her. Besides, he *thought* he was in love at the time. But what could a stupid eighteen-year-old know about love?

And now he found her disgusting. This drinking thing was way out of hand. He knew enough about divorce laws to know he could get custody, Bonnie Jo being an alcoholic. But did he *want* custody? There were many things against it. His job, his hours. And . . . Arizona.

Christ, it always came back to her. He couldn't imagine her wanting to live with his kids. Especially Kim. Clare would've been fourteen had she lived, and how could Arizona handle that? Whoa. He was getting way ahead of himself here.

Maybe the best thing was for his parents to get custody of Jack Jr. and Kim. He tried to picture his children living with his parents. It wasn't a perfect picture, but what was? It had to be better than them living with a drunken mother.

Still, even though his father was older now, and in some ways seemed softer, it worried him that he might use the same form of punishment he'd used on him and his brother,

Buddy. Even now, recalling the beatings made him go dead inside. Going numb, dead, had been the only way he'd been able to handle it. And then there was his mother who turned her back on everything and anything that was unpleasant, went to her Bible instead of dealing. No, that was not a good situation. So what if he didn't try to get custody? What if he just left, let B.J. keep the kids? Abandonment came to mind. And then stuck.

Those kids needed someone other than Bonnie Jo to be around them and it was really only three more years. Holy shit. Three years stretched ahead of him like the road from L.A. to Las Vegas. Endless. By then he'd be forty-one and Arizona would be forty-six.

But this was stupid. Arizona had never given him one inch of encouragement. Fantasy was what this was.

He tossed the cigarette out the window, and at that moment a brown Bronco pulled into the Flemings' driveway.

Jack watched as a tall, willowy woman got out, reached into the back for two bags of groceries. He was out of his car in seconds walking up to hers, and by the time the woman returned for the rest, he was holding two brown bags in his arms.

"Morning, ma'am," he said. "Lieutenant Fincham. Thought I could help."

Her startled expression changed to something more relaxed and Fincham could see she was horsy-faced with a helluva chin.

"Well, thank you, Lieutenant, that's sure kind of you. Guess you want to talk to me about Julie, huh?"

"That's right, ma'am." Naturally the Flemings knew about Julie's disappearance.

"Well, follow me then."

He did, and inside she led him to the kitchen where he

put the bags of groceries next to the ones she'd brought in.

"Let me put away the perishables, then we can talk."

Fincham looked around the kitchen, which was almost identical to the Boyers', except for greenish granite countertops. He thought the Flemings must have more money than the Boyers.

When she was through with her unpacking she said, "Sit, sit. Want a cup of coffee?"

He parked himself at the maple table, decked out with some green-checked placemats. "If it's not too much trouble."

"I'd be making it for myself anyway," and she smiled, changing her look again. It was definitely more appealing.

He said he'd have some and watched her economical movements as she went about preparing the brew.

When the coffee was dripping into the glass pot, she sat down. "Now, how can I help, Lieutenant?"

"Well, Mrs. Fleming . . ."

"Call me Sally, okay?"

"Sure thing. I'd like to know anything you know about Julie Boyer."

"Well, she and my daughter, Augusta, are best friends. Have been since they were five-year-olds, which was when the Boyers moved here."

"I'm most interested in the last year or so."

"Of course. I was just giving you background," she said, as though he'd reprimanded her.

"I know. Just wanted to save you time," he smiled, trying to mitigate any harm he may have done. Had to be careful with this one, he could see.

Slowly, she smiled back. "Uh, huh. The last year. Well, I can honestly say that I didn't notice any difference from the year before, 'cept they, Julie and Augusta, seemed more interested in boys."

Fincham picked up on a flirtatious look on Sally Fleming's face, but chalked it up to that thing some women do when they talk about the opposite sex, even in this context. "How so?"

"Well, it wasn't anything except talk, you know. And I don't spy. But sometimes when they're loud, and God knows teenagers can be, I'd hear parts of the conversation. Boys, boys, boys." She giggled like a teen herself.

"Any particular names you'd hear more than others?"

"I got the impression that Augusta likes Chuck, and Julie one called Buster."

"No last names?"

"I happen to know Chuck is Charles Garnett because we're friends with his parents."

"So Augusta has known this Chuck for a long time?"

"No. We became friends with the parents when Roger Garnett started working with my husband about two years ago. They're insurance agents. Augusta met Chuck at school . . . well, I guess that's where she met him, don't see where else."

"You like him?" Fincham was taking notes, as always.

"Chuck? Sure. I've only met him a few times. They go 'round in groups, don't date. So I've seen them all together at the mall and when Augusta had a party, Chuck was here."

"Was this Buster . . . ? What'd you say his last name was?"

"I didn't. Don't know it."

Fincham did. "Clark sound familiar?"

"Clark's a common name."

"Right. Ever overhear the girls talking about a Lyle Taylor?"

Sally Fleming cocked her head and put a finger to her

lips. Fincham knew this was to indicate she was thinking. He guessed it was also to look cute. It didn't.

"Lyle, Lyle, Lyle. Hmmm. I couldn't swear to it."

"But maybe?"

"Maybe. I think that coffee's done now." She hopped up and went to the counter.

"Julie Boyer ever indicate to you or your daughter that she had trouble at home?" he asked her back.

"Take milk?"

He told her he did and waited for an answer.

She didn't say anything until she'd poured the coffee and brought the cups, spoons, a small green pitcher and a matching sugar bowl to the table, then seated herself.

"I can't truly recall any mention of that. Augusta has said that Mr. Boyer is very strict, but I wouldn't call that trouble. After all, Bob, my husband lays down the law too, if you know what I mean?"

"How did Julie react to her father's strictness?"

"Well, you know how children are. You have any, Lieutenant?"

"Two teens. Boy and girl," he added, to ward off further questions.

"So then you know how they just love to be told anything." She smiled at him, tried to make eye contact as though they shared an important secret.

"Good coffee. Julie's reaction?" he pursued.

"Thank you. Well, Julie didn't like it, naturally. Especially the early curfew, or I should say, what she perceived as an early curfew. Personally I don't think that ten is too early for a girl of sixteen."

Fincham thought of his own curfew when he was sixteen. None. But the nice girls had them. "Was that the only thing that bothered Julie?"

"I don't think she was too happy about not being able to go out at all on school nights. Personally, I agree. Augusta can't either."

"So Julie didn't have any gripes, unusual ones, with her father other than curfews?"

"Not that I ever knew about. Oh, you know, I'd overhear her complaining about the usual things. We," she tapped her chest, "become pariahs when they reach that age. I think especially mothers. They hate even being seen with us. Oh, God," she laughed in a high-pitched way that Fincham felt was false. "Last New Year's Eve they went to this party at the country club, not that we belong," she said. "It was a party held by one of their friends and—"

"Who was that?"

"Hmmm?"

"The friend's name?"

"Oh. Melanie Osborne. Anyway, she gave this party, well, her parents gave it for her, of course. Very rich. And the girls wanted to drive to it. Augusta had her license and we just put our collective feet down and said no way."

Fincham thought sixteen was too young to drive. But that was the law in Virginia. He remembered his own driving at that age and it gave him the willies. Jack Jr. drove and every time the boy went out in his souped-up Ford, Fincham felt a knot in his stomach until the kid came home.

Sally Fleming continued. "I mean, New Year's Eve? All the way out there? Well, first they said they wouldn't go, but finally, after a lot of tears and ruckus, they agreed to let Mrs. Boyer drive them, and me pick them up. Well, when I arrived I made the unpardonable mistake of going inside to get them. You never. Total and complete humiliation. Augusta wouldn't speak to me for a week."

Fincham nodded, smiled. This was getting nowhere. Still, he'd gotten another name, and he'd need a list of who was at that party, because you never knew.

"Anything unusual you can tell me about Julie Boyer?"

"She's a lovely girl. Always has been. I'd say she's your typical teenager, that's what I'd say about her. Except, of course, for the one thing."

He felt his heart give a thump. Calmly as possible, he asked, "And what's that one thing?"

"I feel just terrible telling," she said.

He gave her his biggest smile, the encouraging one. "Now, Sally, this is a missing girl case. You know something that can help, you're obligated to tell me."

"Well, it was a confidence that Augusta entrusted me with."

"I'll never let her know you told me."

"Promise?"

"Promise." It was one he might not be able to keep, he knew, but who gave a shit?

"Well, okay. But I don't feel one bit good about this."

Fincham knew she was dying to tell. "This might be important, Sally."

"I guess that's what counts then. Mind you, no one knows except Augusta and me. Julie's parents don't know and neither does her sister."

"I understand."

"Julie had her nipples pierced."

Chapter Five

Bethany Cobb, the day watch dispatcher, looked up when Dove came in. "Hey, Sheriff?" she said, as if she didn't know who she was addressing, taking a guess perhaps.

"Afternoon, Bethany. Anything for me?"

"Couple calls?" She handed the sheriff a few pieces of pink message paper and Dove noticed they matched the young woman's nails.

"Nice color, your nails."

"Thanks." Bethany smiled, her brown eyes almost disappearing beneath the light brown lids. "You know, Sheriff, you're really somethin'. You always notice stuff?"

"Part of my job," Dove replied.

"Yeah, well." She shook her head, as if to say she knew it wasn't just that.

The sheriff moved on, said hello to this one and that one. The day shift was a lot bigger than the night, but most of the deputies and detectives were working off the premises.

Dove went into her office, sat down behind her desk and spread the four notices out as though she was playing cards.

Two of them, from people she knew, were after her for contributions. She threw them in the wastebasket. Of the other two, one was from the Boyers, and the other from McQuigg, her ex. What the hell did he want?

Mike hadn't been in touch in years. Funny, she'd been recalling him, the short, doomed marriage, the night before. It was odd that he'd phone her after all this time. Out of cu-

56

riosity, she punched in his number, which naturally had a
D.C. area code.

"Agent McQuigg's line," a woman said.

She asked for him, said who she was, but didn't identify
herself as a sheriff. There was a moment of silence and then
she heard Mike's rasping voice. "Hey, Lucia."

"Mike."

"How've you been?"

"What do you want?"

"Oh, friendly, I see."

"Look, we have nothing to be friendly about. You called
and I'm calling you back. So why'd you call?" Dove could
feel every part of her grow tense.

"Heard about the missing girl."

Damn, Dove thought. "What missing girl?"

"Oh, come on, Lucia."

There wasn't much point in playing games. He knew.
She wanted to know how and asked him.

"You forget where I work?"

McQuigg was FBI. "So?" It was much too early for them
to be interested.

"Don'cha know we know everything?" he chuckled.

So much for secrecy, asking people to keep it to themselves. But the next second she knew it must have leaked
through the radios, dispatcher calls. Jesus, did McQuigg
have surveillance on her office? Her? She wasn't going to ask.

"So what about it, Mike? I'm busy."

"Guess you are. Find her yet?"

"You'd know if I had, wouldn't you?"

"You got me there," he said.

"That what you wanted to know, if I'd found her?"

"Not exactly. Thing is when I saw your name, well, it
brought back memories."

He must have seen her name before this. Something was going on. "Mike, that's a crock."

He laughed, more like a cackle. "No, it's true, Lucia."

All Dove could think at that moment was she was so damned glad Fincham called her Arizona.

McQuigg went on. "I've seen your name before but, I don't know, the missing girl aspect and all."

He meant Clare.

"Let's not, Mike." He'd never gotten over the fact that she'd had a child with another man, and even though Clare had died so tragically, he took any opportunity he could to throw it in her face, as though it had been her fault.

"Let's not and say we did?" he asked in a salacious way.

She let out a full-blown sigh. "I told you, I'm busy and I'm not at all interested in going down memory lane with you."

"Hey, I was just concerned. Missing girl must make you think of your own little bastard."

She slammed down the phone, shaking with rage. How dare he?

After she'd given birth to Clare, Mike had found out. They'd been divorced for two years by then. Her having the baby had infuriated him. It was partly because he'd wanted a child when they were married and she hadn't, and partly because he was so moralistic and she'd had the baby as an unwed mother, which was none of his damn business, as she'd told him repeatedly. But he couldn't stand it.

Then when Clare had disappeared, he'd offered to assist. Other FBI agents were in on it, naturally. But Mike hadn't been assigned to her case. After Clare had been missing for three days, Dove was willing to take help from Godzilla. So McQuigg came strictly off the record, and he'd aided in the search.

Six days she'd suffered until one of the local cops had found her child at the bottom of a well. Clare was eight years old. And it had been declared an accident, which she knew it was. But even then, McQuigg had given her a goodbye look that encompassed two things: one, that she was a bad mother, and two, he was glad. He'd called a few times afterwards, then he'd stopped, until now.

She had to calm down, couldn't let that slimeball get her into a state where she couldn't think, concentrate on what was important here. But first things first.

Dove picked up the phone and called George Fells, her electronic genius. "Georgie, porgie," she said. She always called him that, and he always laughed in a good-natured way. Sometimes she wondered if it actually annoyed him, but he was hesitant to say so. She'd ask one of these days, but not now.

"Have a job for you. Want you to check my phones here, also the radios."

"Think you got a bug?"

"Might."

"Is it ASAP?"

"Well, in a way. I mean, not this minute."

"How's tonight after work?"

"Good enough, George."

"Will I see you?" he asked.

Dove knew George, who was a widower and twenty years her senior, had a sneaker for her. "Can't promise I'll be here, got a case going."

"Right, the missing girl."

She felt defeated. "Now, George, how'd you know about that?"

"My police scanner, Lucia."

"Right. Would a scanner reach into D.C.?"

"Hell, you can get this here program on the Internet called Music Match, and it comes with scanners all over the country. You can hear any damn thing you want now. Easy as pie."

"Just terrific," Dove said sarcastically.

"Technology, Lucia."

"Hate it," she said.

"No you don't. No technology I wouldn't be able to track possible bugs in your office," George laughed.

"No technology I wouldn't have any bugs to find."

He was silent for a moment then said, "You got me there. Anyways, I got to tell you, down to the Wayside Diner this morning, pretty near everybody was talking about it."

Christ. She'd be mighty pissed if this made the papers before the twenty-four-hour period was up. "She isn't officially missing yet, George."

"I know that. Told some of them that, too. When she gonna be declared missing, assuming she don't show up?"

"Later today. So, George, Pam'll be here even if I'm not, okay? You find anything you beep me, right? You have that number, don't you?"

"I do. Hope I see you later."

When they hung up Dove started damning the Internet. Then her mind flipped back to Mike. Okay, he could've gotten it through a scanner or any other which way. Maybe she was being paranoid about the phones. Still, it didn't hurt to have George check them. The idea of McQuigg having access to her every conversation gave her the creeps.

Remembering Mike's final words made her burn all over again. There was a time when she thought Clare galled him most because he didn't know who the father was, but then, considering his job, she realized he had to know.

60

Vic Tierney had been her only one-night stand, but he'd inadvertently served her purpose. Clare. Ah, the hell with this.

She looked at her watch. Fifteen minutes until the other two were to meet her here. From her drawer she took a brown paper bag, opened it and took out a plastic container. Her lunch consisted of rice and beans, something she'd made and frozen a week before. She flipped off the top and took out the fork she kept for these occasions, which happened more often than she liked.

It would be nice to go out and have lunch with people in a restaurant having nothing to do with the job. But time constraints hardly ever allowed for that, and during something like this it was impossible.

She dug in. What in the hell did she mean *something like this,* as though she had hundreds of important cases all the time? Even so the small stuff kept her hopping and she couldn't remember the last time she'd had lunch with Dawn or Lucy, a couple of old friends, or especially with her best friend, Kay Holiday. Sometimes she and Fincham would stop somewhere, actually sit at a table or in a booth, order more than a hamburger. But mostly, if they ate together, it was brown-bagging it, or getting some fast food.

Dove scooped up some rice and beans, which were damn good, and chewed. If only Fincham wasn't married. When he'd told her about Bonnie Jo's drinking she'd had a moment of hope. Maybe he'd leave his wife. Dove had wanted to advise him, but she knew her motives weren't pure.

Sometimes she thought he was interested, something in the way he looked at her, smiled. But she ignored him, pulled farther away, sure she was imagining things and not wanting to reveal her own feelings. God, what would he think if he knew? His boss with the hots for him!

So far, her day hadn't proved terribly productive, and she didn't feel any closer to finding Julie Boyer. She dreaded returning the Boyer call but knew she had to and punched in the number.

Mary Lee answered.

"I wish I had something to tell you," Dove said. "Guess you don't know anything more, do you?"

"No. I wish I did." Her voice was strained, sleepless, slight. "Can she be declared a missing person yet?"

"At six o'clock, Mrs. Boyer."

"Stupid."

"Excuse me?"

"I'm sorry, but it seems a stupid rule. Julie would never stay out all night. Never has without us knowing where she was."

The sheriff felt for this woman. She knew what it was like. Maybe she'd bend the rule. "Mrs. Boyer, I know how you feel and . . ."

"No, you don't."

Dove bit her tongue. "I'm going to put an APB on her now."

Silence.

"You understand?"

"You mean you're going to declare her missing *now?*"

"Yes."

"Oh, thank you, Sheriff."

Dove could hear that she was crying. "Hang in there and I'll get back to you just as soon as I know something. And you do the same, you hear?"

"Yes, ma'am. I surely will."

When they hung up Dove sat there, her lunch only half-eaten. She wasn't hungry anymore. What if some pain in the ass decided to go after her for doing this? So what? It wasn't as though she was going to run again. But negative newspaper publicity could hurt the whole office.

Fincham came through the door, followed by Jenkins. They sat down.

"Get anything?" she asked.

Jenkins said, "Got Taylor's phone number. Nobody answered, but I got the number of the people next door, found out Taylor's workplace. He's a gardener."

"How the hell old is he?" she asked.

"Twenty-six."

"Shit," Fincham said.

"Nothing in those e-mails indicated his age," Dove said.

"Nothing. Fact is, if I recall, he said he was a senior in high school."

"That's right."

"Well, he's not," Jenkins said. "Works for Trimble Gardens in Key Largo."

"Did you talk to him?" Dove asked.

"Nope. Wasn't there. Hasn't been in for three days. Nobody knows where he is."

Chapter Six

The sheriff said, "Like I told you, he could've sent that last e-mail from anywhere."

"And did, I guess," added Fincham.

"We have to find out where he sent it from."

Jenkins, who was a little more up on these things than the other two were, said, "If he dialed into his usual provider number and sent it from there, I don't think we can tell."

"Why not?"

"Not sure about this, Sheriff," Jenkins said, twirling a piece of her brown hair. "But, I don't think the number he's calling from would be recorded. Now, if we knew *where* he was calling from, the number he dialed would be recorded."

"I know that much, Dale," she said, irritably. Funny, she thought, how we still say dial.

"Well, we have to find this guy. Get in touch with the county police down there and tell them to put out an APB on Taylor."

"Already did," Jenkins said.

"Good work. How about you, Fincham? Got anything?"

"I re-interviewed the mother. I don't think she knows squat about the girl. But I'll talk to both parents again tomorrow . . . if it's necessary. And also Sally Fleming. There is one more thing. And it'll help with the APB description. But it's weird."

"What do you mean, weird?" she asked.

Jenkins sat forward in her chair expectantly.

"Well, not weird, I guess, considering what kids do these days. But the Boyers don't know about it."

"Hell, Fincham, what is it?"

"Julie Boyer had her nipples pierced."

"I'll be damned," Jenkins said.

Shit, thought Dove. "Let's keep that under wraps."

"Will do. But, Christ, doesn't that hurt?"

"I wouldn't know, Detective," she answered.

Jenkins said, "Gotta hurt." She crossed her arms over her breasts as if to protect them from some mad piercer on the loose.

Dove was silent for a moment, then she said, "Long green fingernails are one thing, but this sort of changes the image, doesn't it?"

Fincham nodded. "My thinking exactly. Not that it makes her bad or anything. But it makes her different than how we thought, how people saw her."

"How'd you find this out?"

Fincham told them.

"You sure it's true?"

"Well, short of seeing them myself," he said. "Look, Sally Fleming had no reason to make it up and neither did the daughter."

"You check with the kid, Augusta?"

"No."

The sheriff said, "I was about to put out an APB. I need to know if that's true, because if it is, it has to be included."

Jenkins looked at her watch. "It hasn't been twenty-four hours, Sheriff."

"I know that. I don't care. Or at least, I didn't. Like you said, Fincham, it doesn't make her bad but it makes her different from who we thought she was."

"Meaning, a kid who would pierce her nipples might skip with a boyfriend?" Jenkins said.

"Meaning . . . I don't know. It looks different now."

Fincham said, "How we going to keep it under wraps, the nipple thing, if we put out an APB and include that?"

Recalling what she'd learned from George, she said, "True. Okay, we don't put that out there. Green fingernails and the rest are enough, I think."

"You find Buster Clark?" Jack asked her.

"No," she said. "Nobody at his trailer. Nobody around knew where he might be."

"So," Jenkins said, "she could be with Clark *or* Taylor."

"Or somebody we haven't even heard of yet," Fincham put in. "So you want me to get a hold of Augusta? Check on the nipple thing? I know exactly where she'll be in ten minutes."

"Then get to her and ask her. It's something we need to be sure of in case the worst scenario is the final one."

"Right." He left.

"Jenkins," she said, "guess you've done all you can on Taylor for now. So you try to locate Clark and when you do, bring him in."

"On what charge?"

"No charge. We want him to help us with our investigation, that's all. Just don't tell him *what* investigation."

"Okay, Sheriff."

When she was alone again she thought about Julie Boyer having pierced nipples. This was something she'd always wondered about. Why did women do it, and echoing the other two, didn't it hurt like a son of a bitch? In this case, where in hell had she had it done? Shit. She beeped Fincham who called back immediately.

"Yeah?"

"Find out from Augusta where Julie had it done, then go there, check it out, then call me."

"Way ahead of you, Arizona."

She knew he meant he'd already thought of this.

"It was probably at Sporty's, place in Spotsylvania. I've heard about it."

"Think you should go there first, then? You have Julie's picture, don't you?"

"What if it isn't the right place and I miss Augusta?"

"Okay. Call me when you know."

"Arizona?"

"What?"

"Nothing. Never mind." He clicked off.

Odd, she thought, replacing the phone in its cradle. Fincham never did stuff like that. She went back to thinking about exactly what kind of girl Julie Boyer was.

Everything they'd heard indicated that she was a conventional kid. Certainly not one who'd have her nipples pierced. What else didn't they know? Was she the kind of kid who slipped out of her house when the rest of the family was sleeping? Had she had sex? These days sixteen was hardly considered young for that, but somehow it hadn't occurred to her that Julie might have, and she realized she'd simply bought everything that she'd been told.

And this was unlike her. But she'd never had a case like this one. She was sure Julie wasn't a runaway because of the way she'd disappeared and the fact that she'd left her belongings behind.

Dove knew she'd been thinking of Julie in a somewhat saintly way because of Clare. Even though her daughter wouldn't have been that old, she'd superimposed Clare onto Julie Boyer. Not good. She had to shake that image loose.

Bethany's voice came over the intercom. "Sheriff, a man from the Days Inn just phoned? Said something strange was going on in one of the rooms?"

"Strange?"

"Weird noises?"

"Get Fincham and Jenkins, tell them to meet me there now."

Dove jumped up and went out to her cruiser. She didn't usually go out on calls like this, but now she had to follow any possible lead, be on the scene, in case. The feelings of anxiety were mixed with excitement. This could be nothing, but it could also be something.

She squealed out of the parking lot, siren going, and headed to 95 where she could pick up 12. It was a short drive. Okay, she had to be prepared for disappointment. But even if this wasn't Julie, it could be something else.

Dove thought of the many false alarms she'd run down over the years and then her mind went to the dozens and dozens that had been involved in the search for Clare.

Right before she pulled into the lot of the Days Inn, she cut her siren. Jenkins's car was in front of her. They both got out and went to the office.

A man in his forties was behind the desk. His dirty blond hair was thin, like an old mouse. He wore wire-rimmed glasses and his skin was sallow.

"I dunno," he said. "I dunno if I did the right thing." He rubbed his hands together as though he was washing them.

"Take it easy," Dove said. "What'd you hear?"

"Noises . . . maybe screams."

"Maybe?"

"Screams," he said definitely.

"When?"

68

"Hour ago the first time. Then a little while back, right before I phoned you."

"What's the occupant's name?"

"He signed the register John Smith."

"Yeah," she said. "Was he alone?"

"Didn't see nobody else."

"What's the room number?"

"Seven."

"You have a key?"

He reached under the counter. "Pass key," he said, gripping it tightly.

Dove held out her hand.

"What if it's nothing?" the clerk asked.

This was typical. "Look," she said. "You called us."

"Will I get in trouble?"

"Only if you don't give me that damn key."

He handed it over, and she and Jenkins left the motel office and bumped into Fincham outside. Dove filled him in quickly.

In the parking slot was a red, two-door Ford with a Virginia license plate. Dove and Jenkins stood on one side of the door to room 7, Fincham on the other, drawing their guns. They listened, but it was quiet. After a signal from Dove, Fincham reached out and knocked.

"Sheriff's office," he said. "Open up."

They listened. Nothing. Fincham did it again.

This time there was a scuffling sound inside and then a man's voice. "Hold on."

"Open up," Fincham demanded.

"Coming."

Scurrying sounds continued and then they heard the unmistakable sound of a chain being unlatched, a lock turned and the door was opened a crack.

Fincham said, "All the way so we can see you."

He did.

The three of them pushed their way in. The man backed up.

Jenkins went into the bathroom, came back out. "Nothing."

Dove noticed that the bed had been hastily made-up to look like it hadn't been used, but there were obvious tell-tale signs. "What's your name?" she asked.

"Why? What's going on?" He was a big man, muscled, wearing a white T-shirt and brown suit pants.

"What are you doing here?" Fincham said.

"What's happening?" he asked, his large eyes blinking rapidly.

"Listen, dumb ass, answer the questions," she said. "What the hell are you doing here?"

"I . . . I was tired."

"You always scream when you're in a motel room?" Jenkins asked.

"Scream?"

Dove moved closer, her gun almost touching the man's chest. "Name," she demanded.

"John Smith," he said.

"Right."

"What's your goddamned name?" Fincham yelled.

"I want my lawyer," he said.

Now Dove knew, as they all did, something was wrong here.

"You can't come in here waving those fucking guns at me. I have rights."

"Mr. Smith," Dove pronounced his name with sarcasm. "Screaming was reported coming from this room."

"That's ridiculous," he said.

"Where's the girl?" she asked.

"Girl? What girl?"

"What'd you do with her?" asked Fincham.

"I want my lawyer," he said, again.

Dove signaled to Fincham to hold his gun on the man and she went to the bed, dropped to her knees next to it and picked up the skirt, looked under.

"Don't shoot," a small voice said.

"Come out of there," she ordered.

"I'm coming."

After some scraping noises a head appeared. It was the flushed, scared face of a teenage boy.

Chapter Seven

Earl Chichester, alias John Smith, was in one of the two cells waiting for his lawyer. The boy, Kevin Bowling, had been let go.

Dove had had a heated argument with Jenkins about the difference between a pederast and a homosexual. Chichester was a pederast, but Jenkins couldn't see the difference. Fincham could.

Fincham had found Augusta Fleming and confirmed Julie Boyer's nipples were pierced and she wore small gold rings through them. Then he'd corroborated this with the infamous Shorty. They'd sent out the APB but didn't include that information. It had only been one hour short of the legal definition of a missing person.

After that Dove called in Hap Orreck, who was their dog handler, and sent him out to the Boyers' with his bloodhound. There he was to meet three other teams of handlers and dogs from Dogs West, a search and rescue organization. They would pick up a piece of Julie's clothing, then cover the surrounding woods and Lilac Park, which was nearby.

She also got in touch with the Divers Association, who were going to search a pond in the area.

Within an hour of the official information release, Dove had heard that a candlelight prayer service was being organized by Julie's Baptist Church.

The phones hadn't stopped.

Now it was eight o'clock and the sun had gone down. The

72

dogs had been called off and the divers could no longer see, but Dove hadn't left her office. She wanted to stay as long as possible, in case somebody, somewhere found the girl.

Her intercom buzzed.

Pam said, "George Fells is here, Sheriff."

She'd forgotten all about him. "Send him in."

"Hey, Sheriff," he said. Fells was a big man, bumbling and awkward.

"Thanks for coming, George."

"You're here anyways."

"Guess so. But I'll get out of your way."

"No need. I can work around you." He smiled shyly.

She didn't need this now. Or ever.

Then Fincham came in.

Surprised she said, "What are you doing?"

"Doing? I'm doing nothing. I'm here, is all."

"You know George Fells, don't you?"

"Yeah, sure." He stuck out his hand and Fells dwarfed it in his own.

"Jack, nice to see ya."

Dove could see that Fells didn't think it was nice at all. Not because he didn't like Fincham, but because he'd hoped to be alone with her.

"You should be home, Fincham," Dove said.

"And you? Why are you still here? Don't answer, I know. You eat any dinner?"

She shook her head. "Let's go in another room so George can do his work."

Fells grunted. With the arrival of Fincham he no longer cared if she stayed or not.

"George, you let me know right away if you find anything."

"Will do, Sheriff."

Dove and Fincham left the office and walked back to an interrogation room. It was stark: a two-way mirror, couple of chairs, one table. They didn't sit.

Fincham said, "Let's go to a restaurant. Pam will call us if there's any news."

"I wouldn't feel right."

"Arizona, that's Arizona talking." He always kidded her this way when he thought some of her ideas had come from Cottage Town, Arizona, where she'd spent those early years. Well, not that they'd come from there, but more from her mother who'd grown up in Cottage Town.

"No, Fincham. I should be here."

"Sheriff at her post and all that?"

"Maybe."

"Come on. You have to eat. What are you going to do here? You want to hang around with Fells? Let's go have a burger."

She sighed. He was right. She should eat and Pam would call them if anything came up. "Okay."

They went to The Apple Tree, a somewhat sleazy burger joint they both liked for reasons they couldn't explain. Seated near the back of the room in a faded blue vinyl booth, she had ordered hers with sautéed mushrooms, he with bacon and cheese. Both had a beer.

"You look tired, Arizona."

"I guess I am. It's the stress." She wondered if she should mention Mike's call. There was no reason not to, no reason she should.

"She's dead," he said.

Dove felt it like a kick in the gut. "Not necessarily," she answered.

He raised his full eyebrows. "Come on. She's not a run-

74

away. Doesn't fit for a kidnap. What other explanation for no word from her?"

"Someone could be holding her. She might still be alive."

"Maybe," he said. "What do you think about Taylor?"

"Maybe he came by, came to the house, and she thought she was going for a ride with him."

"Maybe she did. So what? Why didn't she come back?" Fincham asked. "And if she'd gone with him willingly, I think she might have at least taken her wallet."

"What if he talked her into running away with him, told her not to worry about her stuff? I know this kid seems a little different from what we thought, the pierced nipples and all, but I still don't think she'd go off with somebody she'd never laid eyes on before." She took a healthy swallow of her beer. "On the other hand, it bothers me that she didn't answer that last e-mail from Taylor." They'd downloaded Julie's mail and there hadn't been another from him.

"All he had to do was say who he was to get her to go with him."

"Okay. So, it could be Taylor, but then what?"

"Then he took her somewhere and killed her."

"Jesus, Jack." She hated to admit it, but she knew he was probably right.

The burgers arrived.

"Now, who has the bacon and cheese?" Vivian asked. She'd introduced herself by name as "their waitress for the evening" while flashing a lot of teeth.

Fincham tapped the paper placemat in front of him. It had a map of the area and so-called cute sayings on it.

The waitress placed their dinners in front of them. "Anything else I can get you now?"

"No thanks," Dove said.

75

Vivian showed another toothy smile and left.

"He might have kidnapped her but not for ransom. So maybe she's not dead . . . yet."

Fincham said, "Yeah, yet. But Jenkins didn't find his name on any planes out of Marathon or Miami and the guy's car is still at his house."

"Probably used a different name."

"Sure. But how did he get to the airport?"

"A mystery," she said, lightly.

"Hate mysteries. Okay, let's say he got here somehow and rented a car. What was his plan?"

They stared at each other for a moment, then Dove said, "I guess we know."

"Right." He poured catsup on his burger, added salt and pepper, closed it up and took a big bite. The catsup dripped onto his plate. "And if it wasn't Taylor," he asked, when he'd almost finished chewing, "then who was it?"

"Someone who killed her," she said.

He nodded. "And that could be anybody."

"Anybody. The thing I can't stand, Jack, is not that someone is going to find the body. But who that'll be and when?" She shrugged. "What if a kid finds her?"

Fincham couldn't ignore that Dove had come completely around to believing the girl was dead. "It happens," he said.

"Yeah."

They ate in silence for a while.

Suddenly she said, "Mike called me today."

Fincham stopped his burger midway to his mouth. "And?"

She told him.

"How'd he know?"

"That's why Fells was there. I might have a bug in my

office, but that wouldn't be necessary for him to know the whole thing." She told Fincham what Fells had told her about the Internet and the programs anyone could have.

Fincham slapped his forehead with the palm of his hand. "I know that. Jack Jr. has a program like that on his computer. I've been meaning to tell you about it."

"I guess we can't keep anything secret anymore unless we keep it to ourselves." She wished she'd had bacon on her burger.

"But you have Fells checking for bugs because of McQuigg?"

"No harm in checking. Sweet Jesus. If there's a bug we shouldn't have been talking about the pierced nipples in my office."

"Well, we did. There's nothing we can do about it now. How the hell could McQuigg bug your office, anyway?"

"Ah, Jack, you're naïve. FBI can do anything they want. Get in anywhere, anytime."

"Yeah, but our place is never empty."

"Don't even try to figure it out. Doesn't matter how he did it."

"Yeah. I guess. So, he upset you, huh?"

She started to deny it, then nodded.

"Shithead," Fincham said.

Dove smiled. "Still wants to make my life miserable, I guess."

"But why? Thought you said he'd married again."

"He has. He refers to her as Betty Grable."

"Who's Betty Grable?"

"Oh, come on, Fincham."

"What?"

"Don't you ever watch old movies on TV?"

"Yeah, sure."

"Betty Grable was a big star in musicals. She was the number one pin-up girl in the second World War." God, she felt old. Not that Grable was even making movies by the time Dove was born. But she was a movie nut and watched all the oldies. Mike had been like that, too. One of the few things they'd had in common.

"So Mike's wife is musical?"

She laughed. "No. I think she's got good legs or something. Grable's legs were insured by Lloyds of London."

"Lloyds of London? Never mind. How do you know all this from watching old movies?"

"I read."

"About old movie stars?"

She felt defensive. "Want to make something of it, Fincham?"

He smiled crookedly and she felt it. Their eyes met, lingered and then he looked away and said, "Just wondered."

For a moment she thought he'd given her a meaningful gaze, but now her conviction was that she'd imagined it. "I read everything," she said.

"I never have time," he said.

"And if you did?"

"I like to read. Or I did, when I was younger. But not about old movie stars," he said and grinned. "So he calls her Betty Grable and he still has the hots for you?"

"You call what he said to me 'having the hots?' "

"People show what they feel in strange ways," he said.

Now why did that sound so meaningful? she wondered. As though he was talking about himself . . . maybe in relationship to her. She took a chance. "That what you do, Fincham? Show your feelings in strange ways?"

He didn't answer for a moment, just looked at her.

She looked back, into his eyes, and again she felt something.

Then Fincham said softly, "Sometimes, Arizona. Sometimes."

Now she was sure she wasn't imagining anything. And she remembered something her mother had said to her: *"If you're thinking a lot about some boy, he's probably thinking about you, too, Lucia."* She'd been doing a lot of thinking about Fincham.

"Arizona?"

"Yeah?"

Neither of them was eating now. She couldn't have chewed anything if her life depended on it.

"You know I'm not in love with Bonnie Jo. You know that, don't you?"

She nodded.

"Shit," he said.

"What?" she whispered, and knew she shouldn't be encouraging him, but she couldn't stop.

"Ah, hell," he said. "Forget it."

She wanted to reach out, touch his hand, something. But she knew she couldn't do this. They kept looking at each other, unable to quit. And then a sweeping guilt took over when she thought of Julie Boyer and she broke the look, picked up her burger even though she couldn't imagine eating, swallowing.

The rest of the meal they ate in silence, neither of them able to eat much more than they had when Fincham had started to say the unspeakable. The sound of her beeper made her jump.

She looked at it and saw that it was the office number. "Got to call in," she said.

She took out her cell phone, punched in the number.

Pam answered, then put on Fells.

"Hey, Sheriff, you got a bug here."

"I do?"

"Yep. Took me awhile, pretty sophisticated stuff."

"Any markings on it?"

"No. Never is."

"Was it on the phone?"

"Nah. I would've found that right quick."

"So where was it?"

"Under your desk, a loose floorboard. Way back in the part of the U where your feet can't reach."

"I'll be damned."

"I'll take it with me, see what I can find out," he said.

She thanked him and told Fincham.

"Doesn't have to mean that it was McQuigg, you know."

"Come on, Jack. Who else?"

"Could be anyone," he said.

"Well it isn't. It's that bastard."

Vivian came over. "Everything okay? Ah, ya didn't finish. Something wrong?"

"We're not hungry," he said.

"Well, you wanna take it with you?"

"No," Dove said.

"Whatever. Okay, then. Here's the check. Have a nice evening."

"Yeah, we will," Fincham said.

In the cruiser Dove could feel tension. Sexual tension. She didn't dare look at him and from the corner of her eye she could see that he was looking straight ahead. Why didn't he start the damn car? His hand was on the key in the ignition. She was torn. Half of her hoped he'd say whatever it was he hadn't said, the other half prayed he wouldn't. But she'd never know because the car phone rang.

Dove picked it up. When she put it back she said, "Shit."

"What?"

"Somebody's found a girl's body."

Chapter Eight

By the time Fincham and Dove arrived, the area was lit like a summer's day. Oddly, the spot was only five miles from the Boyers' house, and would have been gone over when the search resumed.

The place was crawling with Snowden cops, and the Crime Scene tape was in place. Some forensic people milled around and there were two sheriffs from other counties where they'd had unsolved crimes of murdered females. A reporter and photographer from *The Jefferson Standard* were also present, and a small crew from station JBC approached her.

Dove knew them and said to the cameraman, "Turn it off, Boggs."

Marcelle Walsh shoved a microphone in the sheriff's face, which she pushed to one side.

"Sheriff," Walsh said, "is this the Boyer girl?"

Dove gave her a withering glance and elbowed past saying, "Later." Then she noticed Jenkins standing next to a young boy, seven or eight.

A worried-looking woman, who was obviously his mother, draped a sheltering arm around the child. The sheriff surmised that he was the one who'd found the body. Damn. Just what she'd been afraid of. Steffey and the coroner had not yet arrived.

She asked the police photographer, "You take some pictures, Pritchett?"

"Yeah, I got them."

Dove checked his feet, saw his shoes were covered.

"Where is she?" she asked.

"Side of the creek bed."

"Better come with us, but stay back a bit until I tell you."

"Right."

After putting protection over their shoes, and latex gloves on their hands, the sheriff, lieutenant and photographer ducked under the tape and slowly made their way down the sloping bank. Dove motioned to Pritchett to stay where he was. Then as she and Fincham came closer to the creek, they could see the body.

The girl was lying on her stomach, her arms tucked under her, legs straight but slightly parted. The hair color was right, but that's all that could be determined from this angle and distance.

Except that she was naked.

Dove had a dizzy moment. The way the girl was in the water reminded her of Clare, even though she'd been fully dressed. She quickly recovered, pushed thoughts of anything but this girl out of her mind.

When they reached her, they bent down and examined the body in that position, as best they could. Fincham started at her feet and Dove at the head.

The sheriff took a pen from her pocket, moved the girl's hair around to search for lacerations, but none was visible to the naked eye. Then, using the pen, she lifted the hair from the victim's neck. Bruises were apparent and at once Dove thought strangulation. She'd seen marks like these early in her career when she was a deputy.

Her eyes traveled downward until she and Fincham came to the same place at the girl's waist.

"Nothing," Fincham said.

Dove told him about the bruises on the back of the girl's neck and they agreed that there were no wounds or unusual marks in any other location.

Fincham said, "Want me to roll her over?"

She nodded.

Carefully, he took her by the left shoulder and turned her onto her back.

Discreetly, Dove drew in her breath, not wanting Fincham to recognize her shock. As a woman sheriff, she always had to be prudent about things like this. Even with him.

"Shit," Fincham said.

Both nipples were bloody, and Dove knew it was from the killer pulling out the rings. There were also bruises on the front of her neck, which made Dove lean even more toward strangulation as the murder method. The green fingernails completely identified who she was. The sheriff quickly noted that none of them was broken as they might be in a defensive mode.

But the most shocking thing was that the girl's pubic area was completely shaved.

"Augusta Fleming didn't mention that, did she?" Dove asked, pointing to the region.

"No," he answered. "Maybe she didn't know."

The sheriff doubted this. If Augusta knew about the pierced nipples, she would have known about the shaving. She remembered what teenage girls told each other. Still, Augusta might not have volunteered the information, finding it too discomfiting.

Both sheriff and lieutenant squatted again and looked over the section of earth that had been underneath the body. To them the ground offered no hint of debris. Later, the forensic team would comb it thoroughly, and if they were lucky they'd find a rogue hair, a thread, something.

Dove gestured to Pritchett.

When he was up close he said, "Holy shit."

"Take the pictures and keep your mouth shut about this, hear?"

"Will do." He began to snap shots, the flashes like miniature lightning bolts.

"Sheriff?"

Dove turned to see Harry Scruggs, the coroner, come lumbering down the bank. He was a big man in every way, his hair a silvery mop that often tumbled over his wide forehead.

"Harry," she acknowledged him.

Scruggs said hello to Fincham then looked past them at the body. "Good Christ," he mumbled. "Is it the girl?"

"Pretty sure."

"Was this the way you found her?" He pushed up his tortoise shell glasses from where they'd slipped to right above the hump in his nose.

Fincham answered. "She was lying on her stomach, arms under her."

"Right." Both the coroner's hands and feet were covered the same way the others were. Still, he tiptoed around the body, in an exceptionally dainty way for a man his size, and viewed her neck from above her left shoulder. In a moment he said, "Looks like strangulation. But that's only my initial impression," he cautioned.

"Yes," Dove said and didn't add, we know the routine about your first impressions.

He moved down the side of her body, looked at her breasts. "Whatever went on here happened before she died." It was said casually, as though he saw this desecration every day. "The blood," he added, as if they wouldn't know.

85

Dove said, "If it's our girl, she had nipple rings."

Scruggs looked up at them. "Nipple rings?"

"Julie Boyer had pierced nipples."

"I see. So the perp pulled them out, is what you're saying?"

"Yes."

Scruggs pointed to her pubic area. "What about this?"

"What about it?" Fincham answered.

Scruggs gave him an unfriendly stare. "What's it mean?"

Dove said, "We don't know yet."

He mulled this for a few seconds, then asked, "Can we turn her over now?"

Fincham leaned down and gently turned the dead girl onto her stomach.

Scruggs scanned the corpse, lifting the hair the way Dove had. "Strangulation, for sure. Nothing else I can determine now. But she hasn't been dead more than twenty-four hours. No decomposition."

They all made their way back up the bank, went under the tape.

Dove said to Jenkins, "Get some more men on the Lyle Taylor thing."

"Yes, Sheriff." She turned away and called to a bunch of deputies.

Steffey was there now.

Dove said to him, "Take some men and pick up Buster Clark."

Steffey said, "Can't find the guy."

"We *have* to find him now."

"Right," Steffey said.

She looked around for her other lieutenant but didn't see him. "Steffey, where's Lieutenant Hutt?"

"Don't know."

"Get him on the radio, tell him to meet me at the office."

"Sure thing."

She turned to Jack. "I want to talk to the boy."

He was standing with his mother and a deputy. She introduced herself and Fincham.

The woman said, "He didn't mean to wait so long, Sheriff. He was scared."

"Of course, I understand," Dove said. She leaned over to be eye-level with the child and asked him his name.

"Nick," he said softly.

"Well, Nick, I want you to know you're a brave boy, no matter how long you waited."

The boy nodded slightly.

"What time did you actually find her?"

When the child didn't answer, the mother said, "He came home around six, late for him, and I knew, I swear I knew then, that something bad had happened, but he kept saying there was nothing. I let it go for an hour or so and then I started asking him again."

Although Dove was glad the mother had persisted, she felt for the boy, being nagged that way.

"And then what happened?" She was still kneeling, looking at Nick.

"He finally started crying and—"

"Did not," Nick blurted.

"Course you didn't," Dove said.

"Well he did," the mother said.

Dove looked up at her with a steely eye.

The woman got the message, sighed, then went on. "He told me he'd seen a girl in the water, but she wasn't swimming." Then she whispered, "And that the girl had no clothes on."

Dove said to Nick, "You did the right thing." She held out her hand for him to shake, and he took it timidly. Then she stood up.

The woman went on. "Well, I knew right off what that meant. So I called it in."

"Thank you," Dove said. "You've given your name and address to the deputy?"

"Yes."

"Fine. You can take him home now. And thanks again."

For a moment she watched them go, then turned to Fincham. "All we have to do is get out of here without talking to the goddamn press."

"In your dreams," he said.

Her dream was over immediately.

Walsh and Boggs were waiting impatiently, as were *The Standard* people. They all started talking at once.

Boggs rolled his camera and Walsh said, "So is it her, Sheriff? Is it the missing Boyer girl?"

"No identification has been made."

"Is there anything to make you think it's Boyer?"

"I told you, there's been no identification made," she said. But she had no doubt that it was Julie Boyer. "I have to go now."

"One more question, Sheriff."

It was always *one* more.

"Are there any suspects?"

"We just found the body, Walsh."

"You still could have a suspect in mind."

Of course that was true, and they did. "No suspects."

As she walked away she thought, in a matter of hours they'd gone from a missing girl to a murdered girl.

Now the true horror would begin.

Chapter Nine

At the morgue, the girl's body was covered. Mary Lee and Emmitt Boyer had identified her face. Dove hated to do it, but she had to ask about the shaved pubic area, and Mary Lee said she hadn't seen her daughter naked in at least four or five years. Dove thought she should have realized this, because she already knew the parents were unaware of the nipple rings.

In Dove's office were Fincham, Lieutenant Gill Hutt and sheriffs from two other counties that had unsolved murders of females on their books. Ernie Cahill from Culpepper and Sanford Dabney from Queen George. They were comparing information.

Dabney said, "She was bones when we found her. No way to know if she'd been shaved. Identified her by her dental records."

"And she was twenty-seven?" Fincham asked.

"Six. Twenty-six." Dabney ran his thumb and fingers down his Zapata mustache. "Married. Two kids. Husband alibied good. He was in New York when she disappeared."

"Cahill?" Dove said. She knew the cases, but needed to hear about them again from the men who were in charge. Men she liked and respected and didn't give her flak because she was a woman.

Ernie Cahill rearranged his unofficial bill-capped hat on his head of red hair. "Mine was bones, too. Same thing, dental shit. But she was only nineteen. You people are damn lucky to have found her so quick. How come it was in the dark?"

"Wasn't," Dove said. She thought about Nick. "The kid found her about six o'clock, but was too afraid to say anything until later. Well, not too afraid, too embarrassed."

"Embarrassed?" asked Sandy Dabney.

Fincham said, "The nude thing. What do you want, he's a kid."

"Jesus," Cahill said. "Poor little bastard." His freckles deepened in color.

Rangy and spare, taller than the others, Lieutenant Hutt was Dove's only black officer. "So what have we got says it's the same perp?"

Cahill said, "Only that they both disappeared suddenly, yours and mine that is," and he turned to Dabney.

"Same. One minute she was in her backyard hanging out wash, the next she was gone."

"Mine was in a mall with some other girls, you believe it. Went on ahead alone to a health food store. That was it. Other girls never saw her again."

"No forensic material about the method?" Fincham asked.

"Oh, yeah," Dabney said. "My coroner found an indentation on the cervical vertebrae."

Sweet Jesus, thought Dove. Why didn't he say this sooner? "Which indicated strangulation," she clarified, to be sure he knew what he was saying.

"Right."

"Same with you, Cahill?"

"Nope. Nothing could be determined."

"This girl strangled?" Dabney asked, rubbing his tired blue eyes.

"Not sure yet, but Scruggs said he thought so."

"Meaning it could be the same perp," Cahill put in.

"Meaning it could be," Dove said. "Not much to go on."

"So what's this then we got? Serial killer?"

Dove said, "Could be."

"Ah, fuck," Dabney said. "Sorry, Lucia."

"I've heard the word, Sandy."

The men laughed.

She knew Sandy never would have apologized if she'd been a man. Wanted to add, "Even done it," but she didn't.

"I can't deal with a serial," Cahill said. "Christ."

"What's that mean?" asked Hutt.

"Means nothing," he mumbled. "Course I can deal with it, don't want to. Everybody'll get crazy."

Sheriff Dove said, "Looks like I'm the one who's going to have to deal with it, Ernie."

"You going to release that speculation?" Dabney asked.

"To the general public, the media? Of course not."

"They'll find out."

Seemed everybody, except Dove, knew how easy it was for anybody to get information. There'd be general panic when they did know. Still, she'd try to keep it quiet as long as she could. "You don't say anything," she said to the two sheriffs, "and we don't say anything." She looked around the room aimlessly, wondering if there were any other bugs that Fells hadn't found, wondering if Mike McQuigg or a cohort was listening right now.

"And nothing about the shaved area," Fincham added.

Dove looked at him and nodded a thank-you.

"How you going to keep your force from leaking?" asked Cahill.

"Maybe it'll stay in this room."

"Scruggs?" said Sandy Dabney.

"His report comes to me."

"What about his big fat mouth?" Hutt said.

"I'll talk to him." She knew this was no guarantee of his silence. Harry had a habit of telling his wife, Faye, everything. And Faye obliged by telling everyone else. Dove saw the skepticism on all their faces. "I know, I know. But I'll tell him the seriousness of this one. Look, we've never had anything this bad. He'll listen." She wished she could be as sure as she sounded.

Cahill looked at his Timex and stood up. "Guess that's it then."

Dabney followed suit. "You keep us up to speed, Lucia?"

She nodded. "And you keep quiet."

"Don't have to worry about that," Dabney said.

When they'd gone, Dove looked at her own watch. It was after one in the morning.

"Hutt, we have to go hard on the parents now."

"Ah shit, Sheriff."

"I know. It's lousy but it has to be done. Family is the first place to look, you know that."

"Before the funeral?" he asked.

Dove said, "Think they're going to be less upset after?"

"No, it's not that, Sheriff. I know you're right. Just seems mean or something to do it now."

"Take care of it in the morning, Hutt. Especially the father. I know it sucks but it's got to be done."

"I thought you already did this, Fincham."

Dove answered for him. "He did. Now I want them questioned by someone they've never seen. Understand?"

"Yeah, okay."

"Best thing we can do now," she said, "is get some sleep so we can get cracking first thing."

Both lieutenants agreed. Hutt left.

Fincham and Dove didn't move, didn't speak. Then she stood up, pushed in her chair against the desk. Their eyes met, locked and she felt herself beginning to tremble slightly. Finally, she said, "I'm going home."

After a moment, Fincham said, "Yeah."

They left her office, plodded past the skeleton crew saying goodnight, went through the door, and walked to the parking lot, careful not to bump each other.

"Any final thoughts?" she asked, and could have kicked herself at the sound of that question.

"I think we got a potential powder keg on our hands."

And that could have been a double entendre too but she knew it wasn't. "Potential? What's potential about it?"

He nodded in agreement. "Front page on *The Standard* this morning for sure."

"And tomorrow the world?" Another old movie title, but apt.

"Christ, I hope not. Not unless . . ."

"Don't even think it, Jack." She knew he was going to say, not unless it happened again.

"Yeah, you're right. See you later." Quickly, he turned, trudged toward his cruiser.

Dove got in hers and sat for a moment. She couldn't get the picture of Julie Boyer's ruined nipples out of her mind.

She watched through her rear-view mirror as Fincham drove out. What would happen between them? She recalled images of Jack across the table from her, the way he looked, what he didn't say. And then there was a knock on her window and she jumped, almost knocking her head on the roof. When she looked she couldn't believe who it was. McQuigg. She rolled down the window.

"What are you doing here?" she said. Her heart thudded, but not because she was excited to see him. It was the thud of fear.

"Thanks for the nice reception."

Dove got out of the cruiser. "Why should I offer you a nice reception?"

"The obvious reply is, why not? But I won't ask."

He smiled, heart-stopping when she was young, but to her now an unsavory expression.

Nevertheless Mike was still a looker. Tall, and resembling Kevin Costner. But the color of his light brown hair was fading to gray and it gave him a seedy look. She sized up the suit he was wearing and figured it cost between one and two thousand.

"So what do you want, McQuigg?"

"I've been assigned to your case, Lucia."

"You're kidding."

"Nope. Me and another agent."

She automatically looked around.

"He's not here," McQuigg said.

"So why are you?"

"I'm more diligent."

"The hell you are. What are you doing here at one in the morning, Mike?"

"Well, Lucia, we've got a few of these in different states and we're very interested."

"A few of what?"

"Abductions and murders. Look," he said, in a conspiratorial manner, "I want us to work together on this thing, not as enemies. I'm well aware of how you cops hate the Bureau coming onto your turf, and you might have special feelings about me on this, but it's an ongoing FBI case, Lucia. There've been abductions and murders like the Boyer case all over the place. Illinois, Florida, New York, New Jersey, and a lot of other states."

"Are you serious?"

"You bet I am."

"So why haven't I heard about them?"

"Since when do you keep track of all the murders in the country?"

This was true. "How long have they been going on, Mike?"

"About five years."

"God Almighty. And it's the same MO?" She wanted to see how much he knew.

"Same. Shaved pubic area nails it."

Sweet Jesus. So he knew the whole thing about Boyer. And the bastard was going to work with her. Take over was more like it. "Has that info about the shaved pubic area ever been released to the public?"

"No."

"You telling me that you've been working on these murders?"

"That's right. If you hadn't hung up on me the other day I might have told you then."

Yeah, sure you would, she thought. "So if we're going to work together maybe you'd better tell me what you have."

"Squat."

"You mean that?"

"Believe me, I wish I didn't."

"Not even a profile?"

"Sure, but you know what I think of them."

"Even so. I'd like to see it."

"Fax it to you in the morning."

"Thanks."

"Anything you can tell *me*, Lucia?"

She laughed. "Nothing you don't already know." Dove turned and reached for the door handle.

McQuigg put his hand on her arm and she instinctively pulled away.

They glared at each other.

"This how it's going to be?" he asked.

"Just don't touch me, okay, McQuigg?"

He raised both arms, bent at the elbows, hands in the air, palms facing her as though he was under arrest. "Hey, no problem. Never again." He gave her a smarmy smile.

The asshole thinks it's because I still care. She could've said a lot of things, but she held her tongue, the better part of valor, she decided. Then she opened the door and got in.

"See you in the morning," he said.

She nodded and rolled up the window. From the corner of her eye she could see that he was walking away.

She waited until she heard his car start, then looked and saw that he was driving the obligatory government car, nondescript, probably tan.

Dove turned on the ignition, backed up and headed out of the lot. She was steaming. Why him? She'd known the FBI would be in on this, they always were. But it never occurred to her that McQuigg would be one of the agents. Of course she hadn't known that Boyer was one of many victims. How could she? "Shit," she said out loud and banged her hand on the wheel.

Later in bed she tossed and turned and finally fell asleep thinking about the horrendous possibilities of having a serial killer loose in Jefferson.

When the phone rang she'd only been asleep for two hours. She picked up in the middle of the second ring.

"Sheriff Dove."

"Arizona?"

She felt her heart thump in her chest. Why was he calling her at this hour? "What's happening?"

"We got Lyle Taylor."

Chapter Ten

When Dove arrived at the station, Lyle Taylor was in a holding cell. The sheriff and Fincham immediately moved him to the interrogation room where they sat him behind the table.

Taylor was a pathetic-looking creature. He had a face that was exceptionally narrow, tapering to a point like a giraffe's. His eyes were small and brown, under eyebrows so fine they were barely visible. The hair on his head was similar, thin, as though he'd had a disease. He had fleshy lips and a long slender nose. Dove guessed he was about six-two and weighed one hundred fifty soaking wet.

His jean-clad legs were splayed on either side of the table like pinchers. Well-worn, New Balance, purple and white running shoes were on his feet. A faded denim shirt was open at the neck.

"Feet down, Taylor," Dove said.

He dropped them, hunched forward and his long meager fingers tapped rhythmically.

They'd gotten him for shoplifting at a 7-Eleven. It was hard for Dove to believe that Julie would have gone anywhere with this man. Still, you never knew.

Fincham began. "Why were you taking food from the 7-Eleven?"

"I was hungry," Taylor said in a shaky voice.

"Ever think of buying it?"

"Run outta money."

Dove asked, "You from around here?"

"No."

"Where you from then?"

"Florida," he said.

Dove remembered that McQuigg had listed Florida as one of the states with an unsolved murder of the same type.

Fincham said, "What are you doing in Jefferson?"

He said nothing, but looked frightened.

"Answer the question," Fincham said.

"I came to see a friend."

"Who."

"Could I have a Coke?"

"No. What friend?"

"Look, I'm hungry. Can I have a sandwich? You have to feed me."

Dove hated television. Goddamn cop shows.

"Answer the question. What friend? Then we'll get you something to eat and drink."

"Okay. I came to see Jeff Miller."

Dove and Fincham glanced at each other, then Fincham said, "Where does Miller live?"

"I thought you were going to get me something to eat," Taylor whined.

"All right," Fincham said. "What do you want?"

"A Coke and a ham and cheese on rye with mayonnaise on the ham side and mustard on the cheese side."

Fincham shot Dove a look as if to say, *can you believe this guy?* "Anything else?" he asked Taylor.

"Chips. *Wise* chips."

"You're some piece of work," Fincham said as he walked toward the door.

The interrogation halted until Fincham returned. He

asked again where Jeff Miller lived.

"I don't know."

"So how were you going to visit him?"

"I don't know." Now he sounded like a four-year-old.

"That isn't who you were here to see, is it, Mr. Taylor?"

"Okay. No, it isn't. I came to see Julie Boyer, but I never got to. And I saw the news so I know she's missing."

Either he didn't know she was dead, or he was acting.

"Why did you lie about who you came to see?"

"I know you're gonna try and pin this thing on me."

Dove said, "What thing are we going to pin on you, Mr. Taylor?"

"Kidnap or some damn thing."

"The only thing we're going to pin on you is shoplifting."

"So why are you asking me about Julie Boyer?"

"You brought her name into the conversation," Fincham said.

Taylor looked completely puzzled.

"When did you and Julie decide that you'd come here?"

He mumbled something.

"Speak up."

"I said, *we* didn't. She didn't know I was coming."

"When did you arrive?"

"The day she disappeared, okay?"

"Did you see her?"

"No. I already told you that."

"How did you get here?"

"I took a plane."

"Under what name?"

"My name."

Fincham said, "No, Mr. Taylor, you didn't."

"Jeez, you know so much, what are you asking for?"

"What name?"

"Keith Jarrett," he said sheepishly. "I like him."

Dove remembered she'd noticed that that was one of names on the passenger lists, but thought nothing of it, figured it wasn't the real singer, but someone with the same name. "Why didn't you fly under your own name?"

"Because . . . because I like to fly under celebrities' names." He flushed slightly.

"Really? What other aliases have you used?"

"Aliases? They're not aliases."

"Whatever," Dove said. "What other names have you used?"

"Shit. Merle Haggard, Marc Anthony. I don't remember any others."

"All right. So you flew here under the name of Keith Jarrett. Then what?"

"I rented a car."

"Under your own name?"

"Yeah. Had to. Credit card."

"Mr. Taylor, I noticed that you had several credit cards among your belongings. Can you tell me why you couldn't have gone to an ATM if you were out of cash?"

"I didn't feel like it."

"You wanted to steal?" Fincham asked.

He paused before answering. "Yeah. That's right. I wanted to."

"Do you do that often?"

"Sometimes. I never got caught before though."

They knew that because Taylor had no record.

"Where's my food?" he asked.

"It's coming."

Dove said, "What did you do after you rented the car?"

"I drove to Julie's house."

"And?"

"I drove by a few times."

"What time was this?"

"I guess about five-thirty or so."

"And did you see her on the stoop?"

"No. Nobody was on the stoop."

If he was telling the truth, this gave them a better time of when she disappeared, Dove thought.

Fincham asked, "Was anything on the stoop?"

"Like what?"

"Like anything."

"I think there was some books."

"So why didn't you stop and go to the door? She wasn't expecting you so you couldn't have expected her to be outside, could you?"

"No."

"But you didn't stop and go to the door?"

"No."

"Why not?"

Taylor pulled in his legs and hunched over. "I, I got scared."

"Scared of what?"

He shrugged. "I dunno."

"Lyle," Dove said. "You saw Julie sitting on the stoop, didn't you?"

He put his head down on his crossed arms and began to cry.

Fincham and Dove exchanged a look and Dove moved closer to Taylor, reached out and put her hand on his shoulder. She didn't want to touch his head.

"It's okay, Lyle. We understand."

"No, no, you don't," he said in a muffled voice.

"All right, then try to tell us what happened so we *can* understand." She felt the rush of adrenaline she always did when she felt something was going to come to an end.

He raised his head, tears streaked his cheeks. "Nothing happened."

"What do you mean?"

"Just that. Nothing happened."

There was a knock on the door. Fincham opened it and a deputy handed him Taylor's food.

"Here's your grub," he said.

This visibly cheered Taylor and he wiped his face with his sleeve, sat up straighter.

"Can I have it?"

"After you tell us what happened," Dove said.

"I told you," he whimpered. "Nothing. I drove by, that's all."

Dove motioned with her head for Fincham to give him the food. Taylor unwrapped the sandwich with fervor, lifted one side of the bread, turned it over and lifted the other. "They got it wrong," he complained. "The mustard and mayonnaise are on the same side."

Through gritted teeth Fincham said, "Sorry. Eat it or don't eat it."

Taylor stared at them for a moment then bit into the sandwich with gusto. He closed his eyes while he chewed, took another bite, then popped the Coke, took a long swallow. "Jeez, that tastes good."

"Great," Fincham said. "Mayonnaise and mustard on the same side not too bothersome?"

"No. It's okay."

They waited for him to get through one half before beginning to question him again.

Dove said, "Lyle, how did you know Julie Boyer?"

"I, I didn't actually *know* her. We wrote e-mail to each other. We met in a chat room. You know what that is?"

"Yes," Dove said.

Fincham nodded.

"Did you exchange pictures?"

"She sent me a picture. I didn't have one."

Having read their correspondence Dove knew that Julie continuously asked him for a photo and he always said he'd have it taken soon. Now she knew why he never sent one.

"Why were you crying?" Fincham asked.

"I dunno. Because she's missing, I guess. Because I'm scared."

"Scared of what?"

"Scared you're gonna try to say I did it."

"Did what?"

"Took her someplace. Kidnapped her."

"Did you?"

"No." It was the first time he raised his voice. "No, I told you. I never even saw her."

Dove motioned to Fincham to go outside, then said to Taylor, "Finish your food. We'll be right back."

"You leaving me in here all alone?"

The question surprised her. "What's wrong with that?"

He looked embarrassed. "Nothing. Never mind."

In the hall Dove asked Fincham what he thought.

"Well, I don't believe in coincidences, Arizona."

"Meaning?"

"Isn't it a little too perfect that this guy should be here at the exact time of Julie's abduction and have nothing to do with it?"

"A little. So you think he did it?"

"How could he not have?"

"I don't know," she said. "But he doesn't seem like he'd

have the guts to do a murder, especially the strangling and the shaving stuff."

"Yeah? Well who seems like a murderer?"

"I know, I know. But he's such a scaredy-cat."

"They're all cowards, killers."

"It's not that, Fincham."

"What then?"

"What about the murders in all those other states? Could he have done those?"

"That's not our problem. I think we should book him."

"Now?"

"Let's book him on the shoplifting charge. Then we get some forensic people to go over the car he rented. Where the hell is it, anyway?"

"Let's find out."

They went back into the room where Taylor sat drinking his Coke and eating chips. The sandwich was gone.

"Where's your car, the one you rented?" Fincham asked.

"I guess it's outside the 7-Eleven."

"What's the make? Keys in it?"

"No. You people took 'em when you took everything else. It's a white Ford."

"Okay."

"We're booking you for shoplifting, Taylor."

"Ah, jeez. I want a lawyer."

Dove said, "Okay. Which lawyer?" She knew he wouldn't know one here.

He stared at her. Then he said, "Public defender."

Goddamn cop shows.

Chapter Eleven

"Dad? Wake up, Dad."

"Huh?" Fincham grunted.

"Wake up, Dad."

Jack slowly opened his eyes. The lids felt as though they had twenty-pound weights on them. "What is it?"

Kim said, "Why are you sleeping on the couch again?"

"Oh, honey," he said to his daughter.

"I mean it, Dad." Her voice was tearful.

"Got home real late, Kim."

"So?"

"Didn't want to wake your mother."

"Bullshit."

"Hey. Stop with the language." Fincham swung his bare legs over the side of the couch. He was wearing briefs and kept the cover across his lap.

"What's going on?"

"Nothing. I don't know what you're talking about. What time is it?"

"You do know. This is the third time this week you've slept here."

"Kim, this is none of your business. Now what time is it?" He couldn't remember where he'd put his watch.

"It *is* my business." Although she was slim, she sat down heavily on the end of the couch, wearing her despair like a poncho. "Are you and Mom breaking up? You going to get divorced?"

"Course not." He reached out a hand but she didn't take it.

"I'm not a baby anymore, Dad. You can tell me the truth."

He looked at her. *Not a baby.* Fourteen years old and looking like forty, with all the makeup and the blond hair puffed and swirling. Her green eyes enhanced by green eye shadow gave her pretty face an extra dollop of artificial beauty. Jack didn't think she needed any of it, but he knew better than to say so. "What time is it?"

"Da-ad. God. It's eight-fifteen."

"Shouldn't you be at school?"

"I have a few minutes. So why are you sleeping here?"

"I told you, Kimmy. I didn't want to wake your mother."

"I know that's not why. You two are fighting, aren't you?"

"Kim. Listen. I got home at about five this morning."

"Well, why?"

"I was working."

"Yeah, right."

"What do you think I was doing?"

She didn't answer, glared at him.

"Kimmy, we got a suspect in the Boyer thing. You can't tell anybody that because we've only booked him on shoplifting, but he looks good for the murder."

"Murder?"

He'd completely forgotten that it was only the night before that they'd found the girl. Kim wouldn't have any way of knowing.

"Oh, God, Dad. I'm sorry. I mean, I'm glad, oh, hell I don't know what I mean."

He put out his hand again and this time she took it.

"Okay, honey. Don't you worry. Go to school."

"You mean Julie Boyer is dead?"

"Yeah. Sorry."

"I didn't know her, but God, Dad."

"Keep that information to yourself. It isn't official yet."

"I will. It's awful and it makes me scared."

"Scared?"

"Maybe there's somebody out there."

"No, I think we got the guy." He wasn't as sure as he sounded.

Kim wrapped her arms around herself as though she had a chill.

"Honey, there's nothing to worry about."

"But you said, you *think* you got the guy."

He thought carefully about what to say to her.

"Dad?"

"Okay, Kimmy. It's true we're not sure yet, and it means you're right, there might be somebody out there. So I don't want you to be alone anywhere, until we're sure. Okay?"

She looked frightened. "Yeah."

"As long as you're not alone, you'll be all right."

"Yeah." After a beat she said, "But Dad . . . something's not right with you and Mom."

He thought she'd forgotten the original thrust of this conversation, but apparently not. "Everything's fine. Don't worry about it."

"Dad?"

"Yeah?" He reached for his white T-shirt and pulled it over his head.

"Last night? Mom was weird."

"Weird?"

Kim looked down. "Drunk."

Fincham sighed. "She's sick, Kim."

"Hell she is. She was drunk."

"That's what I mean," he said. He found his trousers and slipped his legs into them.

"What? You're calling drunk, *sick?*" Now she looked as though he was trying to dupe her.

"It *is* sick."

"You mean she's an alcoholic or something?"

Fincham stood up, his back to her, got into his pants, zipped up and turned around. "Yeah. An alcoholic."

"Oh, God," she cried. "What am I going to tell people?"

Fincham almost laughed at his daughter's self-centeredness, so typically a teenager. "You don't have to tell anybody anything. We'll take care of it. I think you should go to school now, Kim."

She stood up. "She's not going to have to go those meetings is she?"

"That would be good if she did."

"Yeah, but everyone would see her car and know."

Fincham shook his head. "Kim, go to school, okay?"

"This sucks." She picked up her book bag and started toward the door, stopped. "Dad?"

"Yeah?"

"I love you."

"I love you too, Kimmy."

She dropped the bag and ran to him and flung her arms around his neck. He engulfed her in a hug. They stayed like that for a bit and then he kissed her cheek and gently told her to go.

When she'd left, he wandered into the kitchen and began making coffee. Jack Jr. was long gone, he knew. And Bonnie Jo should be getting up fairly soon. He had to talk to her about the drinking. This was the first time either of the kids had said anything. So now the problem with his wife had extended to the kids' problem with their mother. Whole new ball game.

He switched his thoughts to Lyle Taylor. Damn. The guy had to be the killer. Then what about the other murders? What about the ones that happened in Culpepper and Queen George counties? But the only thing they had in common was the way the women disappeared. Boyer's killer didn't have to be the same one in those two cases.

Still, he didn't like it that Arizona wasn't more convinced. Her instincts about people were usually right on. They'd never done a murder case together before, but instincts were instincts.

And then that goddamn McQuigg who'd been watching the interview. He hated the jerk. He knew it was stupid to be jealous, Arizona didn't want him. But the guy was an agent and was going to be on the case.

"What the hell are you doing here?" It was Bonnie Jo.

When he turned around he was shocked. He'd seen her look bad before, but nothing like this. Her hair, usually perfect, was totally disheveled. Dark semi-circles were under her eyes and she was pasty, looking a hundred years old.

"What?" she asked.

"You look like shit," he said.

"Thanks."

"Well, Jesus, B.J., you do."

She pushed past him and poured herself a cup of coffee.

"You have to do something," he said.

"Do something?" Her back was to him. "Do something about what?"

"About your goddamn drinking." He told himself not to lose control.

She whirled around, almost falling, her balance unsteady. "Listen mister, you have a few things you could

109

do something about, you know."

Softly, he said, "We're not talking about me now."

"Well, let's."

"No. Not until we talk about your drinking."

"Fuck you." She started past him, but he stopped her, a hand on her arm.

"Leggo of me, Jack."

"We have to talk."

"So let's talk about you and Sheriff Dove then."

He felt his face flushing.

"What's that supposed to mean?" Shit, he shouldn't have engaged.

"By the look of you, I think you know." She laughed.

"There's nothing going on between me and the sheriff," he said.

"Yeah, yeah."

Fuck. "Kim told me you were drunk last night."

"Kim?"

"Yeah. She noticed, B.J.," he said.

"What she say?"

"You were weird."

"Christ."

"Why don't you sit down so we can talk."

"What's to talk about? What's to say about it?"

"Plenty. Sit down. Please."

Surprisingly, she did what he asked. Fincham sat across from her in the breakfast nook.

"Look, B.J., your drinking has gotten out of control. Are you aware of that?"

She shrugged.

"Well, it has. I haven't said anything because . . . I don't know. But now that the kids have noticed . . ."

"Jack Jr., too?"

"No. At least he hasn't said anything."

"So, just Kimmy?"

"Yeah. For now. Anyway, you got to do something about it."

"Like what? You don't expect me to go to those holy roller AA meetings, do ya?"

"They're not like that."

"How do you know."

"Because I went to one."

"What the hell for?"

"For work. I wanted to understand better." This was true but he'd also had Bonnie Jo in mind.

"I can't go there."

"Why not?"

"That's for alcoholics, Jack. I'm not an alcoholic. I know I drink more than I should, but I'm not an alcoholic."

Denial. "So what are you going to do about drinking more than you should?"

"I'll cut back."

Fincham could've predicted that. He'd done his homework.

"Starting when?"

"Today. I'll cut back today." She looked at the wall clock. "I got to get dressed. I have an early appointment with Mrs. Coe and she's a bitch if I'm not there on time."

"You promise you'll cut back."

"Promise," she said sliding out from the bench.

When she was gone, he thought, yeah, right. Still there was nothing more he could do. He couldn't drag her to AA. But he knew that even if she did cut back for today, soon enough it would start again. So he'd have to wait until she got out of hand or into trouble. He hoped it wouldn't come to that.

Dove waited in the hall of the courthouse for Fincham. He was ten minutes late; unusual.

Forensic had found nothing incriminating in Taylor's car. But that didn't mean he didn't kill her. Still, it puzzled Dove.

The lawyer assigned to the suspect was Darryl Wittman. Dove knew him. In fifteen minutes Taylor would be arraigned for shoplifting and Wittman would ask for bail. The sitting judge was Wally Parker, a good old boy, who wouldn't give bail to the likes of Lyle Taylor, she was sure.

Jesus. There was McQuigg coming down the hall.

"Lucia," he said.

"Would you mind calling me Sheriff?"

He smiled. "Okay, then you can call me Agent McQuigg."

"I'd be happy to."

"Deal," he said.

"I didn't think you'd be here for this, Agent McQuigg."

"Why not? I'll be here for everything." He nodded and went into the courtroom.

This was going to be intolerable, she thought.

"Hey, Arizona. Sorry I'm late."

She turned to face Fincham and saw at once that he looked upset. "What's up?"

"Nothing. Don't know what you mean."

She didn't want to pursue it if he didn't want to tell her. "Okay. McQuigg is here."

"For this?"

She told him what Mike had said.

"You mean, he's going to be around all the time?"

"I don't know. Let's go in."

The courtroom was old. Wainscoting covered the walls part way and big fans hung from the ceiling although they weren't switched on. Large windows lined each side and most of them were open.

The room wasn't crowded and they took seats in the second row on the right. McQuigg was in the back on the left.

Dove told Jack about the initial forensic report on the car.

"They going over it again?"

"Absolutely."

"So what do you make of it?" Fincham asked.

"Got me wondering."

"Maybe she never got in the car," he said.

"Why not?"

"Maybe they went for a walk."

"A five-mile walk?"

"That's nothing for kids."

"Fincham, if they went for a walk, Taylor's car would've been parked in front of her house."

"Maybe she told him to park somewhere else so her folks wouldn't know."

"I guess that's possible."

"More than possible. Likely. Yeah." He was excited by the idea. "Sure, that's what happened. Nobody knew about Taylor and she told him to go around the corner and she'd meet him there."

"So we have to ask if anyone saw the car on the surrounding streets?"

"Right."

"Beep Jenkins and tell her to take some deputies and get right on it."

He left the courtroom because the judge didn't permit phone calls.

Dove was skeptical about Fincham's theory; still she

wasn't about to pass up any idea that had some validity. And this one did. It was plausible, but not probable, she thought. And the likelihood of finding someone who saw the car wasn't in the high percentage bracket.

"All rise," the bailiff stated.

Judge Parker entered in his black robe, sat down behind his bench. He was in his late sixties, flushed face, white hair, big black-framed glasses.

The bailiff called the court into session. Judge Parker banged his gavel and asked for the first case. From a side door, Taylor, in an orange jumpsuit, shuffled in.

Fincham rejoined Dove. They waited silently.

Wittman stood next to Taylor and, after the other things about the case were stated, asked for five hundred dollars bail.

Parker looked at Taylor for a moment, then said: "One thousand dollars bail." Banged his gavel. "Next case."

Taylor's head drooped as he was led out.

Dove was shocked. Parker rarely gave anyone bail. But shoplifting wasn't much of a crime these days.

Wittman came through the gate and up the aisle. Dove and Fincham followed him into the corridor.

Wittman was waiting for them. He looked younger than Taylor, but Dove knew he wasn't. His hair was brown and curly, and he had brown eyes and a heavily freckled face. He wore a blue summer suit, white shirt, gray tie.

McQuigg joined them. Dove introduced him to Wittman. Then she said to the lawyer, "You're not going to get him the bail, are you?"

"You know I can't answer that, Sheriff. What's the big deal anyway? He's a crummy shoplifter."

"Maybe," she said.

"Maybe? What's that mean?"

"You know I can't answer that, Counselor," she said. The lawyer laughed.

"Do you think he can raise the bail money?"

Wittman said, "I don't know. Tell me what's going on."

Fincham gave her a nudge.

"Listen, Darryl, I can't go into it, but this guy might be more than just a shoplifter. We can't afford to let him get away."

"If it's more, then charge him."

"We're not ready to."

"Sorry. Nice seeing you both. Nice to meet you, Agent McQuigg," Wittman said, and walked away.

When Wittman was out of earshot, McQuigg whirled on Dove. "What's wrong with you? You can't tell his lawyer things like that?"

"Excuse me?" she said.

"You've given his lawyer information he shouldn't have."

"I didn't give him anything and I know the guy. This is the way we do things here, Agent."

"Fucked up," he said, and walked away.

Jack said, "Oh, this is going to be terrific."

"We can't let him get to us. We'll just keep doing things the way we do."

"What about you, Arizona? Can you keep him from getting to you?"

"You mean on a personal level? Yeah, I can." But she wasn't sure. "What do you think about the bail?"

"Where's he going to get a thousand?"

"You never know," she said.

And she was right. Taylor was out on the thousand by noon.

Chapter Twelve

Jenkins had found a woman who'd seen Taylor's car parked on her street on the right day at the right time. She was sitting in front of the sheriff's desk. Dove hadn't called McQuigg. If he knew so much he probably knew about this and he could come or not. Fincham leaned against a file cabinet.

Dove had given Lisa Powell coffee and a doughnut, and was trying to make the interview painless and informal. After initial chitchat she began the questioning.

"Mrs. Powell, can you describe the car for me?"

The woman was in her thirties, blond hair perfectly coifed, small features. "Cute" was the word that came to Dove's mind.

Mrs. Powell discreetly wet her lips with her tongue. "Well, it was white." She smoothed down her pink skirt.

"What kind of car was it?"

"I'm afraid I don't know the models of cars," she said, in a *I'm just a girl* voice.

Dove loathed women like this, but she smiled and nodded as though she understood perfectly because she was one of the girls, too.

"How about the number of doors? Was it a two- or four-door car?"

Lisa Powell closed her eyes, scrunching them as if to show she was thinking, trying to remember. "I believe it had four doors."

That was right.

"And what time was this?"

"It was five-ten. I was coming home from the mall and looked at my watch to see how long it had taken me, what with all the traffic we have nowadays."

Fincham said, "What made you notice the car, Mrs. Powell?"

"It was parked in front of the empty lot on the block. We only have one. And it's right across from my house."

"Is it for sale?"

"Yes it is and I bet I know what you're going to ask next." She batted her lashes and grinned.

"What's that?" Dove asked, wishing she could give Fincham the gag sign.

"Why didn't I think it was a realtor's car?" She waited for acknowledgment of her intuitiveness and Dove nodded.

"I didn't think it was because the lot has no hiding spots, no trees or bushes and the like. And no one was there."

"There was no one visible on the lot and you'd know if there was?"

"That's correct."

"And did you notice when the car left?"

"Not really. But the next time I looked out the window, which was near seven when my husband comes home . . . he commutes . . . it was gone."

"Is there anything else you can tell us?"

"Well, what do you want to know?"

Dove glanced at Fincham and he raised his eyebrows.

"I want to know if there's anything else that you may have noticed that was out of place, anything odd that you may have observed?"

"Odd. Let's see." She took a swallow of coffee. "No. Nothing unusual."

"Is there any reason you didn't think that that car might

117

have belonged to someone visiting a neighbor?" Jack asked.

"Well, surely. No one visiting would have parked there. They would have parked in front of who they were visiting," she said, as though Fincham was the dumbest person she'd ever met.

Dove rose. "You've been very helpful, Mrs. Powell."

"I thank you, right much."

"Lieutenant Fincham will see you out."

"Oh. Yes. Of course," she said, embarrassed that she hadn't realized the interview was over. She stood and put her purse strap over her shoulder.

"If there's anything else you remember, you be sure to let us know."

"I surely will."

They said goodbye and Fincham escorted her out. When he returned, Dove asked what he thought.

"Well," he said, batting his lashes, "I surely think she's lying."

Dove laughed. "About which?"

"Everything to do with the car."

"She knew it was white and had four doors."

"Arizona, Walsh had that in her column today."

"Shit. I didn't know that."

"You got to start reading the paper." He flopped into the seat where Mrs. Powell had been.

"Makes me sick. I don't want to read about what a lousy job I'm doing."

"She's not saying that."

"She will."

"Whatever. Anyway, I think Powell is bored and wanted something to do."

"Hell, Jack, it fits your own theory."

"I know."

"The times were good."

"Everybody knows when Julie disappeared. And who's to question the time the car was no longer there."

"On the other hand she could be telling the truth, which could be why forensic found nothing."

"Okay, let's assume that's true. Now what?" Fincham asked.

"I don't know. With no semen for DNA we're up a creek."

"How do you know about no semen? You got Scruggs's report?"

"No, but I called him this morning to ask about that. Sorry I didn't tell you before, I forgot with Miss Virginia sitting here."

Fincham grunted, annoyed.

"Hey, I said I'm sorry."

"Okay. Now—" The phone rang and Dove picked it up. It was Jenkins. "Taylor got a cab sent to him at his motel. He's headed south."

"Toward the airport?"

"Yeah, could be. We're a couple cars behind him."

"Okay, if he goes to the airport and buys a ticket, wait until he starts to board the plane, then arrest him."

"Violates bail, right Sheriff?"

"Can't leave the state. Christ, I guess you'll have to find out where he's headed. If he's going to Richmond or some-place like that, well you have to leave him alone. Let me know if that's the case, if he's going somewhere within the state, and I'll notify law enforcement wherever he goes."

"Gotcha."

"And if he's going out of state, arrest him."

"Will do," she said.

Dove hung up, filled in Fincham.

"Think he *is* going to the airport?"

"Yeah, I do."

"How'd that bastard raise bail, anyway? No bondsman would be giving somebody from Florida money."

"Credit cards."

"Hate goddamn credit cards. So if he's running, why?" Fincham asked. "If the creep didn't do anything, why would he skip?"

"You mean you don't think he'd run on the shoplifting charge?"

"Hell, no. The guy doesn't have a record. What's he going to get? Thirty days or a suspended sentence is my bet."

"Think he knows that?"

"Maybe not exactly. But I bet he knows he's not going to get much. So, I'm asking, why run?"

"Because he killed Julie Boyer?"

"Give that woman a cigar. So what do we do now?"

"What do you mean?"

"While they're following Taylor, what do we do?"

"Wait, I guess. We'll know within half an hour."

"I'm going to find Buster Clark."

"Good idea. Just in case this perp didn't do it."

"I know he did, Arizona, but it's good to keep looking until we can charge him with it."

"Couldn't agree more," she said, making eye contact. They held it and she felt those damn butterflies in her stomach. She looked down at her desk. "Let me know."

"Course." He didn't move.

Eventually, Dove looked up. "What?"

"Bonnie Jo was wiped today. I talked to her about it because Kim said something to me."

"Aw, Jack. I'm sorry."

"Yeah. Well."

"How'd she respond?"

"Not good. Said she'd cut back, but you and I know that's not going to work for long."

"You mention AA?"

"Yeah. But no way."

"They say every person has to hit his or her bottom. Maybe that's what will have to happen."

"Just as long as she doesn't rack up the car, kill herself or somebody else. And I don't want the kids driving with her either. I guess I gotta tell them that."

"And her."

"That'll go over big."

The phone rang and she answered it. It was Jenkins saying Taylor was at the airport and they were right behind him. Dove told her to call when she knew where Taylor was going.

"I think we'll know something pretty soon, Jack."

"Okay." He stood up and stretched. "Tired. Beep me soon as you know anything."

"Course."

"See ya."

After Jack left she started once again to go through the file on the case, and when her mind began to wander toward Fincham she stopped and brought herself back to her work. She'd be damned if she was going to turn out to be one of those women who thought about nothing but the men in their lives. She laughed to herself. What men in her life?

She picked up the phone and called Kay Holiday.

"Hey, Lucia, long time no hear." Kay was one of the only people who pronounced her name correctly, which was probably one of the reasons Dove had loved her ever since college.

"I know, I'm sorry."

"Well, you've got a lot on your plate right now, don't you, kid?"

"You could say that."

"Just did."

"Funny."

"So, what's up, besides that?"

"Not a whole lot." She hadn't told Kay about her feelings for Jack and she wasn't sure why. Now she wanted to, but not on the phone. "I want to have a drink or lunch, but anything I schedule would have to be tentative."

"Okay by me. A drink would be more likely, wouldn't it?"

"Yes."

"Let me look at my calendar. Hey, how about tomorrow?"

"It's open now, but . . ."

"Lucia, I know the drill," Kay said. "So unless I hear otherwise, let's meet at O'Donnell's."

"Good."

"You okay?"

"I . . . yeah, I guess. But I need to talk. And I miss you."

"Miss you, too, toots."

They said their goodbyes.

Lucia thought about their long friendship, that began their junior year in college when Kay transferred from Douglass in New Jersey. She'd been failing everything and Elizabeth Washington was the only school that would take her. So much for E.W.

They'd met in an English Lit class and it was love at first sight. Kay had been Kay Walters then; later she became Kay Meyers, Kay Summers and now she was Holiday. Danny, her husband, was a terrific guy and Lucia hoped this one would last. It had been Kay's longest so far.

122

Bethany was buzzing her when the door flew open and McQuigg stood in the doorway, his face a shade of red that broadcast fury.

Dove stared at him while she told Bethany it was okay.

"You ever hear of knocking, Agent McQuigg?"

"Cut the crap. You interviewed a witness without telling me."

"Did I?"

He slammed the door behind him and strode over to her desk, put his hands on the edge and bent over so that his face was only about a foot from hers. "You'd better start cooperating on this stuff, Sheriff, or I'm going to get you thrown off this case."

"Sit down," she said, evenly.

He took a moment and then did.

"I didn't know you wanted to be in on every little thing." She wondered how he knew. Surely their questioning of Mrs. Powell wasn't on the Internet.

"I thought I made my position clear. And I don't call questioning a witness a little thing."

"I thought you'd be too busy for this one."

"Not too busy for anything. This is a case I've been assigned to, don't you understand that?"

She nodded. "This was a woman who thought she'd seen Taylor's car parked on her street, which isn't that far from the Boyer house."

"And?"

Dove shrugged. "Maybe she did. If so, I'm not even sure it means anything."

"And where's Taylor now?"

"At the airport. I have my people on him."

The color of McQuigg's face was draining, changing back to his natural pinkish white.

123

"If he tries to buy a ticket we'll arrest him." The phone rang. "That's probably Jenkins now."

She picked it up, listened, then replaced the receiver. "He was trying to leave the state. They're bringing him in."

"I'll wait," he said.

"Well, at least we can ask him why he was parked on Kellogg Street."

"I'll ask him," he stated.

"I thought you wanted to observe," she said, trying to keep her temper tamped down.

"I'll ask him," he repeated.

And in her mind she told him to go fuck himself.

Chapter Thirteen

Once again they were in the interrogation room with Taylor: Dove, Fincham, McQuigg and Taylor's lawyer, Wittman.

Dove could tell that Jack was furious about McQuigg running the show.

McQuigg asked, "Why were you going to Texas?"

Taylor looked defeated, like an old rug. "What's the point?"

"What's the point of what?"

"I know what you're gonna do. You're gonna get me for Julie's murder."

"Mr. Taylor, if you didn't do it, you have nothing to worry about."

"Oh, sure. Think I don't know? Think I don't know how many guys get put away, they're innocent?"

McQuigg said, "It happens, but not very often. And it hasn't happened here."

"Here?"

"Did you kill Julie Boyer?"

"See?" He turned to Wittman. "See what they're doing?"

Darryl Wittman said, "Are you charging my client with the Boyer murder, because if you're not, he doesn't have to answer any questions pertaining to that case."

"No, we're not charging him."

"You don't have to answer the question, Mr. Taylor," Wittman said.

"But I didn't kill her."

"Mr. Taylor, please."

Dove said, "You're not being charged with anything other than the charge you already have. And, of course, trying to jump bail."

McQuigg glared at her for speaking. Dove glanced at Fincham. He looked about to boil over and she hoped he'd keep himself in check. She'd already made a mistake by speaking to Taylor; wouldn't be a surprise if Jack did the same, or worse.

"So am I to understand that you were going to Texas because you were afraid we were going to charge you with Julie Boyer's murder?"

"That's right."

"You were willing to jump bail, lose your thousand?"

"You bet. Let me ask you this. How come you were watching me for a shoplifting charge?"

Dove assumed this was more cop show knowledge.

"We watch everyone on bail," McQuigg lied.

"Bullshit."

"Hey," Fincham said.

"What?"

"Watch the language."

"Lieutenant," McQuigg said. "I'm conducting this interview."

Fincham started to say something, pressed his lips together, stopped.

Taylor said, "Look, you don't have the manpower to watch everybody. You were watching me because you think I did the murder."

"If you thought we were watching you, Mr. Taylor, why'd you try to skip?"

"Took my chances."

126

"Is there anything else?" Wittman asked.

"Just a few more things, about his car."

"His car? How does his car pertain to shoplifting or skipping on bail?"

McQuigg said, "It doesn't. But I want to know why he parked his car on Kellogg Street the day Boyer disappeared."

"Good luck," Wittman said. "If that's all, I request that the prisoner be returned to his cell."

There was nothing they could do.

Dove couldn't help noticing that Taylor didn't protest the question, which she was sure he'd do if it wasn't true, no matter what his lawyer said.

They left Wittman with his client, sent in a deputy to take him to his cell and the three of them went into her office.

"I hate lawyers," Dove said.

"What now?" Fincham asked.

"We keep digging."

McQuigg looked at some notes. "Wasn't there a Buster Clark you were going to go after?"

"I haven't been able to locate him yet."

"Keep trying," McQuigg snapped.

Fincham gave him a cursory nod.

"And you, Sheriff?"

"Scruggs is calling me with his report in about two hours. Didn't you say there was a murder in Florida with the same MO?"

"Yes. So?"

"Taylor is from Key Largo. Where was the Florida murder committed?"

"Miami. Murders there everyday, but this one matched," McQuigg said.

"If there's nothing in Scruggs's report to link Taylor, I'm

going to Florida. I assume you'll give me the info on the Miami murder."

"Sure," McQuigg said. "But I've been all over that."

"Not since we had Taylor. I want to talk to people about him. And I want to see if I can find out where he was on the day of the Miami murder."

McQuigg gave her the date the girl was murdered.

"I'm impressed," she said. "You have all the murder dates in your head?"

"In fact, I do. I'm good at this job, Sheriff. Time you accepted that."

Dove didn't respond to his boast. "Anyway, I'm going to Florida if necessary."

"Can't you send Steffey or somebody else?" Fincham said.

She was confused. Why did he care if she went?

"I mean," he said, "why should you have to do that?"

"I want to."

"I think that's a good idea," McQuigg said.

Now Dove doubted it if he thought it was a good idea.

McQuigg walked to the door. "Keep me posted on everything. And I mean that." He left.

Fincham said, "What a shit-heel. How could you—"

"Don't go there," Dove warned.

"Sorry. This thing about going to Florida. You might need help," he said, looking at his shoes.

"You think I should take Jenkins with me?"

He looked up and straight at her. "I think you should take me with you."

She couldn't say anything for a moment. Then, both delighted and frightened she said, "Leave Hutt in charge?"

"Why not? I mean, Arizona, you know the Keys?"

"No. Do you?"

"I was there once on vacation. Thing is, there's a lot of them and maybe Taylor lived different places."

What he was saying made absolutely no sense, but she responded as though it did. "You have a point."

He nodded once and smiled as if he'd won something at an auction. "So when do we go?"

"Tomorrow morning. Find Clark now."

"Right."

When he was gone she let out her breath, not realizing she'd been holding it. Was she crazy? It was clear Fincham didn't want her to go, leave him behind . . . without her? Yes. That's what it was. Why? Listen, Dove, she said to herself, don't play games. You know why. He's interested, just as you thought he was. So going away together could be dangerous. Dangerous? It was suicidal. But she wanted it, didn't she? She wanted Fincham. So what if he was married? He wasn't in love with his wife, and it wasn't as though she'd seduced him or anything.

Oh, stop. She'd always had the lowest opinion of women who went out with married men because they were hurting another woman and that didn't sit right with her. But she could be in control here. Nothing had to happen. If she didn't give him ideas, the trip could be what it was meant to be, part of the job. And that, by God, was what she was going to make it.

Fincham lit up as soon as he got in his car. His hands were shaking. Jesus, a trip with Arizona. What would he tell B.J.? The truth. There was nothing wrong with that. And what would happen in the Keys? Not a damn thing. So why did he have this feeling she was interested? Wishful thinking?

He turned the key in the ignition, started the car.

The first place he went was Clark's trailer. As he'd thought yesterday, it looked like it had been hit by a train. The middle was inverted, the ends forming a U. The thing was painted aqua. Fortunately, the door was near one end. It was painted yellow. Yesterday no one had been there, but today he could hear the sounds of a TV or radio. Fincham knocked, waited about thirty seconds then knocked again. This time he heard footsteps.

The door was opened by a wrecked woman in a stained pink bathrobe. She asked him what he wanted.

He showed his shield and asked if Buster was home.

"What'd the little shit do now?" With a dirty hand she puffed on a cigarette, blew a plume of smoke straight at him.

Fincham said, "He didn't do anything. I just want to talk to him."

"Selling them weeds again, I bet." She swiped at her nose and Fincham could see the black fingernails. There was no telling the age of this woman.

"I'm not interested in that," he said.

"Well, it's neither here or there because he ain't home."

"You his mother?"

"What of it?"

"Nothing. You know where he is?"

"Nope." She started to close the door.

"When's the last time you saw him?"

"Couldn't tell ya. But it's been awhile." She shut the door.

Fincham considered telling the woman he wanted to come in and search, figuring she wouldn't know he needed a warrant, but he believed that Buster wasn't there.

Walking back to the car he was careful to avoid the muddy gulches he'd stepped in on his approach. Still, his soles were caked with mud and he banged them against the inside bottom of the car door before he swung them into place. Some of the dirt stuck. His car would be a mess before the day was over.

He knew of a few kid hangouts and decided to start with The Red Barn, which was big and nasty, selling subs and pizza and catering to a wild crowd. It was a five-minute drive.

When he got there three motorcycles, plus a bunch of ratty looking cars, were parked outside.

Fincham patted his hip as he walked toward the door. Strange he always did that since he knew his gun was there. He guessed it was an unconscious security check. He could hear the loud music before he went in. It was rap, something he didn't understand and hated.

Inside it smelled of beer, onions, garlic and a touch of tomato sauce. The place had been a barn and although it had been converted it still had the same spacious sense. There was a long counter where people could sit and eat or drink. Along one wall were booths with beige vinyl-covered seats. And cheap wooden tables and chairs were in another area. The rest of the room was open and kids danced there or jumped up and down, which is what it always looked like to him.

A jukebox was flashing its lights and a man's voice was saying words Fincham couldn't understand. The thing was blasting.

When he looked around he could see that some of the patrons were staring at him with suspicion. Guess he was obviously a cop. Funny how law-abiding citizens appraised him with no misgivings, but the ones with criminal intent always knew.

Fincham walked over to the counter. A man with

salmon-colored hair and a ruddy complexion said, "What'd you like?"

"Can you tell me if Buster Clark is here?" With so many watching he didn't want to show his shield if he didn't have to.

"Who's asking?" He wiped big red hands on a filthy towel.

"I'm Lieutenant Fincham, Sheriff's Office, Snowden."

"Let's see your badge."

"I'd rather not alarm the patrons," Fincham said.

"Fuck you then," the man said and started walking away.

"All right. I'll show you."

With great skepticism in his hooded eyes the bartender turned back, folded his freckled arms across his chest and waited.

Surreptitiously, Jack took out his shield, flipped the cover back and showed it.

The man reached out but Fincham pulled it back. "You can look, chum, but you can't touch."

"Oh, sorry, *sir*." Leaning over, he examined the shield. "Shiny," he said.

"Satisfied?"

"Yup."

Fincham put it away. "So, Buster Clark here?"

"How the hell should I know? You think I know the name of every bum who walks in here?"

The man had put him through some paces all the time knowing he wasn't going to answer. "Listen, pal, you know who these kids are so don't give me any shit."

"I don't know any Buster Clark," he said loud enough to be heard over the music.

Jack waited a few seconds then whirled around scanning

the room. A guy fitting Clark's description was running for the door. Fincham pursued him. He was out the door before Jack reached it.

Outside, the boy jumped into a rusted Ford, which had been pumped up so it was high over the wheels.

Jack pulled his gun. "Stop right there."

But the driver engaged the engine, and with a roar backed up, turned and started from the lot.

Jack shot at the tires, missed. He ran to his car and as he turned around he put the blue twirling light on the roof. Several cars on the highway kept him from exiting, either not noticing or not caring about the light.

Finally he pulled out, tires screeching. He could see Clark three cars ahead. He hit the radio and gave the information, hoping there would be some cruisers nearby who would help him.

The car in front of Fincham pulled over to the right to let him pass, and the next car did the same. Now he had no one between him and Clark and he pushed the gas pedal down to close the gap. Clark sped up.

Fincham looked down at the speedometer and saw they were doing eighty. A sign showed that an exit was coming up. He had to be ready for Clark to take it.

But instead a cruiser came out of an entrance to the highway, siren going and put himself between Fincham and Clark.

Then Clark's car seemed to spin out of control, crossed the middle island, missed an oncoming car and kept going until it glanced off a tree and came to a stop.

Both the cruiser and Jack followed his path. The oncoming cars stopped for them. They pulled up behind Clark's car. The deputy and Jack, guns drawn, approached cautiously. The deputy got to the driver's door first.

"Out of the car, hands up."

Fincham waited. When nothing happened he moved closer. "Can you see in the window?" he asked.

The deputy moved forward a few inches. "Can now. Suspect looks like he might be unconscious. I'm going to open the door."

"Careful," Jack warned.

"Don't worry." He placed his back against the rear door, reached with his left hand and popped open the driver's door. Then moved slowly, gun in front of him. "Out of the car, hands up. He's out cold."

Fincham approached, saw blood on Clark's forehead and closed eyes.

The deputy moved in to feel Clark's neck pulse. "He's alive, but barely."

"Shit," Fincham said.

Chapter Fourteen

Fincham and Dove stood in the hospital hallway outside of Buster Clark's room. Depressed and angry, Fincham could barely speak.

"Jack, you have to snap out of this. It wasn't your fault."

"Yeah, yeah, it's just . . . hell, I don't know, Arizona, seems like everything about this case is one big screw-up."

"Listen, this is the bare beginning. The fact that Clark ran tells us something."

"Like what?"

"Oh, stop it, Jack." Dove wanted to shake him. But she also wanted to put her arms around him and give the man some comfort.

"Sorry."

"No need to be sorry. Just buck up."

"Yeah, you're right." He looked at her and smiled.

Sweet Jesus, she thought. I have it bad if his smile can do this to me. "Okay, Lieutenant. When the doc comes out we'll see what's what and we'll question the guy."

"What about McQuigg?"

"I called him. He's sending another agent."

"Oh, for chrissakes."

"Frankly, I'm surprised we haven't met Agent Krause before."

"Hard to believe McQuigg would let someone else do this instead of him."

"Out in the field, thank God."

"So what does it mean? We can't question Clark until Krause gets here?"

"That's what it means, Jack. You have to accept this."

"Yeah. And what if Clark stays unconscious and nobody can question him?"

Dove said, "What if it rains monkeys tomorrow?"

He gave a tiny snort for a laugh. "I'm serious."

"I know you are but we have to wait and see and there's no point in writing scripts before we get a report."

He nodded. "Speaking of reports, you get anything from Scruggs?"

"I'm afraid I did. The body was clean as a whistle in terms of anything that could be used for DNA. No rogue hairs, nothing."

"How could that be?"

"Only one way, Jack. Whoever did it knew what he was doing."

"You telling me that that wimp Taylor knew what he was doing?"

"No, I'm not telling you that."

"Clark? Clark would know?"

"Probably not."

"So what are you saying then, Arizona?"

"I don't know. But it seems to me that neither Taylor or Clark would be that smart. Still, they could be lucky."

Fincham rolled his eyes as if to say that was a long shot.

"Yeah," she said. "I know."

"So we got nobody then."

"We have both guys. It's not over yet."

The doctor came out of Clark's room. He was a young man with premature gray hair. His face was egg-shaped, eyes set too close together. Dove read his name tag.

"Dr. Eisenberg, how is Mr. Clark?"

He looked at her as though he was smelling something bad. "He's conscious now. He has a concussion, but that's all. We'll release him tomorrow."

"Then we can speak to him?" Fincham asked.

Eisenberg glanced at one then the other, finally nodded and walked away.

"Friendly cuss, isn't he?" Dove whispered.

"They all think they're goddamn gods."

"Let's go in."

"What about Krause?"

"Shit. I forgot."

"Is he on his way at least?"

"Yeah."

"We going to Florida?"

Dove couldn't help feeling as though they were talking about a romantic getaway. She reminded herself to be professional. "Like I said, didn't get anything from Scruggs, so unless the Clark interview gets us somewhere, I say we go."

Fincham seemed pleased. They were looking at each other when a voice interrupted them.

"Excuse me, you Sheriff Dove?"

She turned toward the speaker. He was obviously Krause. FBI agents were so transparent.

He was tall and wore his inky black hair regulation style. His pale blue eyes were as lifeless as a frozen pond on a gloomy day. Thin, unforgiving lips were above a pointy chin.

They all shook hands and went in to interview Clark.

Buster was in a room with three other patients. He was lying down, his head flat, no pillow. The trio stood over him. Slowly, he turned toward them. When he saw Fincham he groaned, holding his stomach as if that was where he hurt.

137

Fincham said, "We know what your injury is, Clark. We've spoken to the doctor."

"What the fuck they know?" He held his stomach and groaned again. "I'm dyin' here."

"Right," Dove said.

"I'll do this," Krause said. "Why were you running away from Lieutenant Fincham?"

"Who says I was runnin' away? I was leavin', that's all. Goin' to see my girlfriend."

"Julie Boyer?"

"Julie? She's dead, man. And she was not never my girlfriend."

"Who's your girlfriend, Buster?"

"I don' have to tell you that. Whatcha wanna know that for?"

Fincham said, "Listen, Clark, you're under suspicion. I'm going to Mirandize you now."

"Lieutenant," Krause said. He turned back to Clark. "You know what Mirandize means, don't you?" He straightened his very straight, solid blue tie.

Clark didn't say anything for a few moments, then grunted.

"Is that a yes?"

"Yeah."

"Read him his rights, Fincham," Krause ordered.

Dove saw Jack tighten and hoped he wouldn't lose it. But Fincham did what he was told. "You understand?"

"Yeah."

Both Dove and Fincham knew Clark had heard it many times before.

"You want a lawyer?" Krause asked.

"Shit. Know I should, but I ain't got nothin' to hide."

"You can have one if you want one."

Beautiful Rage

"Nah. Go ahead, ask me."

"What's the name of your girlfriend."

"Ask me somethin' else."

"Cut the wisecracking," Krause said.

"I don' wanna answer that."

"Then you weren't going to see your girlfriend when Lieutenant Fincham was chasing you?"

"No."

"So, why were you running?"

"I was scared. I knew you guys would come lookin' for me, cause of Julie. It was stupid. I don' know where I thought I was goin'."

"Why'd you think we were looking for you?" Krause asked.

"Cause everybody thought she was my girlfriend and she wasn't."

Dove and Fincham exchanged a look.

Then Dove said, "Why'd everybody think that, Buster, if it wasn't true?"

"They just did."

Krause nodded for her to go on. Dove guessed that was because he knew she was more familiar with the details than he was.

"You were seen with her a lot."

"Yeah. I know. That's what I mean. Ask me somethin' else except girlfriends." He slowly smoothed down his scrawny mustache.

"Where were you on the night Julie Boyer was abducted and murdered?"

"What time we talkin' about?"

"Between four-thirty and eight p.m."

"How can I remember that?" he whined.

"You'd better remember, Clark," Krause said.

"Or what?"

139

"Or you're in big trouble."

"Well, I know this much: I wasn't nowheres near Julie."

"So where were you?"

"Probably hangin' out."

"By yourself?"

"Lemme think."

"Yeah, you take your time," Krause said.

Dove motioned Fincham and Krause toward the door. "We'll be right back," she said to Clark. "You keep thinking who you were with when you were hanging out, okay?"

"I'm thinkin'," he answered.

Standing near the door, the sheriff whispered to the two men, "It's obvious all his evasions have to do with the girlfriend."

"Right. So how do we get him to give up her name?" Fincham asked.

"We scare the bejesus out of him."

"All right," Krause said. "Do your damnedest." He almost smiled.

They went back to Clark's bedside.

"You remembered anything?" Fincham asked.

"Hangin' out's all I can remember."

"In that case we're going to have to charge you with Boyer's murder," Dove said.

"What?" He quickly swiveled his head and groaned authentically. "Wait a minute."

"We're waiting."

"You can't do that. I never was with her."

"Then where were you, Clark?"

"Shit. I was with my girlfriend from four to about six."

"Guess we've come full circle, Buster. So give us her name," Dove said.

"Ah, fuck. Whatcha gonna do with her name?"

"We're going to check your alibi with her. You know that."

"Yeah. That's the trouble."

"Meaning?"

"She don' want her parents to know cause they'd shit bricks."

"Give us her name, Buster, or you're in trouble big time."

He silently deliberated, then said in a whisper, "Augusta Fleming."

Augusta was crying while her mother stood over her. Dove, Fincham and Krause sat at the kitchen table staring at the girl.

Sally Fleming's face was crimson with anger. "Stop that uproar, Augusta, and answer."

Through her hands, which she held against her face, she said, "What do you want me to say?"

"Answer the G.D. question. Who's your boyfriend?"

"Chuck. You know that."

"Then why are you sobbing around like that?" Sally looked at the others. "Sheriff, I don't know what's wrong with her. Her boyfriend is the son of my husband's business associate, Roger Garnett."

Dove said softly, "Augusta, if Chuck Garnett is your boyfriend and your mother and father know this, I don't understand why you're crying. On the other hand, if Chuck isn't your boyfriend and someone else is, someone your parents don't know about, then I understand why you're upset."

"Who?" Sally yelled. "Who don't we know about?"

This made Augusta cry louder.

Dove looked at the long, black-painted nails covering the girl's eyes. Her brown hair hung on either side of the small face like protective covering. When Dove had first gotten a look at the girl, before the crying had begun, she'd thought she was sweet, attractive. The pink cotton sweater she wore showed that she was well-developed and had a small waist. Augusta hadn't gone to school today in deference to Julie's death.

The sheriff tried again. "You have to tell us, Augusta. No one will hurt you, isn't that right, Mrs. Fleming?"

"Well, of course no one's going to hurt her." She puffed frantically on a cigarette and the image of Bette Davis came to Dove's mind.

"Augusta. Stop it. Answer these officers. Now."

"You'll kill me."

Sally Fleming was clearly embarrassed by this accusation. "Don't be ridiculous. I'm not going to do a thing."

"You promise?" she snuffled.

"Oh, really. Yes. I promise." She rolled her eyes at the others.

"There are witnesses," Augusta said.

"Quit. You'd think we locked you in dark closets or something."

"I know you'll go ballistic."

"Just quit it now."

Augusta stopped crying, let her hands slide down from her face, which was tear-stained and red. Sally swiped a tissue from a decorated box on a counter and handed it to her daughter. She took it and blew her nose.

Dove engaged the girl's tearful brown eyes. "It'll be okay, Augusta."

The teenager looked at Dove as though gauging the truth of the statement. Then she said, "He's a nice boy.

People don't think he is because of, well . . . I think it's because he's poor. But he's real nice when you get to know
him. Gentle and kind. Loves animals."

"Oh, Augusta. Loves animals." Sally couldn't stop herself. "Who is it, Ted Bundy?"

"Who?" Augusta asked.

Dove sighed inwardly at the lack of knowledge this kid
had. But they were all like that. Would Clare have been that
way?

Sally said, "Just answer the G.D. question."

"Your question?" Augusta asked.

"No. The sheriff's question. I'm fast losing my patience
here."

"Sheriff, is something going to happen to him?" Augusta
asked.

"Happen to who?" she responded.

"My boyfriend."

"How can I know that if I don't know who he is?"

"Oh, God. I just know you're going to get him in
trouble."

Dove felt the girl was about to start crying again and
wanted to curb that, so she said in a stern tone, "Augusta,
tell us his name."

It was as though Dove had smacked her on the back and
the words came flying out of Augusta's mouth like pieces of
stuck food. "Buster Clark."

"Oh my God," Sally said.

"You don't know him, Mother. You always said, don't
judge a book by its cover."

"How about his rap sheet? Is that what they call it,
Sheriff?"

Dove nodded. "Augusta, you told Lieutenant Fincham
that you were with some girlfriends during the time Julie

disappeared. Do you still want to stick to that?"

"No. I don't. I was with Buster."

"Where?" Sally demanded.

"We were parked in his car down on Sterling. It's a dead end." She turned toward her mother. "But nothing happened. We were just talking."

"Wait until your father hears this . . . I . . ."

The officers thanked Sally and Augusta. When they were outside, they could still hear the voices raging at one another.

"Hate to destroy and run," Dove said to the men.

They both laughed, making Krause look human.

Fincham said, "Yeah, well, what's really destroyed is a case against Buster."

"Ain't it the truth," she said.

"What's your next step?" Krause asked.

"We're going to Florida tomorrow, check on Taylor further. Especially since you had one of these murders in Miami. Agent McQuigg has approved it." As if she needed approval from him.

Krause nodded. "Okay, keep in touch." He walked toward his car.

"You make the reservations?" Fincham asked.

"No, not yet. I will when we get back to the house. And I have to break a date," she said, remembering her plans with Kay tomorrow.

Fincham opened his mouth to speak and Dove knew he wanted to ask what date, but didn't dare. It made her feel good.

Chapter Fifteen

Should she? Dove wondered, take a bathing suit with her. It wasn't a vacation but they wouldn't be working every minute. And it was Florida. Still, the thought of Jack seeing her in one made her edgy. This was stupid, she decided. She was in great shape, and if he didn't like what he saw, tough. The suit was a black one-piece and she threw it in the suitcase.

Then she remembered she had to call Kay and break their date. How many times had she done this to her?

"So," Kay said, "we're not meeting. What else is new?"

"I'm so sorry."

"Lucia, I know this is part of the deal. You don't have to apologize. You have a helluva case on your hands."

"The thing is I'm going to Florida later today." She knew she didn't have to explain, also that she didn't have to ask her not to repeat this to anyone. "The Keys."

"Will you have time to play?"

Suddenly she had to tell her friend. "Kay, I'm taking one of my lieutenants with me. Jack Fincham."

"And?"

"I think I'm in love with him."

"Well, hell, toots, what's with the grim sound? Hallelujah, I say."

"He's married."

"Ooops."

Dove filled her in quickly.

Kay said, "So do you think he's interested in you?"

Embarrassed, she felt like a teen. "I think so. I think it's why he wanted to go on the trip with me."

"Lucia, if the man is interested and so are you, you'll find out. The fact that he's married to a drunk, whom he doesn't love, makes all the difference. He's going to divorce her, isn't he?"

"I think so. He's worried about losing his kids though."

They talked some more and when Dove hung up, she didn't feel calmer about Jack, but she did feel less like a snake.

For the moment she put it all out of her mind, continued to pack and thought about the case. Buster Clark was now off the list so that left Lyle Taylor. Even though nothing forensic had come up with so far had linked him to Boyer that didn't mean they wouldn't find something later. Besides, it was all they had at this point and she felt obligated to pursue this one lead.

The phone rang. It was Gill Hutt.

"Found Boyer's clothes."

"Where?"

"Buried in a hole way in the woods."

"You send them to forensic?" she asked.

"They're on their way."

"Nice going."

"Thanks. So when are you leaving?"

She looked at her watch. "In about three hours."

"Okay. I got the number where you're staying and I'll call you if forensic comes up with anything."

"Right. Keep everybody running down any possible lead."

"We don't have a one, Sheriff."

"Yeah, I know. But something might come up."

146

"We'll keep up to speed. Don't you worry and you and Fincham have a good time."

Dove cringed. "Hutt, we're not going on a vacation."

"Sorry. Guess I shouldn't have said that. Hope you find what you're looking for."

"Thanks."

When they hung up she realized there'd been a tone in his *hope you find what you're looking for* that was disquieting. Did the whole office think something was going on between her and Jack? Well, so what? There wasn't. She packed some shorts, a few Gap T-shirts and two skirts, one nice blouse, a pair of sandals, then zipped up the case.

Finally she got in the shower and told herself to stop worrying. They were going to solve this murder come hell or high water.

"You bastard," Bonnie Jo said.

"What the hell you talking about, B.J.?"

"Now you're going away with her?"

Fincham looked at his wife. Hung over again. "We're on a case. Nothing is happening between me and my boss, okay?"

"No, it's not okay. You go to Florida with her and I . . . *we* won't be here when you get back!"

"You crazy? What should I do, refuse to go? Quit my job?"

"I'm just sayin', Jack."

"Well what you're saying is nuts." He felt terrible because even though what he was telling her was the truth, he knew what was in his heart. "This is my job, B.J., and you can't threaten me, take the kids anyplace because you haven't got anything going for you."

"That's all you know."

"What's that supposed to mean?"

She gave him a look, smiled. Then, as she tried to bring her cup to her mouth, she sloshed some coffee on her night-gown with a shaking hand. "Shit." She put the cup down and held the material away from her.

"You burn yourself?" he asked.

"No. And no thanks to you." Bonnie Jo turned her back on him and went to the sink.

"What's that mean, no thanks to me? I didn't spill the goddamn coffee on you. You're drunk, hung over."

"I am not," she yelled, whirling around.

"You're goddamn hung over, B.J. Look at you, you look like hell and you're shaking all over. What's that about if you're not hung over?"

"I've had enough of this." She started walking out of the kitchen and he grabbed her. "So what's this now, physical abuse?"

"Oh, shut up. I'm telling you, B.J., you take our kids anywhere and I'm suing for custody and I'll win."

Their faces were inches apart.

"Yeah, well I'll sue for adultery."

"Prove it."

"Don't think I won't."

"You're full of it."

"Leggo of me, Jack."

"Don't do anything stupid. And I don't want the kids riding with you either."

"Go to fucking hell," she said, and pulled out of his grasp.

After she'd left the room, Fincham realized he was shaking with rage. He couldn't remember being this angry at B.J. before. Maybe he shouldn't go. It was his idea, after all, and Arizona would understand if he told her why. But he wanted to go.

And it wasn't just to be with her alone. It was to get away. He couldn't stand watching his wife destroy herself day after day. He needed to get out of here. But would she leave, take the kids? Would they go? He looked at the wall clock. If he left now he'd have enough time to get to the kids before meeting Arizona. He had to talk with them.

Dove paced the living room. It wasn't like Jack to be late. She thought about phoning him at home, but didn't want to have to talk to his wife if she was there. If she remembered right, this was Bonnie Jo's day off. Still, if he didn't come soon she'd have to call.

Ten minutes later she picked up the phone and called Fincham's home number.

Damned if his wife didn't answer. She said hello and asked for Jack.

"Don't think I don't know what the hell is going on, Sheriff. Because I do. And you and Jack can go fuck yourselves." The phone banged down.

Great, Dove thought. Now what was this?

Jack pulled in the drive and honked the horn twice.

She picked up her suitcase, opened the front door, turned the latch and left. In the car she could see his face was stony. She put on her seat belt and he pulled out, headed for I-95.

At least five minutes passed before she said anything. "What's up?"

"Nothing."

"Oh, okay," she said.

"It's Bonnie Jo, of course."

Dove wondered if she should tell him, decided she should. "I called the house when you were late."

"She give you any trouble?"

"I don't know if I'd characterize it as trouble. She said she knew what was going on, we should go fuck ourselves and hung up on me."

"Jesus. I'm sorry, Arizona. And I'm sorry I was late. I had to see the kids at school and it took longer than I thought it would."

"So what's happening?"

He told her about B.J.'s threats but didn't go into her accusations, although from what Dove said, it was clear she could figure it out.

"Oh, Jack. What a mess."

"Yeah. I think when we get back I have to leave her, sue for custody of the kids."

Her heart thumped. He'd be a free man then, even before the divorce.

"What do you think of that idea?" he asked.

She didn't know what to say because her response was so colored by what she wanted herself.

"Arizona? You hear me?"

"Sure. I'm thinking about it. Let me ask you something. Do you really believe she's an alcoholic?"

"You kidding? Course she is."

"And the kids? What did they say when you saw them, told them not to ride with her?"

Fincham took a cigarette from his pocket, held it between his teeth but didn't light it. "Jack Jr. stared at me, hostile as hell. Then he nodded, walked away. I don't know. Kim was different because she knows."

"Because she's female."

"Whatever. Anyway, she agreed."

"Jack, you can light your cigarette. This is your car."

"What about secondhand smoke?"

"It's your car," she said again.

"You sure you don't mind?"

"Go ahead."

He did. Took a deep drag and let it out with the sigh of a contented smoker. "So you didn't answer. What do you think of my plan?"

"If you really aren't in love with her anymore and you honestly think she's a drunk and a danger to the children, then I think you'd be doing the right thing." And she did. She'd say the same to anyone in his position.

"Yeah. Good. That's what I'm going to do."

They rode in silence for awhile, Jack smoking, Dove trying not to choke. Then she told him about the discovery of Boyer's clothes.

"This is somebody who knew what he was doing, Arizona. Bet anything he made her undress and bury the clothes herself. Forensic won't find anything on those clothes to link the killer."

"I think you're right. But they had to get there and maybe there'll be something from the vehicle they used."

"That's possible. Unless they walked."

"Don't you think that would've been a long walk? And the risk of someone seeing them, don't know."

"Guess we'll see."

"Guess we will," she said, and rolled down her window.

They landed in Marathon, the only airport in the Keys, rented a compact car and headed for Coconut Key.

"Palm trees," Dove said, sounding childlike.

Laughing, Fincham said, "You expected redwoods?"

"No. It's just that I've never seen them before."

"Well, that's what they got around here, Arizona. Lots of palm trees."

"God it's beautiful."

"Yeah. Not bad."

They drove through one key after another until they reached Coconut, which was almost near the end of the Keys.

"What does it mean, Mile Marker?" she asked about the signs, which were all along the road.

"Not sure."

"First thing we should do is get a place to stay."

Dove thought he sounded strained. "Right."

They followed some signs to Point Lookout and then found a motel on the beach that didn't look like it would cost too much. They parked and when they got out of the car they realized how hot it was.

"Sweet Jesus," she said. "I want to take off all my clothes." She was immediately embarrassed and felt her face flush, but didn't look at Fincham as they went into the office.

Motel Water's Edge looked like it had seen better days. The office counter was made of Formica and the man behind it appeared as though he was too.

He looked up from the Tom Clancy paperback he was reading. "Help you?"

Fincham said, "We'd like a room. Two rooms."

The clerk snickered, stood up. His comb-over came from both sides and laced across the top of his head like fine fingers. He wore a flowered short-sleeve shirt over khaki shorts. His legs were like hairy stalks.

"Two rooms, huh?"

"That's right," Fincham said.

"Adjoining?"

"It doesn't matter."

"Two floors here. So it don't matter if one's on one floor the other on the other?"

"No," Dove said. "It doesn't matter."

The clerk looked at her for the first time. "Gotcha. Let's see what we got here." He riffled through a book. "Okay then. Got one on the second floor one on the first. Singles then, right?"

"Right."

"Okay then. How you payin'?"

"Credit card," she answered.

"And you, sir?"

"I'm paying for both." She felt incredibly compromised and for no reason. This little weasel was making it as hard as he could. "We're from the sheriff's office in Snowden, Virginia."

"Oh, yeah?"

"I'm the sheriff of Snowden County." She felt foolish but she showed him her shield.

He reached out for it and she gave it to him. Holding it up to his eyes as though he had a jeweler's loupe, he examined it for a long time. Then gave it back to her. "Uh huh. You down here investigating a crime, somethin'?"

"That's right," she answered, putting her shield back in her bag. She indicated Fincham. "This is my lieutenant."

"Oh, I getcha now." But he smiled, implying he didn't believe a word, shield or no shield.

They'd have to live with his suspicions. Who cared anyway? she thought.

"Okay, then. Yer the sheriff lady, guess you get to pick which floor you want to be on."

"The first," she said. She didn't want to lug a bag upstairs and she wanted this to be over.

"Okay then. Sign here. Might as well give me your C.C. so I can run it through while you register."

She dug in her bag and found the little black holder,

pulled out her Visa and handed it to him.

The man turned away and she looked at Jack. He smiled and she knew she'd better go back to signing the register, because if she didn't they'd both start laughing and wouldn't be able to stop. She signed, then gave the pen to Jack.

"Where?" he said.

"Got me."

"Where do I sign?" he called out to the clerk.

"Next line down." His back was to them and he had a phone to his ear. Finally he said into it, "Okay, then," and put it down. When he came back to the counter he said to Dove, "C.C.'s good."

"Oh, joy," she said, unable to stop herself.

"What's that?"

"Nothing." She held out her hand for the card.

He gave it to her, then handed them each a key and said approximately where the rooms were. "Have a nice day," he said.

Dove said, "That's the plan."

Back at the car they got out their bags.

Fincham said, "Jesus, it was like getting into Fort Knox or something."

"Hope the rooms are in a little better shape than he is."

They went to their rooms, agreeing to meet back at the car in half an hour.

When Dove got inside her room, she realized she was on the beach, on the ocean. It didn't much matter what the room was like with a view like this.

It was clear nobody'd been in it for awhile because it smelled stale and was hot as hell. She quickly found the air conditioner, which she set at the highest level. It wheezed to life, then made a sound which was worse than the garbage truck that picked up the trash from police headquarters.

Even though it was a great view, she couldn't have it and have privacy so she shut the blinds. She flicked on a light. The place was furnished with a double bed, a once white, now gray chenille spread, one motel style dresser and an orange chair. She wondered why, no matter where you went, they were always orange? And the carpet was a stained mess that had darkened over the years. But it seemed that the room was clean.

She went into the bathroom because that's how she always could tell. She was amazed. Bright and sparkling. New wrapped soap in the dish and new toilet paper. The towels were thin, but they were clean.

Okay, they'd stay. She flung her bag on the bed and took out a T-shirt which she exchanged for the long-sleeve blouse she was wearing. Then she hung up her things, and stored the other items in the dresser. It didn't matter how long they were staying, she always unpacked.

Out at the car she asked Jack how his room was; he shrugged and said he had a great view but the room was early fifties. She agreed.

"So where to first? House or work?"

Fincham consulted his watch. "Better go to his workplace, it's four o'clock already."

"Okay. Trimble's Gardening it is."

Chapter Sixteen

It took them about fifteen minutes to get to Trimble's. Beautiful flowers and plants lined the parking area. The place was a medium-size cement building, and it was clearly well kept, lovingly looked after.

When they went inside a little bell rang announcing their entrance. It only took a few moments before an attractive woman of about thirty-five stood behind the polished wooden counter. She asked if she could help and Dove showed her shield.

"You're here about Lyle, aren't you?"

"Yes. How did you know?"

"The phone call from your office in Virginia."

"Oh, of course. So what can you tell me about him, Ms. . . . ?" Dove shrugged.

"Sorry. I'm Anita Bell." She ran her fingers through her long red hair.

They all shook hands.

Bell said, "What's Lyle done?"

"We're not sure yet. How long did you employ him?"

"About three years. He was a hard worker. Then one day last week he didn't show up, didn't call. We, my partner and I, thought it was odd but didn't do anything about it until the next day. We phoned him but no answer. He hasn't been back since."

Fincham asked, "Did you do anything more about finding him?"

"Like what?" Her large green eyes were genuinely perplexed.

"Make any other inquiries."

She shook her head. "I wouldn't have known how to start. Lyle was very circumspect. Never said anything about his private life, so I didn't know who his friends were, and he never mentioned having a family."

"Do you have an application form from him?"

She smiled. "We're a two-person operation here, Sheriff. We did it by talking to him."

"How about references?"

"Oh, now that you mention it, we did ask for references and he gave us two."

"Do you have those on file?" Dove asked.

"No. The truth is, we didn't bother checking. He seemed so nice and then we never had a bit of trouble with him, so we just threw away those names. I guess that wasn't too smart, was it?"

"Not too. But lots of people don't bother checking on prospective employees."

"Emma, my partner, would have been the one to do it, but we get so busy." She seemed chagrined.

Dove said, "It's okay. I understand."

"There is one thing. But I've no proof and it's not something we gave any thought to until he disappeared and we got the call from your office."

"What's that, Ms. Bell?"

"Well, every once in awhile the money wouldn't add up right at the end of the day. It wasn't much, ten dollars, seven, sums like that. We didn't think anything about it and it didn't happen often. We simply thought we'd made a mistake."

"And what do you think now?" Fincham asked.

Bell scrunched her lips together, making them look like a scar, and closed her eyes for a moment.

Dove knew she didn't want to accuse Taylor.

Then Bell sighed audibly. "Well, Emma and I began to wonder if those missing sums were . . . if Lyle had taken the money. I hate to say this because we have absolutely no proof."

"We understand. Is there anything else you can tell us?"

She thought a few seconds, then shook her head. "There really isn't. Lyle was a hard worker and never missed a day. Until now."

"What about your partner, Emma was it?"

"Yes, Emma Pike."

Bell blushed, and Dove wondered if Emma and Anita were partners in life as well as in business.

"Do you think Ms. Pike might have any additional information for us?"

"I don't think so. But if you want to talk to her, I'll get her."

Fincham said, "That would be good."

She nodded and went out the door where she'd come from.

"What do you think?" Dove asked.

"I think she's holding something back."

"Me, too. But what the hell could it be?"

"Don't know."

Bell returned with Pike, who was as attractive as her partner but not as young. She was forty-something. Pike had straight blond hair worn about an inch above her shoulders where it turned under at the ends. Her eyes were robin's egg-blue surrounded by thick lashes. A pair of glasses hung around her neck on a gold chain.

After they were introduced, Dove said, "Your partner's

been very helpful, but we wondered if you had anything to add." Then she quickly ran down the list of things that Bell had told them.

Pike looked at Bell, then back at them. "Not anything but thoughts, musings, as it were."

"We'd be interested in those musings," Dove said.

"I don't want to implicate Lyle in anything. You have to understand that I never gave this a thought until we got the call from your department and the boy was missing."

"Implicate him in what?" Fincham asked.

"First, I'd like to know what he's done."

Dove and Fincham gave each other a glance that said yes.

"A girl from our county disappeared and then was found murdered."

Bell gasped and put her hand over her mouth. Pike remained immutable and said, "You think Lyle did that?"

"He's under suspicion."

"But you have no proof, is that it?"

"Not what we call hard evidence, no."

"You mean, Lyle is in your area? Why?"

"He had an e-mail relationship with the murdered girl."

"Lyle wouldn't do anything like that," Bell said.

"Anita, please," Pike said. "Anita liked Lyle a lot more than I did. Not that he ever did anything wrong here. But there was something about him that, well, to put it simply, gave me the creeps."

"How so?"

"Who can ever explain those things? Chemistry or something."

"But feeling that way you still kept him as an employee?" asked Fincham.

"Feelings aren't facts," she said. "He did his job and

never gave us any trouble. So why fire him?"

Dove said, "Then why were you worried about implicating him in something?"

Pike chewed at her bottom lip. "We had a murder here about two years ago. Young girl. Never solved. It happened on Lyle's day off."

Dove wondered why the Coconut Key police hadn't mentioned this. She assumed the MO wasn't the same as with Julie or McQuigg would've put it on his list.

"Have you any reason to connect Lyle to this murder?" Fincham asked.

"As I said, I started thinking about it after the phone call from your office."

"Did the officer tell you there'd been a murder?" Dove was going to chew out Jenkins if she did.

Pike said, "No. The woman I talked with didn't tell me anything. She just asked some questions about Lyle. It got me thinking because obviously Lyle was in some sort of trouble. And I don't know why, but my mind jumped to the murder of Sue Haines. She was seventeen."

Dove felt sick and excited at the same time. "You don't know why you thought of Lyle?"

"I don't. You can't ever say how your mind jumps from one thing to another, know what I mean?"

"Sure. Tell me more about the murder of Haines."

"Although a big deal was made of it, there were no details in the papers because all they had was that she'd been abducted from her backyard and found murdered a few days later. That's what it boiled down to, anyway."

Fincham said to Dove, "I think we'd better go see the police here."

She nodded. "Do you remember the murder of a young girl in Miami about two years ago?"

160

Pike smiled sadly. "Sheriff, there are murders every day in Miami."

Dove gave her the name and date.

"It doesn't mean anything to me."

"Would you know if Lyle was at work on that day?"

"My records don't go back that far. In fact, I don't really keep records. I noted Lyle's absence on the day of the Sue Haines's murder in my mind."

"Right. Ms. Pike, could you tell us how to get to police headquarters?"

Dove and Fincham thanked them, then at the last minute Dove decided to ask them about a restaurant for dinner. The clerk at the motel couldn't be trusted for a recommendation.

Anita said, "The best place in town is Hank's Stone Crab House. Of course they have lobsters and any other seafood."

"I didn't bring any fancy clothes for the best place," Dove said.

"Hey, nobody wears fancy clothes here. The Keys are very laid back, know what I mean? You could go in what you're wearing."

"She's right," Pike added. "The only places that have a dress code are the country clubs."

"Okay. You mind telling us how to get to Hank's?"

When they were back in the car, Fincham said, "What the hell's wrong with these cops down here they didn't tell us about the murder?"

"Why should they tell Jenkins that? I'm sure all she did was ask if Lyle had a record. One thing bothers me. If it was the same MO, McQuigg would've known about it, mentioned it to me. The only Florida murder that matched ours was the one in Miami."

"Yeah, that's true. So what did you think of what the ladi . . . women told us?"

"I think it was very interesting."

"Meaning?"

"Especially Pike's take on things. She saw that there's something odd about Lyle."

"Like maybe he's a murderer?"

"Maybe," she said.

They headed back to Coconut Key. Finally they came to the police station. It was a small cement building that looked like a fort.

"Let's try to be nice, Jack. You know how we hate it when cops from other states come to us."

"No we don't. Not if they can help."

"I guess," she said.

Inside it was cool, two air-conditioners going full blast. The place was one room with a holding cell. A wooden table served for a counter and a blond crew-cut cop in short sleeves manned it. They didn't see anyone else.

Dove introduced them both and asked if he could tell them anything about the Haines murder.

The young cop said, "Well, all I know is it's still open."

"Could we see a file on it?"

"Jeez, I don't know if I'm suppose to do that."

"You are. But if you don't believe me, is there someone you can call?"

"Captain Brush is out fishin' today. And the sarge, not sure where he is. Then there's another officer like me but he couldn't tell me what to do."

Even though Dove was asking the questions, he gave his answers to Fincham. This wasn't new. "What's your name?" Dove asked.

"Clyde Houst."

"Officer Houst, I assure you if you show us the file you won't be going against procedure. Cops from other states come to us all the time asking for information. That's what we cops do, Clyde. Share information. You don't mind me calling you Clyde, do you?"

"No. Not at all. Anyways, I guess it wouldn't hurt nothin' if I showed it to you, you bein' a sheriff and all."

"That's exactly right."

Clyde went to a filing cabinet.

Fincham said softly, "You have the magic touch, Arizona."

He smiled and a rush of adrenaline shot through her the way she imagined a dose of heroin might feel like. She had to stop this. Yeah, right.

Houst came back with a manila file marked Haines. "Everything we know is in there."

"Thanks Officer," she said. Then she looked around and spotted an empty table near the back wall. "Mind if we take it over there?"

"Guess not."

She thanked him again and went to the table, where they opened the folder. There were no chairs so they stood. Dove gave half the papers to Fincham and she took the other half. "Look for the autopsy report," she told him.

He nodded. It didn't take long. It was in Fincham's batch. They read it together.

"Sweet Jesus," she said.

The method of murder was strangulation. But the real kicker was that the pubic area had been shaved.

"How the hell did McQuigg miss this one?"

"Maybe," Fincham said, "he's not as good as he thinks he is."

"It's strange, Jack. FBI is everywhere. This case must

163

have been noticed by them."

"You think they've got someone on every murder of every girl everywhere?"

"I do. We'd better keep looking through these papers, see if there's any mention of an FBI report."

It was Dove who found this one. She showed it to Jack. It illustrated clearly that the FBI had been notified and that an agent was in on the search.

"I'll be damned," Fincham said.

"Why didn't Mike know about this one?"

"Maybe he did. Maybe he just forgot."

"McQuigg forget? Never. A screw-up somewhere. Let's see if Clyde knows."

"Oh, come on," Fincham said.

"Worth a try."

Dove said, "Clyde, I have another question for you."

"Shoot."

"An Agent Tuber of the FBI was in on this case from the moment the girl disappeared, correct?"

"Come to think of it, yeah." He had a look of distaste on his face.

Dove wondered if it was because Agent Tuber was Donna, a woman.

"We're not crazy 'bout the FBI. They try to take over."

"Yes," Dove said sympathetically. "We're familiar with that syndrome. You have any idea if Agent Tuber reported this nationally?"

"Nationally?"

"To the whole bureau."

"Nah. How would I know that?"

Of course he wouldn't know. She looked at Jack.

Clyde said, "But then there was that other agent come down from Washington, so maybe she did report it."

Feeling uneasy, Dove asked, "When was this, Clyde? When did the other agent come here?"

"Couple, three months ago, I guess."

"Man or woman?"

"Man."

"And what did he want?"

"Same as you, wanted to see the file. Captain was here so I didn't have nuthin' to do with it."

"You don't remember the agent's name, do you?"

He chewed hard on his gum and closed his eyes. "Hell, it's right on the tip of my tongue."

They waited.

"It was Mc something, I know that."

Dove and Fincham looked at each other.

"Mc . . . Bain, Mc . . . Mann, Mc . . . Quigg. Yeah that was it. Agent McQuigg."

Chapter Seventeen

Fincham's room had a deck overlooking the ocean. He and Dove decided to have drinks there before they went out to dinner. It was still warm, but the blazing sun didn't have the vigor it had during the mid-afternoon. Still, they both wore hats and sunglasses.

They'd bought the hats in a boutique after leaving the Coconut Key police station. Hers was a tan canvas one with metal snaps and his was the same only in black. Then they'd gone to a liquor store and bought a bottle of vodka, stopped at a grocer's and gotten some tonic water.

Having applied for a search warrant to enter Taylor's apartment, there wasn't much to do but wait. Dove had phoned Snowden to make sure Taylor was still in custody and he was. But the really troublesome thing right now was McQuigg.

"Why did Mike come here?" Dove asked.

"I don't know. But if he was on this case, the whole thing, I mean, it makes sense."

"So why didn't he mention this one?"

Fincham shrugged.

"I have to call Hutt. Throw me your cell phone."

He reached into his pocket, tossed it to her; she caught it and punched in Hutt's home phone number.

He answered on the second ring. "What's up, Sheriff?"

"Did Agent McQuigg call you?"

"Sure did. Said he'd forgotten that there had been a

murder same MO down where you are now. I was gonna call you right soon."

Dove believed that one like she believed the moon was square. "McQuigg say anything else?"

"Nope."

After she asked if there were any new developments, she thanked Hutt, then relayed the conversation to Jack. "Don't you think it's mighty suspicious that he remembers this murder *now?*"

"It's different."

"Different?"

"Well, peculiar then," Fincham said. "Couldn't it be that he *did* just remember this one?"

"No. You don't know Mike."

"And I'm proud of it," he said.

"Yeah, you should be. He's a bastard."

"So you've said."

"He knew all along, Jack."

"Arizona, what are you getting at?"

She mulled this over for some time, then said, "Haven't the vaguest. I just have a feeling."

"Oh, no. The tingle on the back of your neck?"

She laughed. "That's only when I'm in the presence of someone evil. Doesn't apply to thoughts."

"Any tingles around McQuigg?" He took a swallow of his drink and peeped at her over the rim of the glass.

"I loathe him so much I couldn't trust anything I feel."

"What about Taylor? Tingles?"

She thought a few seconds. "No. Not once."

"Then he must be innocent." Fincham grinned.

"It's hardly a proven science."

They laughed and took sips of their drinks.

"I want to hear McQuigg's explanation for only remembering this murder now. I mean, the man came down here. And he knew I was coming to Coconut Key. That alone would have jogged the foggiest memory," Dove said.

"He'll say he only remembered it later and called it in. No way to prove anything about a person's memory."

"You're right. I wish I knew what he was up to, though. It just doesn't compute."

"Forget it for now."

"Right. What do you think we'll find in Taylor's place?" she asked.

"If you mean parts of bodies or frozen heads, I don't think so."

"No, but maybe a notebook, something on his computer." Dove felt dreamy, realized she didn't want to talk about the case. Sitting here, watching the waves roll in, a drink and Fincham were all she cared about.

Fincham said, "Don't get your hopes up, Arizona."

She almost laughed. She knew what Fincham meant, but it was as though he'd been reading her mind. Did he, she wondered for the millionth time, feel in any way as she did?

"My hopes have never been less up," she replied.

He smiled at her in that jagged way of his and it was all she could do to keep from blurting out what she felt. This was almost intolerable.

"It has to be him, though. I don't believe in coincidences."

"Know how many times you've told me that?"

"Sorry," he said and looked hurt.

Oh, God. "Jack, I didn't mean it like that. I was kidding."

"Yeah." He nodded, forced a grim smile.

"Oh, Jack, please. I really was."

"Well, hell. It must be a big bore to hear me say things

over and over. Not that you don't," he added.

She laughed. "I'm sure I do."

"Want to hear them?"

"No, I want to go have dinner. I'm starving."

"Hank's Crab House, here we come."

They clinked their glasses and downed the drinks.

Dove lay in her bed and channel surfed. She couldn't sleep. The meal had been great, crabs and the best fries she'd ever had, a wonderful salad and wine. Fincham had dessert, a chocolate mousse cake, but she'd declined.

She had the same feeling she'd had that last time in Jefferson when they'd had dinner. She couldn't help thinking Jack was flirting with her. And that made her think of Mike.

It wasn't that no one else had ever played the game except the two of them, but they had similarities. And wasn't it said that you are attracted to same type of person over and over?

She stopped surfing, the mute button on, and put her head back on the pillow, stared at the ceiling. Why in the world had she married Mike?

At six-four he'd been an imposing young man, with a shock of brown hair that fell over his forehead in a casual and engaging way. It wasn't until after she'd married him that she became aware of his attention to this detail—nothing random about it. Like everything else. His appearance was studied, his habits, his whole damn life. But she hadn't known that for some time.

Charm was his middle name. Mike McQuigg was a catch. But he had all the trademarks of an abuser, something she didn't know at the time. So she guessed it wasn't so strange that she'd been seduced by his personality. She was young and dumb about men.

McQuigg went right from graduation into the FBI. After he trained at Quantico, they were married and little by little she saw who he really was.

Fincham had the same charm and that's what worried her. Was he an abuser? She couldn't believe that. Still, you didn't honestly know until that first incident. Dove didn't want to make the same mistake twice. Right, she said to herself, as if he was asking her to? Oh, go to sleep she told herself and switched off the TV, picked up her paperback copy of *Cider House Rules* and began to read. It was a long book and she was only 102 pages into it, but it was a wonderful read.

Next thing she knew the phone was ringing. The book was on her chest, the light on. She glanced at the clock. It was quarter after one. She picked up the phone.

"I can't sleep," Fincham said.

"The case?"

"No," he said. "You."

"Come down here," she said, and replaced the phone in its cradle.

He lay on top of her and they kissed.

His kiss was wonderful, like nothing she'd ever experienced. It was soft and encompassing and she felt she could go on like this forever, drifting, even though she wanted more.

Then they made love, urgently, as though they'd lost each other and were now reunited and had no time to wait. Their hands debuted and swiftly learned, and when he moved into her she emitted a contented sound he couldn't recall ever hearing. Jack was conscious of what was going on, because it was almost impossible that this was happening. He couldn't quite take in that it was Arizona ut-

tering the noises, pushing, twisting, her head back, moving
in air, the light leaking from between the blinds, letting him
get a look at her face in a fashion she would never see herself. Jack recognized a hidden Arizona and then, for a
second, her eyes opened.

He said, "I cherish you." Her eyes closed again, but he
couldn't help noticing the tiniest of smiles before he closed
his own.

Lying naked in each other's arms, they were silent for a
long time.

Jack spoke first. "Arizona, I'm in love with you."

"Oh, God."

"What's that mean?" He tensed.

"It means, I'm in love with you, too."

He breathed a sigh of relief. "You had me scared there for
a moment. Thought maybe I was just a sex object for you."

She slapped his chest playfully. "How can you say that?
What do you think I am, anyway?"

"I think you're the most beautiful, most sexy woman in
the world and I don't know what you'd want with the likes
of me."

She laughed. "And I don't know what you'd want with
the likes of me."

"You kidding? My God, I feel like I've never made love
before."

Dove felt the same. She'd never liked the way Mike
kissed, never enjoyed his lovemaking as she had this. And
the few others in her life had been routine. "I don't want to
sound like a parrot, but I feel that, too, Jack. You're a wonderful lover. But it's partly because of the way I feel about
you. Do you have any idea how much I've wanted you and
for how long?"

He raised himself, leaned on his elbow, his chin in his hand. "No, tell me."

"From the first day I laid eyes on you, I think."

"You think? That's not very flattering."

"I just mean, I don't think I knew it, not in the front of my brain. But I knew pretty soon after that."

"I know I knew it. I was ready to hate you. You know, working for a woman and all that junk. And then there you were and I thought I might have a heart attack or something. You just got to me right away."

"Never would have known it, the hard time you gave me."

"Had to or I would've thrown you down on the floor of your office."

"Rape?" she asked, not smiling.

"Me? Never. That's my point, sweetheart. I wanted you so much I had to act like I hated you."

She moved out from under his arm, scooted up in the bed and rested against the pillows, pulling the sheet up with her.

"I've seen them," he said.

"Nevertheless, I'm a modest woman. Jack, we have to talk."

"I thought we were."

"Seriously."

"Are my intentions honorable? Yes."

Sweet Jesus, what did he mean by that? "Jack, what about Bonnie Jo?"

"I'm leaving her; I thought you understood that. Arizona, can I have a cigarette, please?"

She had to laugh. "Sure."

He reached over the side of the bed and found his trousers, pulled out a crumpled pack, extracted one, found his lighter on the night table, lit up. "Ah, better than sex," he said.

"Damned if it is."

"Except with you." He leaned over and kissed her. And once again it seemed as though they might become lost forever.

Reluctantly, she pulled away. "When are you leaving her?"

"Soon as we get back. I'm packing a bag and filing for divorce and custody. Oh, shit."

"What?"

"Custody. Two things. We can't be open about our relationship."

"Didn't think we would be," she said. "What's the other thing."

"You."

"Isn't this where I came in?"

"I mean, how do you feel about living with two teenagers?"

"Living with? Don't you think you're moving a little fast, Jack?"

He looked hurt.

"Wait. I mean, you've got us living together and here we are in Coconut Key in a motel having made love once."

He looked at her for a long moment, then said, "Let's make it twice."

They'd been asleep for only a few hours when the call came.

It was Jenkins. "Find anything, Sheriff?" she said.

Dove looked at the time. Eight. "You calling me at this hour to know that?"

"Yes and no. Wondered what you got because we got something good."

"So are you going to tell me, Jenkins or do I have to beg?"

"Forensic came back on Taylor's car."

She could have easily killed her. "And?"

"Fibers from Julie Boyer's clothes were found in Taylor's vehicle."

"I'll be damned," she said. "Charge him with the murder. Fincham and I need to go to Taylor's house and then we'll take the next plane back. Thanks for calling, Jenkins."

When she'd replaced the phone, Jack asked what was up and she told him.

"Bastard," Jack said. "I'm starving, Arizona, how about you?"

"Could eat a whale."

He leaned over to kiss her.

"Oh, no," she said. "We start that and we'll never get out of here."

"You know what, you're right. For once." And he jumped out of bed laughing, before she could grab him.

"Pancakes," she said. "That's what I want. That's what I need."

"Wanna hear my poem about pancakes?"

"No," she said jokingly.

"Thought you would. Here goes.

Pancakes are a work of art,
With which another day to start.
Dragging out of bed still groggy,
We've just one question, crisp or soggy?"

Laughing, she said, "Where'd you hear that?"

"I made it up."

"You didn't."

"Did."

"Well, what do you know? Not only a great lover, but a poet, too. What more could a girl ask for?"

"A solved case?"

"You betcha," she said.

Chapter Eighteen

The bar that Mike McQuigg sat in was not a usual haunt. Not an FBI place. He'd picked it at random because he had no desire to run into any of his colleagues. There was no way he was going to engage in inter-agency politics or cold cases tonight.

This place, The Broken Down Valise, was a neighborhood bar. And it wasn't his neighborhood so he wouldn't see anyone he knew. No one would find him.

McQuigg ordered a second scotch, the best they had was rotgut, but he didn't really care. He wasn't here to booze as much as he was to think. How the hell had he forgotten the Coconut Key murder? Was he losing it? Was he on overload?

It wasn't routine for him to forget something like that. He'd never failed to recall one single unsolved murder in his life, let alone this batch.

So now Lucia was going to get on his back about it, he had no doubt. Lucia. Why the hell had he ever married the bitch? She was a good-looking woman and he wanted her. Simple as that. He never liked her. She was always too independent. At least Betty Grable behaved like a wife should. Lucia, on the other hand, insisted on working and didn't want kids. Then she changed her mind and had one. Clare. And look what happened. She couldn't even take care of her. She'd had her by either a guy named Vic Tierney or Elliot McBride, Jr. He knew she'd dated both of them, didn't know if she'd slept with them or not, even though they'd both told him she had. He smiled to himself. Amazing what people would tell you when you flipped out your FBI I.D.

But guys, FBI or not, wanted to say they'd made it with a woman. So the father could've been either one. Whore. Lucia was a whore, running around sleeping with these guys, trying to get pregnant. What else could you possibly call her? And now she was making it with that dumb lieutenant, Fincham.

McQuigg swallowed the rest of his drink, but it didn't quell the anger he felt. Or stop the truth. He *hadn't* gotten rid of her. She'd dumped him. And that enraged him. No fucking woman before or after Lucia had ever dumped him. And from that day to this he'd vowed to make her pay. So he couldn't start slipping up now, forgetting murders in this case, losing his edge, his power over her. He was FBI and she was a sheriff of a county. A no-brainer. He was king. Beautiful.

The D.A., Dawson Braxton, was a lithe, thin man in his early forties. But his hairline had receded enough to give him the look of a man ten years older. He sported a full mustache and was known for wearing pink shirts and expensive suits and ties.

Braxton had been elected four years earlier by a landslide. By then he'd been an A.D. for six years and the old D.A. was retiring.

Dawson Braxton was also known to be tough, and wanted all his ducks in a row before he prosecuted.

He sat behind his oak desk and fiddled with a paper cutter. He listened to Sheriff Dove and Lieutenant Fincham with rapt attention. When they were finished, he said, "So all you really have is forensic evidence, puny as it is."

"Why is it puny, Dawson?"

"Fibers from the car. That's it?"

"I know the rest is circumstantial, but don't the fibers from Boyer's clothes mean anything?" Dove asked.

"Sure they do. They mean the girl was in the car. But it doesn't mean he killed her."

Fincham said, "No. Not directly. But, hell, Braxton, he told us he never saw her, never met her, let alone her being in his car."

"You talk to him since you got the forensic report?"

"No," Dove said, "we just got back from Coconut Key, checking him out down there."

"What did you come up with?"

"Aside from the fact that Taylor was absent from work there the day of a murder, one that has the same MO as Boyer and other murders, we got impressions. We tossed his apartment, but there wasn't anything. Not even his computer. He must have stashed it somewhere else. The women he worked for, well, one of them said she always felt uncomfortable around him and thought he stole money."

"Felt, thought. C'mon, Lucia, you know I can't go to court with that. And his absenteeism on the day of a murder is circumstantial at best. Talk to him again." Braxton ran his attenuated fingers across his chin as though he was feeling for stubble.

"We've charged him," Fincham said.

"What? Are you crazy?"

"He was already in jail on shoplifting and trying to skip bail charges."

"So why the fuck didn't you leave it that way?"

Dove said, "Guess we were excited when we got the

news." She felt herself flush, remembering what else had excited her.

Braxton picked up on it immediately. "You're blushing, Lucia. How come?" He cocked his head to one side like a pixie.

"Am I? Can't imagine. It is warm in here."

The D.A. gave a sideways glance at Fincham, saw nothing revealing. Decided to skip the whole thing. He sat straighter in his chair. "Taylor's lawyer object to the charge?"

"Don't know. We came straight here," Fincham said.

"Okay, talk to Taylor again, see if you can break him down. Then talk to me again."

It was clear to both Fincham and Dove the meeting was over. They thanked Braxton and left.

In the hall, Dove said, "I think we may have screwed up."

"Just screwed," he said grinning.

"Is that what it was to you, Jack?" She was sorry the minute she asked the question but she was insecure about this romance.

"Ah, Arizona, give me a break. I was just funning you. I admit it was a little vulgar, but I couldn't resist."

She smiled. "Okay, sorry."

He gently grabbed her arm. "Listen, I love you. You have to know that."

"It's just that . . . well, I'm older than you."

"Oh, what a surprise. You can't be serious. What is it four years?"

"Five."

"Five? Ohmigod. Jesus, didn't know it was five. Hey, we'll have to call this off. You could practically be my mother, no, my grandmother!"

She laughed. "You really don't mind?"

"What's five years between lovers?"

"I don't know. I've never been with a man five years younger."

"Well, now you are. Let's go see Taylor."

Taylor looked like hell. He seemed to have lost weight and his tan was fading, giving him a jaundiced appearance.

They were back in the interrogation room. This time they all stood except for Taylor.

Darryl Wittman, Taylor's lawyer, leaned against the wall, arms crossed.

"So what's this shit that you charged me with Julie's murder?"

Dove said, "You told us you never met Julie, right?"

"Right."

"That's a lie," said Fincham.

"Hell it is."

"Taylor, forensic found fibers from her clothing in the passenger seat," McQuigg said.

"Shit."

"Why don't you start telling the truth, Lyle?" Dove said.

Taylor just kept shaking his head as though he wasn't going to answer.

McQuigg turned to Wittman. "Counselor, would you instruct your client to answer?"

"Well, Agent McQuigg, I will, once somebody asks him a question."

It was true, they hadn't asked a direct question yet. "Taylor, did you kill Julie Boyer?"

"No."

"Did you ever meet her?"

Taylor looked at his lawyer for help.

"The truth, Lyle," Wittman instructed.

"Okay, yes. I met her."

"Why'd you lie about it?" McQuigg asked.

"Because I knew you'd charge me with her murder. I'm not an idiot."

"So tell us what happened," Dove said.

"Oh, God," Taylor said. "I didn't kill her, you have to believe that."

"Tell us what happened."

"Well, it was like I said. I rented the car and when I got to her house, there she was, sitting on the top step. I knew it was her because she'd sent me her picture.

"So anyways, I yelled out the car window to her, told her who I was. Man, she was like freaked. Not in a bad way, just totally surprised. She closed her book and slowly came down the steps. Then she asked me if I was really Lyle Taylor, which I have to say I thought was way dumb. I mean, who else would I be?

"So she said she was glad to meet me and I asked her to get in and we'd go for a drive. She said she should tell somebody where she was going and then I asked her if she told would her mother let her go and she had to admit, she wouldn't. So she came around the passenger side and got in.

"So I was sweating like a pig, I can tell you. Never been so nervous. Don't have a whole lot of experience with females."

Dove found his use of the word *females* interesting.

"Go on," Fincham said. "Tell us more about you and females."

It was clear to Dove that Jack also felt it was an odd word to use.

"So I . . . I just kept wondering if I stunk, you know? I

mean, sweating like that." He started crying.

No one said anything.

Wittman handed him a handkerchief. "It's okay, Lyle. You've got nothing to worry about."

"Shit." He took the handkerchief and wiped his face. "This is humiliating."

McQuigg said, "Julie Boyer can't feel humiliated anymore, Taylor. Think about that."

"What's that supposed to mean?" Wittman said.

"Just the truth."

"I know what it means," Taylor said. "It means you think I killed her."

"It means you're lucky to be able to feel humiliated because you're alive."

"Yeah, right."

"Go on, Lyle," Dove said.

"Well, we went for a drive."

"Where to?"

"I don't know. You got to remember I didn't know where I was."

"Okay. Did you park anywhere?"

"Yeah. On some street near an empty lot."

Dove and Fincham looked at each other.

She said, "Was it Kellogg Street?"

"I don't know, yeah, maybe, I can't be sure."

"But it was definitely an empty lot you parked in front of?"

"Yeah."

"And what time was that?"

"Maybe five-fifteen, five-thirty, not sure."

"How come you're so sure about it being an empty lot?" McQuigg asked.

"I'm not blind. I know what an empty lot looks like for chrissakes."

"But there were other houses around?"

"Yeah, sure. It was like a development area. The lot had a For Sale sign on it."

"Okay," Dove said. "You parked and then what happened?"

"We talked."

"What about?"

"You know, stuff."

"No, we don't know."

"Ah, hell. Us. We talked about us."

"What about you?"

"Like what would happen next?"

"Did you ask her to go away with you?" McQuigg said.

"Yeah."

"What she say?"

"She said no," he whispered, but loud enough for them to hear.

"And?"

Lyle looked at Wittman. "Can't I just cut to the end?"

"Answer the questions, Lyle."

"Okay, she said no and I begged like an asshole, and she asked me to drive her home and I said no and she jumped out of the car and ran through the lot and I got out and yelled after her and that's the last goddamn time I saw her. You satisfied?"

"You expect us to believe that?" Fincham asked.

"It's the truth."

"Lyle, you know that's not what happened," Dove said.

"It is," he whined.

"I think some of it's true. But I also think that when she ran into the lot you ran after her and you caught her. Then you struggled and somehow, I don't know how exactly, but I know it was an accident, Lyle. You didn't mean to do it, but in your struggle somehow Julie died. Isn't that what happened?"

"No, it's not. I didn't run after her, there was no point, even I could see that."

Dove went on as if he hadn't spoken. "When you caught up with her you tried to kiss her, didn't you, Lyle?"

"What's wrong with you? You listening to me, or what?"

McQuigg said, "Taylor, you must think we're fucking idiots. We're supposed to believe that you came all the way here from Florida to see this girl, you find her, get her in your car and then when she runs away you just let her go?"

"That's what happened. Besides . . ." he trailed off.

"Besides what?"

"I knew where she lived, and I thought I'd give her time to cool off, try again the next day."

"Why don't I believe that?" Dove said.

Looking down at the bare table, Taylor shrugged.

"Could it be because it's not true, Lyle? Mighty sophisticated thinking for a man who doesn't have a lot of experience with females." Dove was getting sick of playing it sweet.

"Fuck this." He turned to Wittman. "What am I suppose to do?"

"Just keep telling the truth," the lawyer advised.

"I am. I am."

Wittman said, "Okay. Do you swear, Lyle, that all the answers you've given in this interview are true?"

"Yeah, I do."

"I think that's enough for now. And I'd like you to remove the murder charge and return to the original charges."

"Mr. Wittman," Dove said. "I'm going to let the murder charge stand for another twenty-four."

"This sucks," Lyle said.

"Be quiet, Taylor," Wittman said.

"Twenty-four and then it's off?"

"Or not. Depending what we uncover. By the way, Lyle, where's your PC?"

"I use a laptop. It's in the trunk of the car."

Dove had a sinking feeling. There was no record of a laptop in evidence and she knew what that meant. Someone had stolen it.

Chapter Nineteen

Back in Dove's office, she asked McQuigg about the Sue Haines murder and got the response she'd expected. He'd simply forgotten.

"Even when you knew where I was going?"

"Even then. I'm not a perfect person, Lucia."

She thought that was an odd thing for him to say as he always tried to present himself as perfect.

"It's not like you to forget."

"If you think it didn't give me pause when I *did* remember it, you're wrong. Believe me, I hate my fucking up on this worse than you do." He shrugged, as if to say, what can I do?

It was as futile as she'd expected so there was nothing left but to let it go, and work on what she could.

Fincham had gone to question the deputies who had dealt with Taylor's car, while she went to the forensic building. It was a rabbit warren of a place and she never felt comfortable or welcome there. Except by the clerk at the front desk.

"Lo, Sheriff," she said. Mary Hartmann was a nice woman who had had to put up with a lot of bad jokes because her name was the same as a seventies TV show. Only that was called *Mary Hartmann, Mary Hartmann*. This Mary was a tall brunette with a pallid complexion and bright brown eyes. Today she wore a pink suit, white silk blouse and a gold pendant in the shape of a book embedded with green stones.

"Mary. Nice to see you."

"You, too. What can I do for you today?"

"I need to know who worked on some evidence."

"You have the I.D. number?"

"Sure." Dove handed her a piece of paper and watched while Mary typed the numbers into the computer. From her angle she couldn't see the screen, but in less than thirty seconds Mary had the information. She printed it out and gave it to Dove.

"Any idea where I can find these guys?"

"Let me see if they're working today." Again she did some fast typing on her keyboard. "Yeah, they're both here. First one's in room 131, second in 149. Know how to find them?"

"Well, this place . . ." Dove trailed off.

"Yeah, I know." Mary gave her the directions to 131 and said to ask them there how to get to 149, because it wasn't in the same hall as the number implied.

Dove thanked her and started down the dark wainscoted corridor. She wondered if they used forty-watt bulbs, as the lighting left plenty to be desired. The hallway twisted and turned, but she finally found the right room. She knocked gently on the opaque glass. The door reminded Dove of her elementary school.

"Come in," a female voice said.

She opened the door and stepped into a small dark room which housed bizarre-looking equipment and an even more bizarre-looking woman.

"Officer Copus?"

"That's me." Her hair was dyed the color of a lawn flamingo and she wore striped overalls and a bright red shirt that clashed horribly with her hair.

Dove introduced herself. "You worked on this car,

didn't you?" She handed Copus the piece of paper.

"Oh, yeah, sure." She blew a huge bubble until it popped and splattered across her lips like a spider's web.

Dove watched incredulously as Copus pulled the gum from her mouth and dabbed at her face to remove it. She hadn't seen that since . . . since Clare. Suddenly she felt the blood rush from her head to her toes.

"You all right?" Copus asked.

"I need to sit down."

"You're white as a Klansman."

"Didn't have any breakfast," she lied. Dove had never experienced a feeling like this when she thought about Clare. Sitting in an aqua plastic chair, she started to feel better. Years ago she'd fainted at the sight of her first dead body, which had been discovered after five days and was black and bloated. What had occurred a moment ago was what she'd felt right before she'd become unconscious. Why did a reminder of her daughter put her on the verge of fainting? It wasn't anything she could answer now.

"I'm okay," she said.

"You want a doughnut, something?"

"No, it's okay. Thanks. So you worked on that car?"

"Definitely. What's up?"

"Were you alone or with . . ." she looked down at the paper, ". . . Officer Watts?"

"I was with Len."

"Was there ever a time when one of you was alone with the car?"

Copus stopped chewing. "Hey, Sheriff, what's going on?"

"Could you please answer the question?"

"Well, I don't remember right off. Lemme think."

Dove waited, trying not to return to what had happened

earlier. She didn't want to think about Clare at all right now. Who knew what might happen? She wished this woman would hurry.

"Yeah, I went for lunch."

"How long were you gone?"

"Maybe fifteen, twenty minutes?"

"This is important. Before you went to lunch, did you open the trunk?"

"Yeah."

She could hear the answer to her next question before she asked it. "What was inside?"

"The usual stuff, jack, spare, like that."

"Nothing else?"

"Nope."

"Did you find a notebook computer anywhere in the car?"

"A notebook computer?"

Why, Dove wondered, did they always repeat the question when they were lying? "Yeah, a notebook computer. A laptop."

"Which one?"

Dove smiled. "Why, did you find something?"

"No. No computer." She pressed her fleshy lips together.

"So there's no way Len Watts could've found one while he was alone? While you were getting lunch?"

"No way. We'd already been over the car and we would of seen it if it was there."

Dove stood. She waited a moment before she took a step, still not sure she was steady. "Can you tell me how to get to room 149?"

"You going to talk to Len?"

"Yes. Any objections to that?"

Copus looked startled. "Oh, hell no. Just wondered, is all." She smiled and it made her look like a clown: the hair, the blouse, the lipsticked mouth.

Dove asked for directions again and got them. Oddly enough, 149 wasn't even on the same floor. It was on the fourth and there was no reason for it that Dove could see. She slowly made her way to an elevator, testing her steadiness. She was all right now. As soon as this interview was over, she had to go back to the station and assess what happened to her in Copus's office.

She knocked on 149 and a man told her to come in. He was just replacing his phone when she entered and she couldn't help wondering if that had been Copus. After introducing herself she said, "You been on that phone long, Officer Watts?"

"Beg your pardon, Sheriff?"

She knew it was an odd question to ask, so she smiled. "Just curious if that was your partner, Copus, or someone else."

He stared at her. Watts was a nice-looking young man, about thirty, with a full head of brown hair, a part on the left, neatly groomed. His brown eyes were his best feature, large and heavily lashed for a man. The clothes he wore were conventional: shirt, tie, gray slacks.

"I don't see who I was talking to . . . I mean, what is it you're here for, Sheriff?"

"I'm asking the questions," she answered.

"Sorry." He pulled on an earlobe. "I was actually talking to my girlfriend."

His phone rang and he reached for it.

"I don't want you to answer that, Len."

"But . . ."

"No."

"It might be something important."

"*This* is important."

Watts withdrew his hand. "Okay."

It was irritating that it kept ringing.

"You have voice mail?"

"Sure."

"Put it on."

"It is on. It'll pick up on the fifth ring."

And it did.

"Okay, I'm here to ask you about this car." She handed him the paper.

He stared at it. "What about it?"

"I want to know what you and Copus did with the notebook computer."

He didn't look up. "The notebook computer?"

"Yeah. Did you sell it, split the profit, or did one of you take it home?"

"She tell you that?"

"Just answer the question, Len. Where's the computer?"

"I . . . I gave it to my girlfriend. Oh, Christ."

"I want it back and I want it now."

Fincham had turned up nothing with the deputies who'd found the car. They hadn't gone inside or opened the trunk. He had figured before going back to work, he'd better check his house, his wife.

Now he sat in his car for a moment and stared at his house. How normal, how perfect it looked, as though it belonged to regular people with *family values,* the American dream. He recalled when they'd bought this, their first house. Before that they'd rented an apartment over a garage, which was fine for the two of them, honeymoon cottage in a way.

191

Then B.J. got pregnant and it was clear that they needed to buy a house. Smiling, Jack remembered how B.J. had started out wanting the Taj Mahal. They'd spent hours discussing it, sometimes fighting, until she was convinced that what she had in mind was out of their reach. So they went out again, with different expectations. They must have looked at twenty or more houses, but when they saw this one, they knew it was right.

They were still paying off the mortgage, but now the payments were minimal. They'd bought at a very good time. If they sold, they'd double their investment.

That wasn't going to happen. He didn't know the outcome of his decision, but he did know the honorable thing was to let B.J. keep the house. He'd miss it. Still, it was just a thing. What was important was to get custody of the kids.

Fincham got out of the car and walked up the drive. He tried the back door but it was locked. Having left the keys in the car, he went around to the front. That was locked, too. It was odd because they always left one door open. Living in a close-knit neighborhood like this, it was safe. Someone always had an eye out for strangers.

He got the keys and went back to the front door where he found that the dead bolt was in place. That could mean B.J. was inside. He hoped not. He used a second key and the bolt slipped easily out of its home.

Inside it felt cold but he knew that was his imagination. The stillness was unusual. It was rare that he was ever in his house alone, something he only now realized. He looked around as though he were seeing the place for the last time, which might be true.

He called out, "B.J.?" and didn't know why. She'd probably been hung over and gone out the back door, locked it forgetting the bolt was in place on the front. But the kids always used the front door. Still, they left before B.J. Why would she bolt the front after they left, then lock the back door?

Fincham took the stairs two at a time and went into their bedroom. The bed was unmade, but that wasn't odd. She often didn't deal with it when she was hung over. But the room was a total mess, as if there'd been a struggle. Chairs were on their sides and lamps on the floor. Fincham felt angry that she'd left the room in this condition. Then he opened the closet door and saw that her nightgown and robe were not hanging on their hook. Could she have thrown them in the wash? Sure, that was it. So why didn't he feel convinced?

He sat on the bed, picked up the white phone and punched in the numbers to B.J.'s salon.

Iris picked up. "Hair and Now," she said.

Christ. "Iris, is B.J. there?"

"No, Jack. She's not in yet. Did you try her at home?"

"I *am* at home," he said.

"Well then, she's probably on her way."

"Yeah, probably. Ask her to call me when she gets in, will you? Thanks." He hung up before she could say anything, because the idea of B.J. being on her way suddenly gave him an idea.

He rushed down the stairs and through the kitchen, which he noted was also a mess, and out the back door to the garage. Then he realized he needed the goddamn opener and ran to his car, grabbed it from the glove compartment, and trotted back up the driveway. He pointed it at the garage and clicked the button.

Slowly, the door raised and his heart sank. B.J.'s car was there. At least it wasn't running and there were no gas fumes. Still, he looked inside, but it was empty.

Leaving the garage door open, he went back into the house. He stood in the kitchen and Dresden came to mind. Dirty dishes everywhere: sink, table, counter. And the cabinets were all open as if someone had been desperately looking for something, too rushed to close them again. Then he spotted it. A chair was missing from the table.

He hadn't been in every room so he looked now, both downstairs and up. No B.J. No kitchen chair. There was one last place and he dreaded going there, but he had no choice.

Fincham opened the door to the basement. It wasn't a finished one, for sitting around, but it wasn't creepy either. So why did it feel creepy? The basement stairs were wooden, in good shape, and the space itself ran the whole width and length of the house with cement walls and floor. When he reached the last step he didn't see anything except what he was accustomed to seeing: a washer/dryer and many storage boxes. He stood at the bottom of the stairs, afraid to turn and see the rest of the cellar behind him.

But he knew he had to. And he did. "Oh, shit," he said.

Bonnie Jo was there all right. She was swinging from a beam, the kitchen chair knocked over, and Jack knew immediately that he was far too late.

Chapter Twenty

Dove sat behind her desk, staring. While waiting for the notebook computer to be delivered to her by a deputy, she looked into the middle distance, and into her self.

Why had her body reacted that way to the thought of Clare? Then she almost laughed, realizing she was blaming it on her body, not willing to take responsibility for her mind, her self. Having been in counseling for almost two years after Clare's death, she certainly knew enough to understand that her body was reacting to thoughts. But what were they?

It wasn't as if she'd never before thought of her child, her death, her funeral. She'd replayed them countless times over the years. But she'd never felt anything like that. What was it that triggered the feeling?

She tried to remember and a picture of Officer Copus came to mind. And then the gum, the blowing of a bubble, the splat, removing the sticky tentacles from her face, just the way Clare had. Okay, that made her think of her daughter, but so what? It was some inner knowledge, so buried it wasn't available to her conscious mind. Perhaps she should go back to Alana. But what if it got out that the sheriff was in therapy? If mob bosses could go to therapy, why couldn't a sheriff? But that was TV and movies. This was real life. She could think of a number of people who would make hay with that one if they found out. So what, she—

There was a knock on the door. It was the day dispatcher, Bethany.

"Sheriff, sorry to come in like this, but I thought you'd want to know and I didn't want to do it on the phone?"

Sweet Jesus. What now? "Spit it out, Bethany."

"Lieutenant Fincham radioed for an ambulance and police cars?"

Dove was out of her chair and walking toward the door of her office. "What happened?"

"I don't know. He didn't say. But I thought you'd want to know?"

"You're right, thanks. Listen, Bethany, Deputy Massey will be bringing in a notebook computer, and when he does lock it in the safe."

"Will do."

"And thanks for telling me. You did the right thing."

Dove ran down the hall and out to her cruiser. She started up before she even closed the door.

When she pulled up at Fincham's house, the ambulance and three police cars were there. She ran up the front path, her heart thudding. But at least she knew Jack wasn't dead because he'd made the call. Bonnie Jo. It was bound to be something to do with her. The door was open.

Inside a lot of officers she knew were milling around. "Where's the lieutenant?"

"In the basement with the coroner and the body."

The body. She hadn't even noticed the coroner's car. Dove didn't ask anything more, went through the kitchen and down the stairs to the basement. More officers were at the bottom of the steps. They saluted her and one motioned with his head to the other end of the cellar. When Dove turned she saw Scruggs, Lieutenant Hutt and Jack walling off what they were looking at on the basement floor. Their backs were to her, but she saw the swinging rope that had clearly been cut. Pritchett was taking pictures.

Oh, God, she thought, please don't let it be one of the children. "Jack," she said softly.

He turned, looking surprised.

When she got closer she said, "What happened?"

"B.J.," was all he answered.

And she couldn't help feeling relieved it wasn't a child, if only for a moment. "Oh, Jack. I'm so sorry."

"Yeah. I found her. Scruggs says she's probably been dead about two or three hours. She wasn't due at work until three."

"Do the kids know?"

He shook his head. "I want the body removed first."

"Yes. That's better." She could see he'd been crying. And a wave of guilt engulfed her. Had Bonnie Jo done this because of them? But how could she have known? She suspected, thought it was true before it really was. How much of that made her take her life?

Jack touched her sleeve. "There were bottles all over. I'm sure she was drunk."

"Can I do anything? Want me to stay when you tell the kids? I mean, I don't know them well, but sometimes a woman . . ." she trailed off.

"I don't know. Maybe." He turned back to Scruggs. "Harry, how soon can she go?"

Scruggs, his lock of silver hair fallen above his bushy brows, looked back at Jack with what Dove thought was an expression of sympathy she'd never seen on the man before.

"I think she can go now, Jack."

Jack nodded and walked over to one of the deputies near

the steps, spoke to him and the man hurried upstairs. Then he came back to Dove.

"Going to take her now."

She wanted to hold Jack, but she couldn't. What would she do if they were as they'd been before Coconut Key? She certainly wouldn't have embraced him. At least not in front of the other professionals. But she might put an arm around his shoulder, like two good buddies. Shit. Anyway, she did it and he let her.

"I'm so sorry, Jack." What else could you say, even if you'd said it before? She gave his arm a squeeze and let go quickly, perhaps a little too quickly.

"I guess I should call the school, ask the kids to come home. You think that's the best way? Or should I go get them?"

She wondered what she would've done had it been Mike and she'd had to tell Clare? It was a ridiculous comparison; he wasn't even her father. "Won't they be panicked if they don't know why they're being sent home?"

"That's right. I'd better go. And I think I should do this alone. Hope you understand."

"Of course I do, Jack." And she did. "Go. I'll stay until the situation is under control."

"You don't mind?"

"No. Go on. I'm sure things will be settled down by the time you get back."

"Thanks." He smiled at her.

She felt it and for a blinding moment reality was gone.

Then he said, "Should I take them for ice cream?"

"Oh, Jack," she said. It was so typically a man's question in a situation like this. "I really don't think they'd want that. I think you have to tell them right away, in the car."

"Yeah. That's right. Tell them soon as I have them alone. Not in the school."

"Yes."

"Okay, thanks. Will you be here when I get back?"

"I don't know, do you want me to be here? Will it help?"

"Don't know. I guess if you're here, you're here. I'll talk to you later."

She watched him go, feeling helpless, useless and guilty. She'd slept with Bonnie Jo's husband and it didn't matter that the woman was a drunk. Guilt was going to have its way.

"Sheriff?"

"Yes, Harry."

"I'm sure it's a suicide. No reason to believe otherwise right now. I think she was drunk as a skunk."

"Probably."

"But I'll have to do an autopsy, no matter. Make sure."

"Naturally."

"Yes. Well. Just checking."

"You do what you'd do in any case like this, Harry."

He pushed his glasses back up over the hump in his nose to where they belonged and nodded.

The EMT people came down the stairs with a folded gurney. Solemnly they made their way back to the body, lifted her onto the canvas, then pulled the whole thing up and the legs popped into place. They covered her from toes to beyond the top of her head with a blanket, then asked if there was another way out besides the stairway.

"There's a door back here," one of the officers said. "Don't know where it goes though."

One of the EMT people, a tall, strapping woman, went to the door and tried it. Locked. She turned back to her partner. "Stairs, Jim."

He looked disappointed, but determined. Together, they lifted the gurney up, the legs retracted and they slowly carried the body up the stairs.

There was no point remaining in the cellar. Dove went up, followed by Scruggs, Pritchett and the remaining officers.

In the kitchen, Scruggs said, "What a mess."

"Keep this part to yourself, Harry," Dove said.

"Why're you always saying that to me, Sheriff? You think I go down to the bar and tell stories out of school?"

"No, course not. Habit, I guess. Didn't mean to insult you."

"Yeah, well."

"Really, Harry, I didn't mean anything personal," she said. But, of course, she couldn't help thinking of Harry's wife, Faye.

Harry said, "Pritchett you get pictures of this kitchen?"

"Is that necessary?" Dove asked.

"It might be. You never know."

"What do you mean, Harry?"

"Look, you and I know Jack had nothing to do with this, but you never know when maybe Bonnie Jo's family or friends might want to say it was murder."

Dove knew from experience that he was right. She was too personally involved in this to think straight. "Of course."

Scruggs said, "You keep this part to yourself, Pritchett."

Dove checked a smile. "Anyone look in the medicine cabinet?"

"Don't know," he said. "Good idea, though."

"I'll do it," she said.

"You know where the bedroom is?" Scruggs asked.

"I imagine it's on the second floor and that the master

bedroom will be obvious," she said.

"Yes, of course," he said, looking chastised.

"See you later."

Dove went through the kitchen and out to the main hall where the staircase was. Everyone was clearing out now and she listened to the ambulance siren as it faded away. In moments she'd be alone in this house. She'd only been here a few times, when the Finchams had had a Christmas party, or something like that.

Only the door to the master bedroom was open. The others were closed and she gathered they were the children's rooms, shouting privacy.

The master bedroom was in disarray, as if there'd been a brawl or struggle. But with whom? And what did that mean? Bonnie Jo was murdered? She shook her head as if to rid herself of stupid ideas.

In the bathroom, which had pale yellow fixtures, the door to the medicine cabinet was open, and items from it had tumbled, or were thrown, into the sink. She reached in her bag and put on the rubber gloves. It was true that you never knew. Then she carefully picked up each item and read the labels. There was one open and empty pill container. The label read: Seconal. She put it in an evidence bag then into her purse. Her guess was that Harry Scruggs would find Bonnie Jo's body full of the stuff.

If it was in the medicine cabinet, why was the room tossed? Something wasn't right here. She had to get forensic to go over this room. She called them and then shut the bedroom door behind her.

It was unfortunate that the forensic people might be here when the kids and Jack returned. But there was nothing she could do about it. And for that reason she decided to stay.

★ ★ ★ ★ ★

When the Finchams arrived, Dove was sitting in the living room. The forensic people were upstairs working.

Jack, Jr. gave her a filthy look, didn't say hello as he usually did and went immediately upstairs.

Kim said, "What the fuck are you doing here?"

Fincham grabbed her by the arm. "Are you nuts, Kimmy? Don't you speak that way to the sheriff."

"It's all right, Jack. She's upset." But Dove didn't understand it herself.

"You bet I'm upset and I hate you," she screamed at Dove.

"Why?"

Kim turned away from her and looked at Fincham. "And I hate you, too."

Jack held onto her. "Stop this. What are you talking about?"

"I know," she said bitterly. "You might as well have killed Mom yourselves."

"What?"

"She told me about the two of you, so don't fucking pretend." She pulled out of Jack's grasp and ran up the stairs.

After she was out of sight, Fincham looked at Dove. "I'm sorry, Arizona. I don't know . . . B.J. must have . . ." He shrugged.

"Yes, she must have. But it wasn't true. Don't forget that."

He nodded.

"Do you have any idea why the bedroom looks the way it does?"

"No. I wondered, too."

"And what about the medicine cabinet, all the stuff in the sink?"

"Sometimes she'd hide pills from herself and forget where she'd hidden them. Especially if she was drunk."

She didn't know why, but she didn't believe that's what happened.

Chapter Twenty-One

After Arizona left, Jack wasn't sure what he should do. She had told him why she had the forensic people going over the bedroom and why she wanted them to tackle the kitchen, too. He thought she was being over-cautious, but she was right in that you never knew. Still, in B.J.'s case he was sure that she'd just forgotten where she'd hidden her pills.

Worse than that was this stuff with the kids. He had to talk to them. Even though what B.J. had obviously told them wasn't true at the time, it was now. So what could he say? He had to go with the truth.

Reluctantly, he climbed the stairs. He decided to take the hardest one first and knocked on Kim's door.

"Go away," she said.

"No, Kimmy. I need to talk to you."

"I don't fucking want to talk to you."

She'd never used this kind of language before. At least not to him. He guessed that she knew under the circumstances she could get away with it.

Fincham opened the door anyway.

"Get out," she screamed. "This is exactly why we wanted locks on our doors."

Jack and B.J. had denied them this in case of fire and promised never to come in without their approval. But this was different.

"Kim, we need to talk."

She was curled into a ball on her bed. "I never want to talk to you again, you cheat."

"Listen to me . . ."

"Do you deny that you're sleeping with her?" Kim asked.

"Let me explain something."

"See, you don't deny it."

"Kim. Shut up and listen."

"What then?"

He sat at the end of her bed, not too close.

"What your mother may have told you wasn't true."

"Why did she say it then?"

"Because she thought it was true."

"And it isn't?"

Shit. This was what he was afraid of, she'd ask him in the present. Oh, God. He couldn't lie, he'd always preached to these kids about honesty. But it was so much to take in one day. Still . . .

"Yes. It's true now, but it wasn't true when she told you."

Kim sat up and screamed. "What the fuck does that mean?"

"Kim, calm down."

"Why should I?"

"I don't know, don't calm down." He was at a loss. "The thing is, nothing was going on between me and the Sheriff when Bonnie Jo told you it was."

"But it is now?"

"Yes."

"So what difference does it make, you shit? It just means she knew before you did. She killed herself because she knew it was *going* to happen even if you didn't. That's the way women are."

"Yeah, I know." He got up. "I'm sorry, Kim."

"Get out."

"I'm going. You need me, I'll be here."

"I'm never going to need you again."

And women know what to say to really hurt you, he thought, as he closed her door behind him.

When he knocked on Jack's door, Fincham decided to tell the truth from the top.

"Yeah?"

"It's Dad."

After a few moments of silence the boy told him he could come in.

"What?" Jack Jr. asked.

"I want to talk to you about what Mom told you."

"What about it?"

"When she told you that, it was something she thought and it wasn't true. But it's true now. Your mother didn't know because it wasn't happening then. Do you understand?"

"Like which word do you think I don't get?"

"Don't be a smart ass, Jack. We all need to pull together now. Understand?"

"Right. Mom didn't tell me anyway. Kim did. And I think you're splitting hairs. I mean, Mom didn't know because it wasn't true, but now it is? Get real, Dad."

"I just wanted you to know the truth."

"Yeah, well thanks right much."

Fincham knew there was nothing else to say about it. "I'll be here if you need me."

Jack didn't answer and Fincham went into his bedroom. The forensic people were still working, black dust everywhere. He knew from experience that they weren't the ones who were going to clean up. He'd have to call in a cleaner, because he couldn't do it.

"Find anything?" Jack asked.

A young man Fincham knew as Blackshirt Bob, because that's the only color he ever wore, said, "The usual."

"What's that mean?"

"Prints everywhere, but my guess is they're yours and hers, Mrs. Fincham."

"That would be right," Jack said. "You finished in here?"

"Just about. Sheriff said to do the kitchen, too."

"Yeah, do that."

Jack left them and went downstairs. He picked up the hall phone, dialed the station, got Bethany, who gave him her condolences and put him through to Dove.

"It was hell with the kids, Arizona."

"You have to give them time, Jack."

"Yeah, I guess."

"Forensic find anything?"

He told her. "When do you think we can be together again?"

When Dove put down the phone she was worried. Thrilled that Jack wanted to be together, she couldn't help wondering how he could think of that at this time. On the other hand, it wasn't as though he'd been in love with his wife.

Although suicide could be the only answer, if the autopsy showed murder, the D.A.'s office might uncover their affair and ascertain Jack's threat to take the children, B.J.'s determination to keep them. Dove had no doubt she'd confided all to her coworkers, not to mention her children. What a mess.

She eyed Lyle's notebook sitting on her desk and took it out of its case, found the power cord and plugged it in. It was a nice, new-looking Sony Vaio, very slim and light. She discovered the catch to open it on the front, pulled it to the right with her nail. Then she pushed back the top which was the screen. At the back of the keyboard it said: PCGF160, which identified the model. She found something on the side that looked like it might be the on switch and pulled it forward. Yes. She listened as she heard the thing power up, and soon it said *Windows 98*. It went through its dance and finally there was the screen, clouds in the background and little icons covering them. She'd never seen so many. They all had names underneath.

Finally she found what she was looking for. A mail program. She tapped twice on the touch pad and it loaded, then opened. She clicked on *Read Mail* and there was the program. She was sure Lyle had Julie in a separate folder so she clicked on the Inbox and it opened to show all the folders. Bingo. There was one named Julie and she tapped for it to open. But these were all *from* Julie. She went back and saw it. She'd been in too much in a hurry. The label was *To Julie* and she opened that.

All his letters to her were there. They were listed by date and his last to her was at the top. She clicked twice on it and it opened to a full screen. It was the same one she'd seen on Julie's computer.

She was looking in the wrong place. The wrong program? She minimized this one and was back on the desktop. She double tapped the icon for *Word*. It appeared and on the program's toolbar were many icons that Taylor had obviously colored in some paint program. Dove was mighty glad she'd taken the time to go to the computer course the county offered.

She tapped on the *Open* icon and what came up was a box marked *Personal* and many folders within. She opened the one that was labeled *Thoughts.*

Inside that were various documents that had only dates for labels. She went to the most recent and it bloomed on the screen.

She read:

> *I hate those fucking bitches. Always after me to do something they think a "Man" should do. I'd like to take their dyke heads and smash them together. Maybe I will. But, fuck, I'm never going back there. I'm going to Virginia and I'm going to see Julie even though she doesn't know it and if she doesn't like me I'll smash in her head. I'll take it and bash it against a tree until her brains run out on the ground and the ants eat them or the flies get them and lay their maggot eggs in them. I fucking don't care anymore.*

That was it. And it was plenty. She carefully shut down each program and hit the Start button, which brought up the *Shutdown* icon, clicked on that and watched as the computer went to sleep, and then she shut the case, clicked on her intercom.

"Sheriff?" Bethany said.

"Get me someone from Evidence, Beth. Get them here right now. I need something bagged and tagged."

"Right."

She sat back in her chair. They had the sick bastard now. Then her smile died like a fading flower. Christ, how could she have been so stupid? It was Jack's situation that made her forget procedure. She could easily be accused of writing that piece of filth herself. No witness. She'd have to do it again with someone standing by. Sweet Jesus. She hit the intercom.

"Bethany, did you get through to Evidence yet?"

"Sorry, Sheriff but they've been busy, busy . . ."

"Never mind. That's fine. Forget it."

"I was just gonna buzz you anyway. A missing person call just came through?"

"And?"

"Well, it's two girls? Sisters? They were in their backyard and now they're gone?"

"And?"

"It's been hours, I guess, and the mother says they'd never go off like that without telling her?"

"What else?"

As Bethany went down the list of things, Dove slowly sank in her chair, sickened. With every word the dispatcher said, it sounded more and more like the Julie Boyer case. And if it was, no matter what he'd written in his computer, it couldn't be Lyle Taylor, who was sitting in jail. If it was the same thing, if those sisters turned up dead, she was way off track and didn't have one damn lead.

Chapter Twenty-Two

After Dove called McQuigg and left a message with his secretary, she'd asked Gill Hutt to go with her to the Scotts, the family of the missing girls. She felt an unusual tension emanating from Hutt.

"What's up?" she asked.

"Meaning?"

"You're tense, not the usual way we all are, something else."

"Boy, you're good, Sheriff." He made a sound that was almost laughter. "I was just thinking, I hope to hell whoever's doing this isn't a black man."

"I think I understand," she said.

"It's a white guy, the public's going to go crazy, it's a black guy they going to go berserk, you get my drift."

"You really think so? I mean things have changed."

This time his laugh was ironic. "Well, Sheriff, no offense, but that's what white people like to think. Truth is, not that much has changed. White people still hate us and I don't mean only here in the South. Everywhere. Regular folks can maybe sit in the front of the bus, eat where we want, some other small stuff, but that's about it."

Dove knew what he was saying was true. She'd seen it among her colleagues at closed political meetings, and she'd observed the subtle ways that her fellow whites had of showing their contempt and hatred. It sickened her, but she couldn't change everyone.

"I think most serial killers are white, Gill. Wayne Williams is the only black guy I can think of."

"Jesus, Sheriff, you think we got a serial?"

Dove was immediately sorry she'd said it. "I was thinking about the murders in the other states that resemble Julie Boyer's killing."

"Yeah, there's that, I guess."

They rode in silence for the rest of the way. Dove was sick at her stomach. The personal reasons: Jack, Bonnie Jo's death, McQuigg's intrusion. But underneath, like so many worms, the overriding nausea probably had more to do with what lay ahead of them. Two girls missing from the same family spelled twice the horror.

There was still daylight when they pulled up at the Scotts, so the windows of the houses didn't appear to be alive. Two cruisers were parked at the curb.

Dove and Hutt walked up the path and when they got to the opened doorway, a worn-looking woman stood there puffing on a cigarette.

"I'm the neighbor," she said, as though this was the name of a character in a play. "The Scotts are in the living room."

Dove took a deep breath and they went inside. It was *déjà vu,* except another child wasn't sitting with the devastated parents. She introduced herself and Hutt, then started the questioning.

This time Dove ordered an APB immediately. Too many details matched those in the Boyer case. Girls, thirteen and fifteen, outside in the yard, backpacks and bags in their rooms. All I.D.s and money were intact. No history of going off without telling someone. Both exemplary students and both well-liked by peers. No boyfriends, or none that the parents knew about. There was one computer and it was in the family room. A quick check revealed nothing. Even while Dove was scanning the material she knew no kid would put anything personal on a family machine. She'd wondered if kids still wrote diaries, then recognized her old-fashioned self, realizing they would now call them *journals*. They'd searched each girl's room but nothing of that nature was discovered.

Back at Dove's office McQuigg arrived and joined Hutt, Jenkins, and Steffey.

"You know what, Sheriff?" Jenkins said. "We have to just wait."

"What you talking about?" said Steffey. "We got the dogs out, people lookin', we're not waitin'."

"I meant us."

Dove said, "We have to canvas all the neighbors, the school friends, everybody these girls knew, and that includes teachers." This time she wasn't doing any of it herself. "And it's important to treat this case as one of a kind. No assumptions. We don't know if we're looking for the same killer or not."

"We all know what's what here," McQuigg said.

"No. We don't. We suspect but we don't *know*."

"You going to parse words with me, Sheriff?"

"I think we should approach this situation on its own. Leave the Boyer case out of it. When we go over your notes, if anything matches, we're going to see it pretty quickly."

"It will," McQuigg said.

"Do you want to do something different, Agent McQuigg? Go at this some special way?"

"No. But it's clear to me that one person is responsible for the Boyer killing and these."

Dove took a beat as she looked at him. "Do we know the girls are dead?"

He shook his head derisively, as if to say she was the fool she'd always been. At least it was how Dove interpreted it.

McQuigg said, "Give it a rest, Sheriff. You know that's what this is."

She ignored his remark. "Jenkins, you canvas the neighbors; Steffey, the friends. Hutt, school and anyone else they'd know."

As they rose they groaned, stretched and mumbled, each one hating their assignment. This work was tedious, but if you made a hit, nothing was more rewarding.

When the others left, Dove turned to McQuigg. "What are you going to do?"

"Want to put money on the fact that these two new ones are dead?"

She felt shocked at his words. And angry. "You disgust me. 'Two new ones?' They're young girls, Mike, not *things*."

"I didn't say they were *things*."

"Sometimes I wonder about you," Dove said.

"What's that supposed to mean?"

"Nothing. So what *are* you going to do now?"

"Wait. See you." He slammed the door on his way out.

She stared at the door a moment, thinking about what she *had* meant. Sometimes he didn't seem authentic at all, as though he'd read a book on how to appear human.

Dove picked up the phone and called Fincham. She was relieved when he answered instead of either of his kids.

He said, "What's going on? I heard two girls disappeared."

"Right." She filled him in as much as possible.

"You think it's the same guy?" he asked.

"I do," she said. "But I'm not saying that to anyone else.

214

I want them looking at this with fresh eyes. But how are you, Jack? That's what I want to know?"

"My wife is dead, maybe murdered, and my kids hate my guts. How do you think I am?" he asked.

"Terrific."

"Arizona, you know I didn't kill B.J., don't you?"

"Of course I do."

"Christ, I know how it must look."

"Not to me. Anyway, nobody's said she was murdered. So what are you talking about?"

"I know, but in case it turns out that way. The husband is always the first suspect."

"Not you, Jack."

"Then who?"

"You have to stop this. Let's wait and see what Scruggs comes up with, okay?"

"Yeah, you're right. Arizona, what're we going to do?"

She bit her top lip, then said, "Want me to come over, Jack?"

"What I want and what I can do are two different things, Arizona."

"The kids, huh?"

"Yeah. I told them about us, but that B.J. didn't know. Didn't make any difference, that part."

"I'm so sorry." Selfishly she couldn't help wondering if this was going to queer the whole relationship. What relationship? They'd slept together once.

"They'll come around," he said. "Thing is, now I have to plan a funeral. Jesus, I wish Scruggs could do things a little faster. If it does turn out to be a murder, you think I'll be arrested?"

"We're back there again. Listen, when Scruggs comes up with a timeframe, I think that'll prove where you were when it happened, won't it, Jack?"

"I was with the deputies who picked up Taylor's car before I went home. Before that I was in your office and before that, with you on a plane."

"Which is fine."

"I don't want to compromise you."

"You won't. We were on official business."

"You think Scruggs is over the hill?"

"I think Scruggs is Scruggs. I'll call him, hurry him up."

"Good. I'm going bonkers here."

"I know. This is so hard."

"It is. So where does this Scott thing leave Taylor?" he asked.

She'd been trying not to think about that. "It leaves him in jail for the moment."

Jack said, "You think the girls are dead?"

She took a breath. "I don't know."

"But do you *think* they are?"

"Probably."

"So far everything looks the same as the Boyer case?"

"I'd have to say yes to that. Still, that doesn't make it true."

"Right. So when should I come back to work?"

"After the funeral. Wait until that's over."

"Yeah. I don't like being cut out of this investigation."

She wished he'd given a more personal reason.

"This is not my thing, to be home while everybody else is doing their job, running down leads."

"You can't have things your way right now. You've got plenty to do there."

"Yeah, I guess. Gotta be here for the kids, anyway. But I sure wish I could see you."

"Soon," she said.

"Soon," he repeated.

Her intercom buzzed. "Got to go, Jack."

"Let me know, anything develops."

"Sure thing. Talk to you later." She'd wanted to end on a more intimate note but the buzzer was insistent and she was nervous about saying anything more than she already had.

"Sheriff," Bethany said over the speaker. "Could you pick up the phone please?"

"Sure thing. Yes, Bethany?"

"Sheriff, I . . . they found the two girls."

"And?"

"They're dead."

Part Two

"The cases are beginning to emerge as too coincidental, and Sheriff Dove of Snowden County hasn't taken any action. Only Agent Michael McQuigg of the FBI appears to be on top of things."
Tom Matthews

— JBCTV News

Chapter Twenty-Three

She turned off Crawford Boulevard onto Hickory Avenue, made a left onto Oak Drive, and as she turned the corner she saw the cars. Closing in, she noticed that Fincham's car was among them. He'd probably heard it on his police scanner. She parked behind Hutt's cruiser and got out. McQuigg pulled in behind her. He immediately ran up beside her and started talking.

"Good thing I heard."

"I don't know what you're talking about," Dove snapped.

"Well, you didn't fucking call me."

"Didn't have time."

They walked into Wilson's woods, so named for William Wilson who had owned three hundred acres at one time. Now most of it was developed, but Wilson had kept seventy five acres in the family, designated it as a preserve for wildlife. It was a dense and dark place.

The print and TV reporters were there already. This time Tom Matthews for JBCTV, along with Marcelle Walsh. Matthews, who looked like he might be putting on some weight, approached her.

"This another one, Sheriff?" He stuck a mike under her nose.

"How would I know?" she said. "I haven't been to the crime scene yet. Now please get out of my way, Matthews, and go have another candy bar or whatever it is you're eating these days."

He looked incredibly hurt and Dove felt awful. "Sorry," she mumbled and kept on walking. When she glanced back she saw McQuigg speaking into Matthew's microphone. What the hell was he telling him? She wanted to go back but knew she couldn't. It wouldn't matter anyway; she couldn't stop him. Besides, she had to get to the crime scene.

A deputy stood at the edge of the woods where the path began.

He saluted her. "Just follow the trail, Sheriff."

"Thanks."

The path was dark and twisting and gave Dove the creeps. Eventually it opened into a clearing where people, including Jack, were standing around. She nodded at Fincham, but didn't say anything, or ask him why he was there. She went directly to Hutt.

"Where are they?"

"Down there a ways. There's a stream."

"Have you seen them?"

"Yeah." His eyes betrayed the anguish he felt.

Dove touched his arm and asked him to come with her. Silently, he led her down the heavily forested slope.

Two hours later, back in the office, once again the senior officers stood around. Dove sat behind her desk, McQuigg leaned against a wall. No one questioned Fincham's presence. They could all understand why he'd want to be here. Clearly it was the same killer who'd murdered Julie Boyer. The MO was exactly the same. Except this time there were two of them.

Dove said, "We have to tell the parents. We know they're innocent, but we're obliged to question them again anyway. And you never know what information they give us will help. Hutt, will you do that?"

"You want me to tell them?" he asked.

"Something wrong with that?"

"I thought you'd . . . it's just that . . ." he shrugged.

"You're a lieutenant, nothing wrong with you telling them, unless you have a problem with it."

He did, but he wasn't about to say so. "No, I'll do it."

"Good." Dove assigned other officers to different tasks. When they were all gone she was alone with Jack. On cue the phone rang. It was Scruggs.

"Sheriff, I have the results on Mrs. Fincham," he rasped.

"What's wrong with your voice?"

He cleared his throat. "Got a tickle in there, I guess."

"What did you find?"

"There are definite finger indentations on the jaw. Thumb on the left side and on the right it looks like two fingers, first and second."

"Want to spell this out for me, Scruggs?" She understood, but she wanted to hear him say it.

"It looks like someone grabbed her that way, probably to hold her jaw open."

"For what reason?"

"In this case I'd say to get the pills down her throat."

"You're saying this is a homicide?"

"I'd say so."

"Prints?"

"Gloves. But the size of the indentations indicate a large hand, most likely a man's."

"Timeframe?" She looked up at Jack, who appeared worried.

"I'd say between noon and two. Could be a four-hour frame, one on each end, of course."

Dove wondered why he didn't call it four. "So what

you're saying is eleven to three."

"Could say that."

"Then why aren't you?"

He cleared his throat again. "Well, Sheriff, I'll say that then. Timeframe eleven to three."

He hung up before she could ask him anything else. And then she realized he'd been trying to help Jack. She told him what Scruggs had said.

"That's crazy, Arizona. Who'd murder B.J. and why?"

"You sure she didn't have a boyfriend?"

"How can I be sure about that? Seems unlikely, unless he was a drinking buddy."

"Not unheard of for two drunks to make a couple."

"And she did get home late lots of times. Those women at her salon would definitely cover for her. Then there was that thing she said before we left."

"What was it?"

"I was mad and she was threatening to take the kids away. So I told her she was a drunk and didn't have anything going for her. She said, 'That's all you know,' and gave me a look."

"What kind of look?"

"Like I was wrong . . . that she did have something going and I didn't know."

"It could be our answer. A lover."

"Then why don't we believe it?"

"Right," she said.

"So I'm back to who and why?"

"But we really can't rule out a boyfriend." She purposely didn't say lover again because she knew how most people reacted, even if they didn't care for the person anymore.

"I'm not ruling out a boyfriend. We have to look into that. We also have to think about someone else."

"I agree. But we do have to start with a boyfriend, Jack."

"I can't cover that and neither can you. Everybody else is on other things."

"It can wait a day."

"What about putting McQuigg on it?"

Dove didn't know how to explain to him that McQuigg would love to see Jack arrested for the murder. The only thing to do was to say it flat out. She did.

"He doesn't even know me."

"But he knows me. And for sure he knows about us. He wants me to be unhappy; don't ask me why, because all I can say is he's a miserable sonuvabitch."

"Sounds like he's still in love with you."

She was surprised by this remark. "You call that being in love?"

"I didn't say it was healthy, Arizona. But you left him, remember. Some guys never get over that. Doesn't matter he's married again."

"Just don't start getting jealous."

He laughed. "Hey, I'm sane. I know how you feel about McQuigg. What he feels about you is another matter. Okay, we can't use him. Two of the deputies will work."

"I'd rather use Steffey or Jenkins even though they have their hands full."

"You're right."

"Tomorrow," she said.

As Hutt drove to the Scotts' house he could feel fear thumping in his chest. Or was it anger? He often got those two emotions mixed up, never knew which was which. He banged the flat of his hand against the wheel. That looked like anger to him. Still, he could be angry because he was afraid. Afraid of what? he asked himself.

But he knew. It had been there since he'd met them, and he didn't want to face it. The Scotts. They hated him. Hated him because he was black.

Reverend Hill had counseled him about this, calling it Gill's personal paranoia. That had made him furious. What was wrong with Hill that he didn't know the whites still hated them? It was like some of these people lived in a cave or something. The reverend said Gill was hanging on to old ideas, living in the past, still angry over Cubby's death. Death? Murder was the truth. Everybody knew it and nobody cared. It was twenty years ago, way before Dove's time, and Gill was only fifteen and couldn't do anything about it. Today it would've immediately been labeled a hate crime and sure as shit the press would've jumped on it like fleas on Lassie.

Jesus. Cubby would've been forty-five now. Hutt wondered what his cousin would've become. At twenty-five he'd been a quiet guy working for a local paint company and taking night courses to get a college degree so he could teach history. He'd been engaged. A nice girl, Mary. Everything going along just as Cubby planned. And then it happened.

On a Friday night he and some friends left a bar where they'd stopped for a couple of drinks after work. It was something they did at the end of every week. But this particular night, five white boys were waiting for them. With guns. Why they picked Cubby, no one knew. Hutt's guess was that it was just the luck of the draw. No meaning at all.

After punching him stupid, they threw Cubby in a truck and drove to an isolated place where they stripped him, poured gasoline over his body and set him on fire.

Hutt felt sick thinking about it. He'd gone with his aunt to identify the remains. Of course it was impossible, but dental records proved who it was.

The Sheriff's Office today would never have had anyone

come in and look at a burned body where there was nothing left to identify it. More cruelty on the part of the white police.

Nothing ever happened to the boys who did it. Cubby's friends were too afraid to identify them. As for an investigation, Hutt seriously doubted there was one, no matter what the police said.

Cubby's murder and the police conduct were what had led Gill Hutt to law enforcement. He'd figured if there was a black man on the force maybe there'd be a chance to help his people. It had been tough at first, but he'd minded his p's and q's and little by little he'd climbed the ladder. It was Sheriff Dove who'd promoted him to lieutenant.

She was a great lady, he thought. Not just because she'd promoted him, but he believed she truly wasn't prejudiced. And she was fair. Tough, too. Still, sometimes she didn't get it. Like the conversation they'd had about his concern that the killer might be black. Maybe because of her own views, she didn't realize what it was really like out there.

Again, he said a silent prayer that the killer was white. If he turned out to be black, anything could happen, including a lynching. This was still the South, after all, and some things are always lurking in the background.

Hutt pulled up outside the Scott house. It wasn't as nice as the Boyers' and neither were the Scotts. He walked up the path to the brick and white siding house. Next to a window on the second floor, one green shutter hung crookedly, about to drop. Gill rang the bell.

Mrs. Scott opened the door. She was a small woman, with blue eyes set too close together and a thin, unyielding mouth, like a strip of tape.

Hutt could feel her fear, see it in her eyes.

She looked past him, saw he was alone and almost imperceptibly closed the door a few inches.

"Yes?"

"I'd like to come in and talk to you, Mrs. Scott."

"Did you find them?"

"May I please come in?" When she said nothing, simply stared at him, he said, "Is your husband at home?"

She nodded. "Did you find them?"

"Your husband. Why don't you get him?"

Hutt was in a rage and trying not to show it. He knew she was afraid to let him in because he was black and he was alone. He didn't want to be cruel because these people were about to learn both their daughters were dead. That had to be his priority.

"Mrs. Scott, I'd like to come in and talk to you both."

"Yes. I'll call Dennis." She shut the door, leaving Hutt on the doorstep.

"Fucking honky," he said in an angry semi-whisper. This wasn't good, his fury mounting like this. There were ways to tell people what he had to, and then there were other ways.

Then Dennis Scott filled the doorway, wearing a T-shirt and jeans, arms tanned from outside work. His brown hair was clipped close at the sides and top. He had a reddish face as though he drank too much.

"What's up? You find them?"

Hutt took a deep breath, counted rapidly to ten. "I'd like to come in, Mr. Scott."

"Yeah. Okay." Scott stepped back, the door opening further.

Gill walked in and waited until the door was closed.

"I'd like to talk to both of you," he said.

"Listen, boy, you find them or what?"

Hutt lost it. "Yeah we did. They're dead."

Chapter Twenty-Four

Bonnie Jo's funeral was in an hour. Dove lay on her bed wondering what to wear. She couldn't decide. It wasn't like her to have trouble choosing clothes because basically she didn't care about things like that. And she suspected that she didn't care today either. It really wasn't a tough decision. A light blue linen suit, a white blouse, low-heeled blue shoes.

Almost everyone from the force was attending. Certainly all the main people who worked with Jack. Bethany had even brought in a temp and she was sure Pam would be there too.

The reason she felt immobilized had to do with B.J., but not her funeral. It had to do with her murder. Who would kill Bonnie Jo? And why? Was it related to the other murders, somehow? But that made no sense. Still, it appeared that someone killed her. And it wasn't Jack. It couldn't be Jack. He'd been with *her* and then checking things with the deputies until going home. He hadn't had time. Oh Lord, *hadn't had time.*

The truth was there was a small window of opportunity . . . very small, maybe fifteen minutes . . . if he'd wanted to kill her. But Jack wouldn't have done that, no matter what. And to connect B.J.'s murder to the three girls made no sense.

Was she to conclude that there were two murderers on the loose in this area when there'd never been one on her watch before this? Not like these.

Why would anyone want to kill Bonnie Jo? When she declared her death a homicide after the funeral, Jack would be the prime suspect. And even though it would be easy enough to clear himself, the aroma of guilt would linger. The press would grab hold, and until another suspect was found they'd milk what they had. Poor Jack. What would those kids do now?

Dove checked her watch. She'd better get ready. Her body felt leaden as she hauled herself from the comfort of her bed. She took the clothes from her closet, tossed them on the bed as she took off her robe and began to dress.

Fincham paced the living room waiting for his children. Neither had spoken to him unless it was absolutely necessary. Neighbors had brought food in casserole dishes the last few days so meals hadn't been a problem. As for after the funeral, his next door neighbor, Alice Hussie, had organized some of the other women and they'd made a spread with so much food Jack didn't think he'd have to worry about what to eat for a month. Alice and Ceil Raynor were in the dining room now. Tired of waiting for the kids, he joined them.

Alice, who was tall and thin, was the exact opposite of her friend, Ceil, who was round and short. They both were pleasant looking women in their early sixties.

"Jack, do you think we have enough?" Ceil asked.

"For an army," he said.

They'd covered the table in a white lace cloth and put demure flower arrangements at either end. The food was displayed in various dishes, many of them silver. All were covered with Saran Wrap to keep them fresh.

Alice said, "What do you think?"

"It looks just great," he said. "Very nice, pretty." He didn't know what the hell he was saying.

"Where are those kids of yours? We have to get going." Ceil pushed up her glasses.

She was right. "Would one of you mind seeing what's keeping them?"

The women exchanged a look, then Ceil left to get them.

"They're taking it very hard, aren't they, Jack?"

He nodded.

"You having trouble with them?"

"Yeah. They're blaming me for some damn reason."

"I could put 'paid' to that," she said. "Many's a time I saw Bonnie Jo in her cups, no disrespect, Jack."

"None taken."

"I was always afraid something like this would happen. That woman worried me so. But there was no talking to her about her addictions."

"No. There wasn't. Alice, I know this might be hard for you to answer, but it's important. Did you ever see B.J. with another man?"

"Oh, Jack."

"I have to know."

"What difference does it make now?" Alice busied herself at the table, pushing dishes around needlessly.

"It makes a big difference, even though I can't tell you why. Not yet anyway. Please," he implored.

"Well, yes."

He felt a kick to his belly. Was it jealousy? "When and who?"

Alice was obviously uncomfortable and Jack wished he could help her, but there wasn't any way if he wanted some answers.

"I don't know who. What his name was, I mean. I only saw him twice."

Thank God, Fincham thought. This would give them someone to go after. How could he have been so oblivious to what was going on with his own wife, while a neighbor knew?

"Tell me about it," he said.

"He brought her home a few times. Well, twice, as I said. Late," Alice added.

"Did you get a look at him?"

"I wasn't spying, Jack. I couldn't sleep and I was sitting in my chair near the window, smoking."

"Sure. I know you wouldn't spy." And he did. She wasn't the type.

"I just don't want you to think I'm a nosey parker or anything."

"Alice, I don't. I swear. Did you get a good look at him?"

She tortured her bottom lip with her teeth for a moment or two. "It was dark. He got out of the car to open her door. I remember thinking how courtly it was in this day and age. I can only tell you he was tall and wore a suit."

"Hair?"

"I couldn't tell the color."

"Anything else?"

"No. But he didn't kiss her and he didn't walk her to the door. It was the same both times I saw him."

"How about the car?"

"Oh, dearie, I don't know makes of cars."

He smiled. "Didn't think so. But could you tell the color? Two or four doors? Anything like that."

"I'm pretty sure it had four doors. And I'm guessing, but I think it wasn't dark, not black or dark blue or anything like that. Still, I wouldn't say it was white. Maybe in between."

"When was this, Alice?"

"In the last month."

"Is there any way you could figure out the exact dates?"

"Oh, I don't know. Maybe. I'll have to think about that."

In the background they heard the sound of feet coming down the stairs.

Ceil shouted from the hall, "Okay, folks we're ready."

"Thanks, Alice. You'll never know what a help you've been. And if you think of anything else, or remember when it was, please tell me, okay?"

"I surely will, but I don't think there's anything else. I'll work on the dates though."

Jack gave her arm a squeeze and her cheek a chaste peck. In the hall Kim said, "I'm going with Aunt Ceil."

"Okay," Fincham said.

"You go with your father," Alice ordered Jack, Jr.

He looked annoyed but nodded.

"You want to go with Ceil, too, Jack?"

"It's all right, Dad," he mumbled.

"Okay then, let's go."

The funeral had been well attended. Their neighbors and friends, most of the Force and many customers of Bonnie Jo's, and her coworkers.

Afterward, at the Fincham house, people milled around, talking and eating as though they'd been starving. Dove wondered about this, having seen it at many funeral receptions. If bread was the staff of life, this was perhaps the reason people ate this way, to declare to themselves that they were still among the living.

Dove stayed away from Jack, thinking it would be better in regard to his kids, who were, for the moment, on the sun porch with some of their friends. But either one of them could come into the main room at any time and if Dove and Jack were standing together, well, who knew what effect this might have on Kim or Jack, Jr. She had made eye contact with Jack several times and she thought he understood her distance.

"Penny?"

The sheriff turned to see Hutt. "Guess."

"The murders." He was holding a plate piled high with food.

"You got it."

Hutt nodded and looked uncomfortable.

"What?"

"I did something lousy," he said.

She raised her eyebrows as if to say, *you?* "I doubt it."

"Yeah. I did, Sheriff."

"Okay, I'll bite. What did you do that was lousy?" She smiled.

"I spared the compassion when I told the Scotts about their girls." And he explained it to her, the way it happened.

She didn't say anything right away, mulled it over. "The bad news is that they're racists. The good news is, they were probably so upset they didn't notice *how* you told them."

"What if they make a complaint?"

"I'll deal with it, Gill. Don't worry about it," Dove reassured him.

"Thanks, Sheriff. You're not eating?"

"Not hungry."

"Want something to drink?"

"Thanks, but after this I still have to work."

"Right. Me, too."

They chatted in a desultory manner for a few more minutes and then Dove said she'd better get going. She went over to Jack, who was talking to someone she didn't know.

"Excuse me," she said. "Something work-related."

The man understood and moved away.

"I'm going back to the station," she said.

"I have some information about B.J. and a guy." He told her quickly.

"Can you come into the office later?"

"Much later," he said. "The kids don't want me anyway."

"I'm so sorry, Jack."

"Bummer," he said.

Dove kissed him on the cheek, as she would have if nothing were going on between them, and made her way through the room to the front door. God, she hated deception.

It was a little after four when Jack came into her office. He sat in the chair opposite her desk, remaining professional, and she was grateful for that right now.

"What have you got?" she asked him.

He told her everything he'd learned from Alice Hussie.

When he was finished she said, "It's not much to go on, but it sure as hell is a break."

"Think we should try to track him down?"

"You bet," she said. "Jack, don't you think it's peculiar that we should have a second murderer running around?"

"What are you saying?"

"Could it be the same person?"

Jack looked at her oddly because to him it didn't make sense. "Think about what you're suggesting, Arizona. The guy who murdered these girls all over the country, and probably murdered the girls here, has murdered B.J.? I don't think so."

"Yeah, it is pretty lame."

"Crazy as it is, or peculiar, as you put it, I think we *do* have two murderers."

"Coincidence?"

"I know how we feel about that, but it's the only explanation. The first perp likes his females to be girls, kids. And how would he know B.J.? Why kill her? Jesus. Poor B.J. I hope she was so drunk she didn't know what was happening. But that's unlikely, isn't it? If somebody had to hold her jaw open hard enough to leave impressions, then she must've been fighting."

"That's what it says to me."

"And of course she'd let him in if she'd been seeing him. Listen, I think I'm the best person to interview her friends. They may not like me, but I think they cared enough about her to talk to me. They probably have a goddamn name."

"Okay."

"But they're going to think I killed her."

"Maybe at first. Wouldn't you?"

"You bet I would. Especially if I knew about you and me. Have you made that she was murdered official yet?"

"Not yet."

"The sooner you do it, the better, I think."

"You're right. We have to start looking for her killer."

"Her killer," he said to himself as though he couldn't quite fathom the words.

She stood up and walked around the desk to his chair.

When he stood, they moved into each other's arms. It was more comforting than anything romantic.

"I'm so sorry, Jack."

"I know. We have to get this bastard."

"We will."

Chapter Twenty-Five

The FBI had faxed a profile of the girl's killer. As Dove sat at her desk with it in front of her, she thought, spare me from profilers. Then reconsidered, knowing that they were often right.

This one had a Before the Crime and After the Crime.

Before:

This person may have experienced some stressful event in his personal life.

After:

Changes in the consumption of alcohol, drugs or cigarettes. Avoidance of family, friends and associates; absence from school, work or appointments.

Before:

The stress could have been a problem with teachers, at work with managers or co-workers, at home with parents, spouse or girlfriend, or with law enforcement.

After:

Unplanned disruption of daily activities. May attempt to leave the area for plausible reason such as a work-related trip, or to visit a distant relative or friend, etc.

Before:

He would have displayed a preoccupation with adolescent girls but an awkwardness or lack of success in establishing relationships with them.

After:

Highly nervous, irritable, short-tempered disposition. Disruption of normal sleeping patterns. Changes in physical appearance, such as hair coloring or new cut, removal or growth of facial hair. Lack of pride in appearance.

Before:

He would spend time driving in areas young girls could be found and be seen staring at them to the point of the girls becoming uncomfortable.

After:

Unexplained injuries such as scratches or bruises.

Before:

He may have displayed an avid interest in TV shows, movies or magazines featuring young girls, especially in athletic roles.

After:

Uncharacteristic turn to or away from religious activity. Physical sickness.

Intense interest in status of the investigation through discussion, media monitoring, etc.

Changes to his vehicle. May clean or change appearance of vehicle (paint, removal of accessories). May hide, sell or dispose of it.

"Thanks a bunch," Dove said out loud. Most of these things applied to knowing the person. Or questioning everyone in Jefferson about their husbands, fathers, sons, brothers.

They'd already questioned every known sex offender. That had been a lot of fun. It gave her the creeps to be in the same room with them.

Usually the profilers said something about intelligence. No clue here. But Dove didn't believe in that part either.

Maybe the Feebs were dropping this part of the profile, as it so often proved wrong. The research and reading she'd done indicated a serial killer's intelligence had nothing to do with it. Sometimes they were dopes and sometimes brilliant. She would hunt for a person growing a mustache or beard, or getting rid of one or the other. Yeah, that would do it!

Gradually, she became aware of a faint din somewhere. The more she listened the more it seemed to have a rhythm to it. As the sound moved closer, there was a knock on the door.

Dove told the person to come in.

Bethany stood there looking ashen. "It's a demonstration?"

"What is?"

"Don't you hear it, Sheriff?"

The din. "I was wondering what that was. What kind of a demonstration?"

"About the murders?"

"Already?"

Bethany shrugged.

"Right."

Dove followed her out to the main office. Everyone was clustered at the windows, looking out. She moved in between two clerks who acted like kids caught in a lewd act, and she waved a hand to let them know it was okay.

Outside, a band of thirty or forty people were marching toward the station and chanting. Some carried signs. And now she could hear them.

"Catch the child killer, catch the child killer."

Oh, God. Nobody wasted a moment these days, she thought. As they came closer she could read the signs.

Do Nothing Police
Sheriff Resign

Catch Him Before He Kills Again
We Want Justice

Over on the side the sheriff spotted Tom Matthews with the cameraman from JBC. And Dawson Pratt and his photographer from *The Standard*. Obviously they'd been alerted. This was great. It would bring out the mayor, the commissioner, maybe even the governor. She was going to be on the spit and it would be hot as hell.

"Sheriff?"

She turned to see Fincham.

"What are you doing here?"

"I work here." He smiled.

She nodded.

"I was on my way to interview B.J.'s coworkers and I heard about this on the radio. You have to go out there," he said.

"I know."

"Better do it now. Want me to come with you?"

"You think it's okay?" she asked softly as they moved away from the window.

"Sheriff, you have to stop thinking of our personal lives."

She knew he was right. "Okay. Yes, come with me. I could use the moral support."

They walked down the hall in silence, exchanged a quick smile, their eyes meeting, and they were infused with a longing to be alone together. Quickly, they looked away before Dove opened the heavy front door and they stepped outside.

It was a hot, muggy day and she felt like she was walking straight into a wet towel. The chanting stopped as people began to yell at her. She couldn't make out whole phrases, just an unkind word here and there. Jack lightly touched her sleeve.

Dove held up her hands, palms outward, the way she'd seen politicians and movie stars do. "Please, please," she shouted.

It took about a minute for the crowd to quiet down. And then she experienced raw fear because she didn't have a clue about what to say. But she opened her mouth and words came out.

"I know how you feel. I feel the same way. But I assure you we're doing everything we can . . ."

"How do we know that?" a man yelled.

"Because I'm telling you." She mustn't get angry. Firm but not mad. "Murders like these don't get solved overnight. There's a great deal of work to do, evidence to sift."

"You got any evidence?"

She ignored the question. "We have leads to follow, suspects to question."

"You ain't got no suspects."

"As soon as we know something, you'll know. I promise."

"Why the hell don't you resign, give yer job to a man who deserves it."

"Excuse me, sir. I ran for this job against two very qualified men, and I won. I would hope the voters here would support me."

"I didn't vote for ya."

"I'm sure you didn't. But the majority of people in this county did. Now go home. Let me do the job I was elected to do."

She didn't wait to hear responses but walked back into the station. Jack followed.

"You were great, Arizona."

"I don't even know what I said."

"I do and it was perfect."

"Aren't you a little prejudiced?"

"Could be," he said.

The staff gave her a round of applause as they reached her floor and she gave them a mock bow.

Jack said softly, "You okay?"

"Fine."

"Have you made B.J.'s murder official yet?"

"I'm about to."

"Can you give me an hour to question the salon women?"

"Sure. They're going to give you flak whether it's official or not," she said.

"I know. But I'd rather try before you do."

"You're sure you don't want me to send someone else?"

"Only if I don't get any results."

"Okay. Good luck, Fincham."

"Thanks, I'll need it."

Hair and Now was in the middle of a refurbished block. Every building was meant to appear quaint, but to Jack it looked too programmed, unreal, like the reproduction it was.

He easily found a parking place. As he walked toward the shop he found himself tossed around by conflicting emotions. So many times he'd gone here in so many different moods. He remembered the opening of the shop when B.J. was so proud and happy. Had he loved her then? Was she drinking alcoholically? Were there signs then of fissures or even cracks in the marriage that he had failed to recognize? He couldn't recall now what their life had been like.

A bell tinkled as he opened the door. Two of the three

working hairdressers looked up at him. He could see the surprised, then angry, expressions on their faces.

Behind the reception desk was Trinity, a blond, beautiful but blank-faced young woman about twenty. She had what the kids called "big hair." And it was.

"Hey, Trinity."

"Hey, Jack." She stared at the appointment book.

"I'd like to speak to Debbie, or any of the others."

"They're all busy now, Jack."

"I can see that. But when the first girl is finished with her customer, I'd like to talk with her."

"Oh, I don't know about that, Jack. Tight schedule."

He took a breath, didn't want to lose his temper before he started these interviews.

"Trinity, I'm here officially."

She finally looked up at him, her blue eyes reflecting nothing. "What's that mean?"

"It means I'm here on police business. You want me to show you my shield?" he added.

"No."

"Okay. So you tell them I want to talk to whoever's free first. And I'll wait." He went to the wicker couch near the window.

This was going to be hell, he thought. If a little twit like Trinity was dismissing him, what the hell was it going to be like with the partners? Although he was tempted to glance at *Newsweek* he didn't pick it up. He wanted them to see he was waiting. And he needed to watch them and let them know that that's what he was doing.

Debbie was finished first. "Mrs. Whiteside?" she called for her next client.

Fincham stood up. "Excuse me, Debbie?"

"Yeah?"

"I'd like to speak with you. This is official."

"Now?" she whined.

"Now."

Smiling, sounding sweet, "Would you mind waiting a moment, Mrs. Whiteside?"

"Will it be long, dear?"

"No, not at all. Thanks." She motioned for Jack to come to her station. "What's official?"

"The questions I have to ask you. And you don't have to act like this toward me; I didn't kill B.J."

"You might as well have."

"There are two sides to every story, Debbie, but I'm not here to discuss that. When did she start seeing the last boyfriend?"

"What's that supposed to mean?"

"This guy she was seeing . . . when did it start?"

"I don't know what you're talking about."

"I think you do. You were the closest to B.J. She'd tell you about him."

Debbie pulled hair from one of the brushes and dropped it to the floor like a floating coil. "This is official?"

"Yes."

"What difference does any of it make now?"

"Just answer my questions," he said gently, but feeling like a bear.

"Wasn't it a suicide, Jack?"

"Debbie, please answer. Do you know the name of the man she was seeing?"

She nodded almost imperceptibly.

"What is it?"

"His name is Bernie Zanville."

"With an S or a Z?"

Raising her voice slightly she said, "Who the hell

knows?" Then she looked around, saw some customers glancing her way, lowered her tone. "Ya think B.J. spelled his name for me?"

She had a point. "I assume his name was Bernard?"

"Yeah, I think so."

"Did you ever see him?"

"You know, I never did. B.J. said he was handsome, but he'd never come in to pick her up."

Because he didn't want anyone to know who he was, Fincham thought. But why? Married?

"Anything else you can tell me about him? B.J. ever say he got violent with her, anything like that?"

"Never. And guess what? She was going to divorce you and marry him, Jack," she said defiantly.

"You know anything else that might be helpful?"

"Helpful for what?" She tossed her curly brown hair in an arrogant way.

"I'd like to talk to Mr. Z."

"Bet you would."

"Officially," he reminded her.

"Yeah, right."

He wanted to shake her. "So you have no idea how I can contact this man?"

"Nope."

"B.J. ever say what he did for a living?"

"Salesman, something like that. You might want to try the phone book, Lieutenant." She smiled in a profoundly nasty way. "That all?"

"Yeah. Thanks. Any of the other women know anything?"

"Far as I know B.J. didn't talk to nobody but me. I got to go now. My appointments are all backed up."

"Thanks."

Jack sat in his cruiser, thinking. So there definitely was a lover. He'd had a stab of jealousy when Debbie confirmed it, but he knew it was ego and had nothing to do with his feelings for his dead wife. He was amazed that his pride, or whatever, gave a damn.

And now Fincham would have the job of finding this man. A man no one ever saw. A man who clearly didn't want to be seen or known by anyone other than B.J.

A man who was going to be hell to find.

Chapter Twenty-Six

Betty Grable flipped an egg over easy as McQuigg watched from his seat in the breakfast nook. He wondered why in hell he'd ever married her. Sure she was pretty, and she might look like Betty Grable, but she wasn't Grable. Not that he knew what *she'd* been like.

"Here you go, Mike," Eleanor said.

Same thing every day. *Here you go, Mike.* Couldn't she say something else for a change? It was old.

"Thanks, babe," he said. He was getting a late start today.

"More coffee?"

She could see his cup was empty, why did she have to ask? "Yeah." He wasn't sure how long he could stay in this marriage. On the other hand, he didn't want it to get around that he'd fucked up again. The Bureau liked it better if you were married. Another divorce could hold him back, derail his career. Maybe she'd die. No. She was healthy as a horse. He stopped eating for a moment and wondered where that expression had come from. Horses weren't always healthy.

Eleanor poured his coffee and some for her, put the carafe back on the Mr. Coffee, and sat down opposite him.

"You got in late last night, Mike."

Why the fuck did it sound like an accusation? "Yeah. Working."

"Something interesting, I hope."

"Eleanor," he said in a patronizing tone, which she never seemed to hear that way, "it's *all* interesting. I'm not some clerk in an office. I have cases and I work them and when they get to my level, they're all interesting."

"Sorry. I was just making conversation."

He ate the last bite of egg, washed it down with a gulp of coffee and his beeper went off.

McQuigg looked at the number and saw it was Dove. He pushed back his chair and went to the phone in his study.

"What's up?" he asked when he got through to her.

"Thought you'd want to know that we're bringing Lieutenant Fincham in for questioning about the murder of his wife."

"What's that got to do with us, Lucia?"

"Not a damn thing, McQuigg. But I figure you'll make it your business sooner or later, so why not sooner?"

McQuigg smiled to himself. "You mean you think this murder and the others are connected?"

"I don't know."

"Then you think your boyfriend offed his wife?"

"Come in or don't." She hung up.

Well, that would be the end of Sheriff Dove's love affair. Too, too bad. He returned to the kitchen.

"You going now?" Eleanor asked.

"Yes."

"You think you'll be home for dinner?"

She asked this every day and he answered the same way. "I don't know. I'll call you." He gave her a perfunctory peck on the cheek, picked up his briefcase and left the house.

He unlocked the door to his tan Chevrolet. Everyone knew government employees drove tan or beige cars, so why did they keep issuing them? The car started immediately and McQuigg backed out of his driveway in this small subdivision of Fairfax.

When he remarried he'd given up his apartment in D.C. and moved to this house. It had been her idea. He wished that he'd kept the apartment, too. It would have made things so much easier, but he couldn't afford it, so there was no point in dwelling on that.

On the car phone he called Krause and told him to meet him at the Snowden station and why.

He drove into the small town, passing the old courthouse. He'd gotten into the habit of buying *The Washington Post* at a small shop here instead of wrestling the hordes in D.C. Besides, there was always a parking space.

God knew how long the little store had been there; the owner was a man in his late seventies and he'd owned it for fifty years, he'd told Mike.

"Hey, Arnie."

"Mr. Mike," the old man said.

McQuigg smiled and picked up his newspaper, put the money on the marble counter.

"How's Betty Grable?"

"She's just fine," he said. "Your wife?"

"Oh, well. Good days and bad days," Arnie said sadly.

Arnie's wife had Alzheimer's and needed a nurse when he wasn't around. Mike never let Arnie get too far into his answer because he didn't want to hear about it.

"Guess you have to be thankful for the good days, Arnie. See you tomorrow."

"Take it easy, my boy."

Mike waved a hand, almost like a salute, and was out the door, the old bell chiming behind him. He glanced at the headline as he walked to the car. Same old same old.

Inside the car he scanned the first section and on page twelve there was a squib about the Scott girls' murders. He hoped like hell he could make Fincham for these as well as his wife. Throwing the paper on the passenger seat he started up and headed for Jefferson.

Dove, Hutt, McQuigg and Krause walked to the interrogation room where Jack was waiting. It broke her heart to see him, sitting straight up in the wooden chair, this time on the other side of the table.

"Why doesn't this man have a guard?" Krause asked.

"He's a lieutenant and he hasn't been charged with anything," Dove said.

"Yet," McQuigg added.

The agents declined chairs, preferring to stand and be threatening, she thought. After going through the opening formalities, McQuigg tried to ask the first question, but Dove stopped him.

"I let you in on this for the reason I told you. I don't expect you to take charge of the interrogation."

McQuigg said, "You want to do it, Sheriff? I think you'd be better off recusing yourself under the circumstances, don't you?"

"That's why Lieutenant Hutt is here."

The two agents looked at Hutt as though they'd never seen him before.

"He's a member of your staff. I'd expect him to be loyal to you, Sheriff."

Dove glanced at Fincham, who nodded.

"Oh, go ahead," she said.

"Thank you." He turned to Jack. "After you got back from investigating in Coconut Key, where'd you go?"

"We drove back here. Had a meeting. Then I went to

251

interview Deputies Gruen and Johnston about towing the suspect's car."

"And what time was that?"

"That I went to question them? Maybe about two o'clock."

Dove said, "I think it was—"

"Sheriff," McQuigg said.

"How long did the questioning take?"

"About an hour."

"So we're up to what time?"

He hesitated only a moment, but enough for Dove to take notice.

"About three, I guess."

"Deputy Gruen says it was two."

Dove was furious. McQuigg had known about this and had questioned those deputies days ago.

"Two?"

Agent Krause took out a notebook and flipped the pages. "Yes, one-fifty-five to be exact. Deputy Johnston concurred."

"I'd like to know when and why you questioned these men?"

"Covering loose ends, Sheriff." He gave her a fake smile.

It wasn't a satisfactory answer, but there was no point in going off on this tangent. What was clear to her was that McQuigg had had his eye on Jack from the minute B.J. was found dead. And she hadn't missed him calling Fincham her boyfriend that morning or what he'd meant by "under the circumstances" she should recuse herself.

McQuigg asked, "So how long did it take you to drive from the deputies' office to your home?"

"About fifteen minutes."

"So according to you, you left the deputies at quarter to three?"

"I thought it was about that time, yes."

"I think we have a discrepancy, Lieutenant Fincham."

"About forty-five minutes are unaccounted for," Krause said.

Dove could see a fine line of sweat beginning to form above Jack's lip. What the hell was going on?

"Well, I don't know," Fincham said impatiently. "What difference does forty-five minutes make?"

McQuigg raised his eyebrows. "You're a law enforcement officer and you ask that?"

"Okay. I was driving around before I went home. I forgot at first."

Dove was concerned. How could he have forgotten something like that?

Krause said, " 'Driving around?' What's that mean, 'driving around?' "

"Driving around. Thinking."

"About what, Fincham?"

"What does what I was thinking have to do with anything? You think I killed my wife in those forty-five minutes?"

"According to the coroner, it could fit the timeframe."

"Bullshit," Jack said and pounded a fist on the table.

"Lieutenant," Dove said.

"Sorry. But I didn't kill my wife."

McQuigg asked, "Did you love your wife?"

"No," he said without hesitation.

"Why were you still with her?"

"In fact," Fincham said, "I was planning to divorce her. I told her that before I left for the Keys."

"And how did she respond?"

"We argued about custody. My wife was a dru—an alcoholic. I didn't want her to have the kids."

"Was she planning to fight you for them?"

"She said she was."

Dove knew they would consider this a motive.

Krause looked at some notes. "Your wife took a lot of drugs, didn't she?"

"You mean in general?"

"Yes."

"She did. They were mostly tranquilizers and sleeping pills."

"And you knew where they were?"

" 'Course I knew," he answered, irritated.

Dove didn't want Jack to lose his cool, give them anything to go on.

"Tell us what happened when you got home."

Jack did.

Back in her office, Fincham said, "Why are you looking at me like that, Arizona?"

"Like what?"

"I dunno. Suspicious, maybe."

"I guess I'm wondering why you said you left the office at two?"

"I thought it was."

"All right."

"You don't believe I drove around before I went home, do you?"

She wasn't sure what to say. It was true that she wondered why he hadn't said anything about this earlier. But that didn't mean she thought he killed Bonnie Jo. "How come you didn't mention it before, Jack?"

He laughed. "I knew it."

"Knew what?"

"You think I'm guilty."

"No. I don't. I asked you a question, that's all."

"I didn't mention it because I forgot."

"It's not like you to forget something like that."

"So what are you saying, Sheriff?"

"Truth? I don't know."

Fincham took out his pack of cigarettes, shook one out, put it back. Then, fondling the pack, he said, "Okay. I didn't drive around. I got home when they said. But I didn't kill her."

"Of course you didn't. Jack, how could you believe I'd think you killed her?"

He shrugged. "I haven't had a chance to tell you, but I found out that B.J. *did* have a boyfriend."

"Who said so?"

"Debbie, at the salon. Guy's name was Bernard Zanville."

Bernard Zanville. Why did that name ring a distant bell? "Where can we find him?"

"She didn't know. Never met him. B.J. talked about him, that's all. This guy operated like some sort of phantom."

Dove spoke into the intercom. "Bethany, get someone to check for a Bernard Zanville."

"Call the FBI?"

"Not yet. Have one of our people do a DMV computer check first."

Fincham said, "It was a mistake, wasn't it, to lie to those guys?"

"Yes, it was. You have to rectify it, Jack."

"How's that going to go down?"

"Not good. But better than if you leave it like this. I mean, what time did you call the salon the day of B.J.'s death and speak to one of the girls there?"

"I don't remember exactly, but it won't time out right."

"That's my point. Tell them the truth. You knew it would look bad so you fudged the truth a little."

"Yeah, right. What would we think if someone said that?"

Dove knew he had a point. "You have two choices. Tell or don't."

"But it's going to come out, isn't it?"

"I think so. I can't imagine that it won't."

"Okay, I'll tell them. But if I get arrested, Arizona, you'd better bake me a cake with a file in it."

"Deal."

Chapter Twenty-Seven

A month had gone by since Bonnie Jo and the two little girls were murdered, and almost two months since Julie Boyer was killed. Taylor had been let go right after the second homicides. None of the murders was solved. They'd worked every lead they had, often covering the same ground again and again.

The only good news was that the murderer of the girls hadn't killed again. At least not anywhere close to Jefferson. Dove knew it was possible that he'd moved on. If he was the serial killer they'd all come to believe in, he could have gone anywhere; he could have disappeared from Virginia forever. Which meant the murders would never be solved. And she hated that.

Bonnie Jo's murder remained unsolved too. They'd had no luck in locating Bernard Zanville. No one by that name was listed in any county in Virginia, nor in D.C. Neither Bernard or Bernie. The name plagued her. An odd name for this someone to choose if it wasn't his own, and if it was, why couldn't they find him? Dove knew she'd either heard it or seen it before. Not Bernie, but Bernard. Whoever he was, he hadn't left any trail to his whereabouts.

Professionally, the whole thing was a hot potato. There had been the obligatory press conferences with government officials, including a senator, along with a dressing down by people in high places, accusing her of not doing enough. And more requests from citizens for her resignation.

Dove would be damned if she was going to give into that. What she wanted to do was to solve the damn murders and then resign. And she wanted to marry Jack. But that would take more time, too. He was trying to work things out with his kids himself and that was rough going. Now certainly wasn't the time to bring her into the picture.

Jack was still under suspicion for B.J.'s death, but there wasn't a shred of proof. He'd voluntarily matched his thumb and fingers to the plaster cast made of the indentations on his wife's neck, and unfortunately for him, it was too close to call.

He'd corrected his statement to the FBI, and despite what McQuigg thought, a minor time discrepancy and a possible motive didn't add up to a case, let alone an arrest.

But that hadn't protected Jack from being treated like a criminal. Both his own car and his police vehicle had been impounded by the state. When Dove tried to find out why, she got stonewalled. And Jack wasn't standing up to the pressure very well. He smoked continually now . . . jokes about that were a thing of the past. And he was drinking more than usual. Sometimes he showed up for work as though he'd slept in his clothes, or not at all. She thought of her conversation with Jack a few days before.

"What the hell do they think they're going to find in my cars, Arizona?"

"I have no idea."

"They going to find B.J.'s hairs or something? Course they are. And the Feebs came to the house again this morning. Planned to go through it all over again. The kids are scared and upset and it's too much for them. My God, they just lost their mother."

"I'd do something if I could, Jack. You know that."

"Hey, I'm not expecting you to *do* anything. I need to talk about it, is all."

"I understand. And it's not only the kids who've had a loss, you have, too. No one's taking that into consideration. And I hate the way you've been treated."

"You're right. It is a loss . . . bigger than I would've expected. Christ, I lived with this woman for seventeen years, better or worse."

He ran a hand through his unruly blond hair as he paced back and forth. "The thing is, I can't understand why the hell they're focusing on me. Even if nobody can find this Zanville turkey, I have an alibi. So I had forty-five minutes, but they ruled that out."

Dove knew better. "They didn't exactly rule it out, Jack. But, without other evidence they couldn't arrest you on that alone."

"You knew this?"

"I thought you did, too."

"Guess I didn't think about it." His face fell like a collapsed cake. "So you mean I've been under suspicion all this time?"

"It seems that way. I had no idea. Jack, I have to tell you something."

"Oh, what the hell now?"

"You have to do something about your appearance."

"Huh?"

"You don't even know, do you? You look like hell."

"Thanks very much, Arizona. I knew I could count on your support."

"Shut up and listen. Half the time you don't comb your hair, your clothes are wrinkled, sometimes stained, and you've come in here unshaved a few days.

"Do you think they look at you and see a man distracted

by grief? A man who's worried about protecting his kids?"

"I don't care what they see."

"Well, you'd better start caring because they look at you and see a man who's losing it, someone they're getting to, and that'll just make them try harder. You've done it yourself, sweating a suspect—"

"I know it, Arizona. I know you're right. But I'm so fucking depressed." He slumped into the chair in front of her desk.

"Oh, Jack. Let me help."

"That's part of the problem. There's nothing you can do, nothing we can do together. When I go home I've got these two kids who still barely talk to me. I've got these guys on my back who never let up. And where the hell is Bernie Zanville, if he even exists? I feel like everything's down the toilet."

"You and I aren't, Jack."

He moved to the edge of the chair, put his arms across her desk, offering her his hands, which she took.

"You sure?" he asked.

"I've never been surer about anyone in my life. Even though I *am* robbing the cradle."

He managed a laugh as they squeezed each other's hands.

Last night Jack had been with her and they'd made love. He'd had to go home because of the kids. She understood that, though she didn't like it. Dove knew she could win over Jack's kids if she were given a chance. But that would have to wait.

She snapped on a light. At times like this she wished that she still smoked. Slapping her pillows into shape she sat up to think. Dove could never think properly, rationally when she was lying down.

She didn't have a thing to go on except instinct, and it made no sense, but she believed that the same person who did the murders of the girls also killed Bonnie Jo.

It was a long shot, but no worse than believing they had two murderers in the same area. The MOs were different, but he might have been trying to burglarize the Fincham house and came across Bonnie Jo drunk and unable to fight back, though still sentient enough to get him arrested. And if he had killed the girls, the idea of apprehension could have panicked him.

Dove stared at the ceiling. Why didn't she buy the scenario? Was it too flimsy, or was it that this serial killer had never had a connection to burglary before? Was it too coincidental that he would kill the wife of one of the cops on the case? Still, the murders were connected. She knew it.

She asked herself what the murders had in common. All of the vics were female. Three were in their teens and one in her forties. So that didn't jibe. And . . . oh, hell, she had to face it; the vics didn't have anything in common except their gender.

Even so, in her mind the illusive Bernie Zanville, whom she was convinced murdered B.J., was the killer of the girls. The connection eluded her, but that didn't squash the feeling, intuition.

Dove threw back the covers and got up. It was only five-thirty but she knew she wasn't going to sleep anymore, so she might as well get going.

Downstairs in the kitchen she clicked the on button for her coffee. She always set it up the night before. Though it was still dark outside, light was beginning to flicker through like a faulty bulb.

She got out her large Arabia ware mug. It was off-white with a hand-painted wide blue band of flowers. She'd had it for years. When she was with Mike they'd bought two of these and they'd been special, reserved for the weekends.

The coffee wept its last drops into the carafe. Dove got her cup ready by putting in one packet of *Equal*, one of *Sweet and Low*, and a splash of milk. She removed the glass coffee pot and poured the brew over her mix. This way she never had to stir it.

She sat at the round kitchen table. It was a small one that seated four. These were hard to find, but she'd come across it at an antique store while she was hunting for a glass lampshade. The minute she'd seen the table she knew she had to have it.

The urge to phone Jack was almost overwhelming. But she couldn't because of the kids. A snake of resentment coiled through her. She quickly banished it. Her attitude toward Jack Jr. and Kim had to be one of understanding, putting their feelings first. Most of the time it was. She could easily picture herself as a mother to Kim, even though at times the girl made Dove wonder about Clare and what she would've been like had she lived.

Oh, hell, her ruminations were getting her nowhere. With her cup of coffee in hand, she left the kitchen and headed back upstairs. She'd take a shower, and get dressed for work.

Before she could turn on the water the phone rang. It was Hutt.

"What's up?"

"I hate to tell you this, Sheriff, but Fincham's been arrested."

"Oh, hell. They think they have evidence for him killing B.J.?"

"Well, maybe, but that's not what he's been arrested for."

"Then what?"

"The murders."

262

She couldn't take it in. "What murders?"

"The girls. Boyer and the Scotts."

"You're kidding?" The towel she'd had around her slipped to the floor.

"Wish I was, Sheriff."

"Who arrested him?"

"Damn state troopers."

"How'd they get in on this?"

"Got me."

"What's the evidence?"

"Don't know. Fincham made his one call to us. Guess he knew he'd be sure to get somebody."

"Who took it?"

"Pam was still on. She was sort of hysterical-like when she called me."

"Why didn't she call me?"

"Don't know."

"What did she say?"

"Just that Jack called and he'd been arrested for the murders."

"Where is he?"

"Station three. You know where that is, don't ya?"

"Yes. Thank you, Gill." She hung up the phone and stood there, naked, numb, and then she was on the move.

What in hell was going on? Had the FBI lost their minds? Why hadn't they arrested him themselves? Why bring in the troopers?

And Jack a killer? It was absurd. But she knew inside they wouldn't arrest him on a whim—they could have done that any time in the past weeks. They had something concrete, even if she couldn't imagine what it was. Still, whatever they had, it had to be a mistake. And no doubt McQuigg was behind this.

Fifteen minutes later she was starting up her cruiser. It would take her twenty to thirty minutes to get to station three. She hated to do it but she hit the lights and the siren. Jack wasn't going to spend one second more in jail than he had to if she had anything to say about it.

And she had plenty.

Chapter Twenty-Eight

Dove hated going to the troopers' station. They acted so damn superior, you'd think they were Canadian Mounties the way they behaved. But she was wearing her uniform, hoping for a little more respect than a civilian woman entering their territory.

A beefy, red-faced man in his late twenties sat behind a high desk. His brown shirt was crisp, the black tie perfect and spotless. He was writing in a ledger of some sort and after his initial glance at Dove when she'd entered, he didn't look up again for what felt like minutes but was probably seconds.

"Ma'am?"

His bleached blue eyes were hooded, giving him the appearance of a lizard, she thought. Her uniform wasn't going to get any recognition from him. "I'm here to see about Lieutenant Jack Fincham."

"See what about him, ma'am?"

"What's your name?"

He nodded toward the bronze nameplate to his right on the desk.

"Well, Trooper Sherman, I'm Sheriff Dove of Jefferson County and Lieutenant Fincham works for me. I'd like to see him."

"Fincham, you say?"

"Fincham, I say." She bit back the impulse to scream her words. How many people did they have in custody, after all?

Sherman began to look at the ledger, running his sausage-like finger down the page, then swiping it across his tongue, turning pages. It was ridiculous.

"Fincham, Fincham," he said. "Yeah, here it is, ma'am."

"Would you please address me correctly?"

He looked at her as though he had no idea what she meant.

"Sheriff," she said.

He continued to stare, then finally said, "Fincham is here, *Sheriff.*"

"I know he's here. I want to see him."

"Says here only his lawyer can do that." He smiled.

"I'd like to see your superior."

"Ma . . . Sheriff?"

She wanted to slap him. "Is there a word in that sentence you don't understand, Sherman?"

He twisted his fleshy lips to the side, then picked up a phone. "Captain, there's a sheriff out here to see you. Jefferson County. Wants to talk about that lieutenant we booked. Fincham. Yes, sir. Yes, sir." He hung up.

To Dove he said, "If you just take a seat, the captain will see you in a few minutes." He immediately dropped his gaze back down to the ledger.

Dove wasn't going to waste any more energy on him. She took a seat on the wooden bench. Looking around, she saw that there were no magazines. What did she expect? This wasn't a doctor's office.

When twenty minutes had passed, she approached the desk again and she and Sherman went through much the same thing as before. At forty-five minutes, she demanded to see the captain. After an hour, he saw her.

Captain Kennedy was a tall thin man, the comb marks

still visible in his gray hair. His large sympathetic brown eyes might be misleading if you were caught unaware. The uniform was perfect, not a crease out of place as he rose and walked toward her, his hand extended.

"Sheriff, nice to see you," he said. "Have a seat. Balmy weather we're havin' for November, wouldn't you say, hmm?"

"Very balmy." She dropped his warm, dry hand and took a chair across from him as he seated himself behind a plain wooden desk.

He rubbed his hands once as though washing them, then tented his fingers, elbows on the arms of his chair. "Now, what can Ah do for you on this lovely day, Sheriff, hmm?"

Oh, sweet Jesus, she thought. She repeated what she'd told Trooper Sherman but added a question. "What evidence do you have against my lieutenant?"

"Now, now, little lady, you know better than that."

"Excuse me?"

"Well, Ah can't be given out those pahticulas to just any ole person."

"Captain Kennedy, I'm fed up to here," she said, drawing a finger across her throat. "I am not *just any ole person*. I'm the Sheriff of Jefferson County and Lieutenant Fincham works for me. As he's been booked for murder, I have a right to know what evidence you have. So stop jerking me around."

Kennedy blinked and clenched his jaw. "Now, now, no need to get so upset." He leeched a smarmy smile at her, shook his head as though to say she was a little lady after all. "I suspect you have a point."

Huzzah, she thought.

He riffled some papers and came up with one, perusing it for a long time before he spoke. "Forensic evidence taken from one of his vehicles turned up hair that matched a murder victim. Also, some thread samples matched a blouse."

"Why wouldn't his wife's hair and a thread of her clothing be in his car?"

"Not his wife's. Murdered girls."

"That's impossible." Planted, she thought. Someone had planted evidence in Jack's car. But why and who? "I'd like to see that report."

"Ah'll have it faxed to you; you give me your fax number. You got one, doncha?"

She wanted to squeeze his scrawny neck. "Yes, Captain, we have several. Is that the entire thing. All the evidence?"

"No. In his house was found a throwaway razor with minute traces of pubic hair matchin' both murdered girls' DNA. Apparently the FBI's been after this man for some time."

"Why is he here? Why didn't the FBI pick him up?"

"This is temporary. FBI's coming to get him real soon."

"I'd like to see him now."

"Ah'm only supposed to allow his lawyer in, but seein' as you're a sheriff, I'll make an exception."

"Oh, thank you, Captain Kennedy, that's surely gracious," she said.

"You betcha," he said, missing her verbal joust.

They smiled at each other falsely and then Kennedy picked up the phone.

They'd let her in his cell. Fincham looked like hell. Worse than he had on his recent bad days. "Jack, what the hell is going on?"

"I feel like I'm in some sort of nightmare."

"You are. This is unbelievable."

"How can they get away with this?"

Obviously they hadn't told him what they had, or what they *thought* they had. She had to tell him. "They say they have fibers and DNA evidence."

"That's bullshit."

"I know."

"What do they say they have exactly, Arizona?"

As she told him he shook his head silently.

"The FBI's picking you up."

"Oh, joy. McQuigg, huh?"

"Probably. What time did they arrest you last night?"

"About nine."

"McQuigg probably didn't feel like driving back from Washington, so he used the troopers. I guess they'll take you back to the field office in D.C. If McQuigg wasn't on this, it'd probably be Richmond."

"But he is. And he's pissed at us being together."

There was no point in going all through this again.

"Jack, can you think of anyone who'd do this to you? Any enemies?"

"Not off the top of my head. Maybe someone I arrested in the past? Somebody who got sent up?"

"Maybe."

"I have to think about this. Right now I can't think about anything except the kids."

"Where are they?"

"My neighbor, Alice, is taking care of them. She's going to sleep at the house."

"I wish things were different, Jack. I'd take care of them; you know that, don't you?"

"Sure I do. I wish things were different, too." He took her hands in his.

A guard outside the cell said, "No touching."

Jack dropped Dove's hands.

"Jesus, what's this going to do to the kids? You think I should take them out of school?"

"No. Why?"

"Won't they go through hell when this hits the papers?"

"They might. But taking them out of school makes them look like criminals, cowards, something. They're strong kids, Jack. They'll survive this. And you're innocent."

"Yeah. You do believe that, don't you?"

"Of course I do, how can you ask?"

"Thank Christ for that."

"We all believe you're innocent, Jack. Everybody does."

"Do you think Kim and Jack do?"

"I'm sure they do. I wish I could talk to them. Anyway, do you remember where you were when the Scott girls disappeared?"

"I was probably working."

"I'll take a look at the records. If you were and we can establish exactly what you were doing during those times, then all the DNA evidence should mean nothing. Everyone knows things can be planted."

"You think?"

"I know."

"But who?"

"That's what I'm going to find out. There must be a link somewhere. Something we can't think of right now. Believe me, I'll have your whole life gone over."

"That's a little scary," he said, smiling.

"Nothing I shouldn't know, is there?"

"Well, there was this girl in tenth grade."

"You're kidding me," she said.

"Maybe more than one."

"You womanizer. And what about now?"

"Now there's only one, Arizona."

Nothing was said for a time as they looked into each other's eyes and spoke the silent language of love. Finally Dove stood.

"I have to go. I want to get on all this as soon as I can."

"Okay," said Jack, standing as well.

"I'll be notified when the Feebs pick you up, Jack."

"You going to come to D.C.?"

"Not sure if they can keep me out or not. There's not a whole lot of reciprocity between them and us. But if they book you, I'll know."

"Book me?" he said.

"Who's your lawyer, Jack?"

"Hey, call me crazy, but I don't have a criminal lawyer."

"How about Larry Wagner?" They both knew him through the system.

"He's a good man. Sure."

"I'll give him a call."

"Thanks, Arizona."

"I love you, Jack."

"Me too, you."

They said goodbye and Dove walked back through the long hall, up the stairs, past Trooper Sherman and out the door.

Sitting in her car, she felt sick. She was, after all, a cop. And a cop always had doubts about any arrested person claiming innocence. But this wasn't just anyone. This was no serial killer. This was Jack and she was in love with him.

And because of that, she had to be very careful, Dove reminded herself. Her judgment could be impaired, and her credibility. Someone else would have to go back over the roster and check Jack's whereabouts. She didn't want anyone accusing her of anything, like tampering with the records to protect him.

People knew about the two of them. She had to assume it was common knowledge. They hadn't announced anything, but in the last month they hadn't hidden much either, except from the kids.

Still, she felt nagged by doubts. Why would anyone kill those girls and then take the trouble to plant evidence in Jack's car? But maybe it wasn't the murderer who planted evidence. Then who had?

There was something fishy going on and Sheriff Dove didn't like the smell.

Chapter Twenty-Nine

Fincham couldn't believe this was happening to him. He sat in the FBI field office with McQuigg and Krause. The room was air-conditioned, turned way up, and even though he wore a long-sleeve shirt he was cold. He knew there was no use asking for the air to be turned down.

There was no table in the room. Three chairs and a desk in a corner. Jack sat facing the other two. They'd yet to start questioning him, and had been silent on the drive from the jail.

McQuigg stared at him in an openly hostile way, while Krause continued to look like an embryo, no expression, no one there.

"Want to tell us the truth, Fincham?" McQuigg asked.

"I have told the truth."

"That was then, this is now."

"I didn't kill my wife."

"And you didn't kill any nice little girls either, huh?" Krause said.

"I don't know what the hell you think you have, but I didn't kill anybody. Jesus, McQuigg, you can't believe I'd do that."

"I believe evidence, Fincham. I believe forensics. DNA. All that good stuff."

"You don't have anything to connect me to those murders. And if you do, it was planted."

A bored and knowing look passed between the two

agents. Fincham knew how lame that sounded. How many times had he heard this claim himself?

"Listen," he said, "let's start with my wife. Did you know she had a lover?"

Neither agent showed anything in his expression that he knew or didn't know.

"And?" McQuigg asked.

"You find him, you'll find who killed her."

"Name?"

Fincham was surprised that Arizona hadn't told them. "Bernard Zanville."

"Bernard?"

"Maybe she called him Bernie, I don't know."

"And where is this character, Fincham?"

Jack shrugged. "He's not in Virginia. Why don't you run him through?"

"Delighted to," said McQuigg. He picked up a wall phone and gave the order. "So while we're waiting for the results, why don't you tell us how the hair of Rose and Iris Scott got into your car?"

"I have no idea. Look, are you going to charge me, because if you are I want you to do it now so I can get a lawyer in place."

"We're asking the questions, Fincham," Krause said.

How many times had he said the same thing to a suspect? "Ask, then." Jack couldn't believe he was on the other end of this. It made him feel as though he were guilty. Innocent suspects that he'd questioned must have experienced the same feeling.

"How did you know the Scott sisters?"

"I didn't."

"How did you get them in your car?"

"I didn't." Jack sighed. He knew it was going to go on

274

and on like this. There was nothing he could do until he was booked, so he settled in for the duration.

It was late afternoon when McQuigg called Dove.

"We're bringing Fincham over and we want you to book him. Technically, he's your collar."

"Exactly what would you like me to book him for?"

McQuigg laughed. "Almost anything. You and I both know he killed his wife. But what we have evidence for are the Scott murders."

"Know something, McQuigg? I *don't* know that. And I don't think he killed anybody else, either."

"You wouldn't, would you, Lucia?"

"Meaning?"

"Let's just say you have an unprofessional interest in the suspect."

She wanted to let him have it, but kept her cool.

"Moving right along. We've located two Bernard Zanvilles. One lives in New York, the other in Pennsylvania. This is another reason I'm not booking him on his wife's murder. Got to clear these Zanville men."

"What makes you think you can clear them?"

"Well, the one in New York is seventy-five and the one in P.A. is twenty-four."

Unlikely choices for B.J., she silently agreed. "So you're sending someone to interview them?"

"An agent in the area will do that."

"Meanwhile, what?"

"Meanwhile Fincham is on his way to you with Agent Krause."

"Swell," she said and hung up. She sat staring at the wall for a moment thinking about Bernard Zanville again. Why the hell was that name familiar to her? She'd never even known a Bernard. Dove picked up the phone again and punched in Kay's number. She'd had to cancel their last date so they hadn't seen each other in ages. This time she'd make it if Kay was free. She absolutely needed the company of another woman, Kay in particular.

Krause, looking sour as usual, stood in front of her next to Jack. His wrists were cuffed behind his back.

"Take off the cuffs, Agent."

"When he's in a cell."

"You're on my turf now and I said, take off the cuffs."

He worked his jaw back and forth hard enough to dislocate it. "He's been booked for the two homicides," he mumbled as he unlocked the handcuffs.

"Thank you," Dove said. "You can go now."

"Sorry, but Agent McQuigg said to wait 'til he was in a cell."

"Sweet Jesus," she said. "Okay, Lieutenant, let's go." She gently turned Fincham so he was in front of her and in a line the three made their way back to the small cell block.

Dove said to the deputy, "Open a cell, please, Deputy."

"Yes, ma'am."

The sheriff rolled her eyes heavenward. She couldn't count the number of times she'd asked him to call her Sheriff. It wasn't just habit with those who called her ma'am, it was a way to withhold respect.

When the cell was unlocked, Jack walked into it alone and the deputy locked it behind him.

Dove turned to Krause. "Okay?"

"You're not going to let him out after I leave, are you, Sheriff?"

If she'd been a man she would have socked him. "He's booked, isn't he? Why would I let a booked man out of jail?"

"Just checking, that's all."

"Well, now you can check your way out of this building."

He started to say something, his mouth opening like a fish, then he changed his mind and left.

Dove said to the deputy, "Take a break."

"Yes, ma'am."

When he was gone, Fincham said, "Why do you let him talk to you like that, Arizona?"

"In the grander scheme of things it's not too important. How are you?"

"You mean aside from looking at you through steel bars?" He laughed cheerlessly.

"I called Larry Wagner."

"I can't afford him."

"Pro bono."

"How come?"

"He likes you."

"You mean he likes *you*."

"Whatever. Anyway, he should be here any minute. He'll get you out of here on bail."

"And is that money going to be pro bono too?"

"You don't skip, the fee isn't that bad." She smiled at him.

"Depends how much bail is set at, doesn't it, Arizona?"

"Don't worry about it, Jack. I wish I could kiss you," she said.

Although there were surveillance cameras here, there was no microphone.

"Me too," he said. "I wish—"

Fincham didn't finish as the door opened and Larry Wagner came toward them. He was a good-looking man with a full head of brown hair. Behind round wire-rimmed glasses, his eyes were brown, and he had the pink flawless skin of a baby.

"Hey," he said.

They greeted him and he reached through the bars to shake Fincham's hand. "This settin' doesn't suit you, Lieutenant."

"Not my favorite," Fincham said.

"I'd like to talk with the lieutenant now, Sheriff."

"Sure." She knew he had to be alone with Jack. "I'll send the deputy back with the keys so you can be together."

"Fine."

Dove left them and found the deputy, gave him instructions and went back into her office.

An hour later Wagner knocked at her door. She'd asked for coffee for them both. They'd recently gotten a cappuccino machine so that's what they had as they sat opposite each other.

"Sheriff, I wanted you to know that I really believe in Fincham's innocence. I mean, sometimes you don't, you know, but as a defense lawyer you have to act as if. Know what I mean?" He touched a forefinger to the wire bridge of his glasses and unnecessarily pushed upwards.

"I'm glad, Larry. I believe him, too. But I don't know what this forensic evidence is going to do to him. It had to be planted, but I don't understand that."

"Right now, I don't either. But I reckon between the two of us we'll get to the bottom of it."

"We will."

"He's mighty depressed, Jack is. I know about the two of you, by the way."

"I was sure you did."

"Betcha didn't know I'm real glad." He smiled.

"Didn't. That makes me feel good, Larry."

"Trouble is, of course, it gives him a motive for killing Bonnie Jo."

"Yes. I know."

"When did the relationship start, Sheriff?" He sipped his coffee and beads of foam dotted his upper lip then popped, leaving a tiny brown stain, which he wiped away as though he could feel its weight.

"When we were in Florida. He would've had to make a very quick decision, and in a very short time period."

"I know."

"He told you the same thing?"

"Sorry. I had to be sure about the timing."

She nodded, knowing he *did* have to know. "When will he go for a bail hearing?"

"I'm going now to try for tomorrow. We're not supposed to have to prove he's innocent, but you know, well as I do, that's a crock."

She nodded in agreement. "We're working on it now." She'd called Hutt before going to court and given him instructions.

"I mean," he said, "it's all so dumb. Jack goin' around killin' little girls. Thing is, Sheriff, we got to find the real killer."

"Larry, you have to understand something. If he was a drifter or the serial, he's probably gone and we may never know."

"I thought of that. But does the drifter idea make sense? The serial killer even? I mean in Fincham's wife's case?"

"No. Nothing makes sense."

"Hell, Sheriff, why would a drifter or a serial put evidence in Jack's car?"

"Exactly."

"But there is another explanation."

"What's that?"

"Somebody other than the killer, plantin' evidence."

"Thought of that," she said. "Any ideas?"

He shrugged. "Guess somebody who doesn't like Jack and who had access."

"That'd be for sure. Starting with who had access is the first step, I think."

"That's how I'd go." Wagner finished his coffee.

"Right," she said.

They shook hands and he left.

After thinking a minute or so, Dove buzzed Bethany and asked if Jenkins was around. She was and the sheriff gave her the job of looking into who had access to the evidence that turned up in Jack's car.

Jenkins said, "I'm real sorry about this, Sheriff."

Dove considered whether to play this out and ask her what she meant or just acknowledge that Dale knew as well as everybody else what the situation was between Jack and her.

"Thanks, Dale."

"Anything I can do? I mean on a personal level?"

"No."

"You wanna talk I'll be there. You can trust me."

"I know I can." And she might have talked things over with her, if she hadn't had a lunch date with Kay. "Best way to help right now is get on this assignment."

"Will do."

When she'd gone, Dove took her purse from where it hung for her lunch with Kay, but first went to talk to Jack about his new lawyer.

Chapter Thirty

Dove waited for Kay at a table in Bistro Blue, one of the nicer restaurants in Jefferson. She sipped her Perrier. Drinking in the middle of the day was no longer an option. She could do it in her thirties but no more.

"Hey, toots." Kay kissed Dove on the cheek, then pulled out a chair and sat across the small table from her. She wore a smart blue suit that brought out the color of her eyes.

Kay Holiday was a striking woman, a tall, natural blonde, though now she needed to "freshen" it every so often. Her skin was smooth and wrinkle-free, except for laugh lines.

Dove said, "You look great."

"Thanks. You look like shit."

"Why, thank you, dear."

"Think nothing of it." Kay smiled. When the waiter appeared she ordered a glass of house white wine. When he was gone she said, "Seriously, what's wrong?"

Dove told her about Jack's situation.

Kay listened intently as she always did. "What do you think?"

"You mean about his innocence?"

"Yes."

"I know he's innocent, Kay," she said.

"Okay, okay. I wanted to make sure. You also have to remember, Lucia, I've only met him once or twice and never in the new capacity as your lover."

"Sorry. I guess I'm a little sensitive to that particular question."

"Now don't kill me. Is that because you have the tiniest doubt?"

Dove started to say no, stopped. "It's not a doubt. I just can't understand why this happened, why somebody planted evidence in Jack's car."

"Yeah, I can see that. The thing is, being a cop himself, if he'd done it, he would certainly have gotten rid of any forensic evidence, wouldn't he?" Her wine was placed in front of her.

"Would you ladies like to order?"

"No. We're not ready yet," Kay answered.

Dove said, "He wouldn't have used his own car for starters. I can hardly speak about it this way. The idea of Jack being a killer is so ridiculous."

"So either it was the real killer, or someone who had access to this evidence gathered from the bodies and wanted to hang it on Jack, is that right?"

"Exactly right."

"So who's on the list? The coroner, of course."

"Harry Scruggs? No way. No reason and no imagination."

"What about the people who work with Jack?"

"We're looking into that, even though it's very unlikely. The thing is, Kay, anyone we think of is unlikely. But Lieutenant Hutt is running it all down, even as we speak, and maybe someone along the chain will turn out to have a motive for doing this to Jack."

"You don't sound very convinced."

"I'm not. Nothing about this makes sense to me, Kay."

"Maybe it's what doesn't make sense that's the most important. Maybe you're overlooking something because you want it to make sense."

Dove stared at her. Nothing fell into place, no bolt of lightning or thump of the heart. But she knew what Kay said had merit and she had to start thinking in a different way.

"Thanks, Kay. I think you're on to something."

"Really?"

"I do. Maybe I've been limiting my focus somehow. When I get back to the office I'll take everything I've got and rethink. I love you," she said.

Kay smiled.

"How's Danny?"

"He's fine. Next week is our sixth anniversary. Every day better than the one before," she said.

"Right."

"Marriage is hard, Lucia. I ought to know after so many. But it's been worth it with Danny. And maybe it'll be worth it with Jack."

"I don't know if we'll get married."

"Oh, of course you will. I know all the problems, the kids and you thinking you're robbing the cradle (which you're not) and working together and on and on. But I've never known you to sound the way you have these last weeks, even in the midst of what's been going on. Don't forget, I knew you when you were married to the maniac."

Maniac. Mike. And Kay often referred to him like that. But this time Dove did feel a thump of the heart and thought she saw a bolt of lightning.

"Lucia? What's the matter?"

"Nothing. Let's order, okay?"

"You sure you're okay?"

"I'm fine," Dove said. "Just fine."

★ ★ ★ ★ ★

Back in her office, Dove called Scruggs. An assistant answered and she asked for him. She felt shaky and she could hear the tremulous sound of her voice. Closing her eyes, she concentrated on making it sound normal.

"Yes, Sheriff?"

"Harry, how are you?"

"Elbow deep in entrails." He laughed.

She drew in a breath. "Sounds like fun. Anyone I know?" She played this game because she knew Harry liked it. And it was probably the only way he stayed sane dealing with corpses day after day.

"Don't think so, Sheriff."

"Good. How's Faye?"

"Oh, she's good. The same as always. So, what can I do you?"

He knew she wasn't calling for chitchat. "Harry, when you were working on the Scott girls, was there anyone around who normally wouldn't be there, or shouldn't have been?"

"Whatcha mean, Sheriff?"

Dove bit her bottom lip. She knew this was going to be hard, going to take explaining to him, because it was his way, probably unconscious, to draw things out. Harry Scruggs was a lonely man.

"Not your assistants, Harry. Not anyone who works there, but somebody who you were surprised to see?"

"Lemme think."

She could hear him talking to himself, but she couldn't make out any words.

"Well, I don't know if this is so strange, but there was that guy who I'd never seen around an autopsy before."

She closed her eyes. Scruggs was forcing her to ask who, and she did.

"That agent fella. Nice enough."

"Agent?"

"FBI. Let's see now, what was his name?"

Dove's heart was doing the tango, but she didn't want to put any words in his mouth.

"Wondered why he was there, actually. Agent . . . oh, hell, Sheriff, I can't think of the fella's name."

"You must have written it down somewhere, Harry."

"Hey, you're right about that. Hold on a sec."

It seemed like hours while she waited and she knew she wasn't going to be surprised; still, you never knew until you had the fact.

When Harry came back to the phone he said, "Here we go. Fella's name was Agent McQuigg."

Dove thanked him and replaced the receiver. Technically, there was nothing out of order in McQuigg being at the autopsy, but why would he *want* to be there?

She picked up the phone and punched in Larry Wagner's cell phone number. He answered immediately.

"Is this a bad time, Larry?"

"I'm in the hallway of the courthouse. Got Jack a bail hearing tomorrow morning."

"Great."

"Can this wait? About to go in to the courtroom."

"I'll make it fast. I have some information. FBI Agent McQuigg visited the autopsy of the Scott girls."

"Is that so unusual?"

"He's on the case so he had a perfect right to be there. But it doesn't make much sense that he would be. Anyway, I think he did it."

"Did what?"

"Took samples and planted them."

"Forgive me, Sheriff, but why would Agent McQuigg do that?"

"I used to be married to him. I thought everyone knew that."

"Everyone does. I still don't see why he'd want to place evidence . . . oh, I see, I think. He's still in love with you?"

"No. He hates me."

"And that would be his motive?"

"It might be. I don't think Mike wants to see me happy."

"So he knew about you and Jack?"

"I can't prove that he knew at the time. He knows now."

"Don't want to rain on your parade but the fact is, Sheriff, you can't prove anything."

"No. No, I can't. But I know it's true, Larry. He's the only one with opportunity *and* motive."

"Hey, maybe he's the real killer."

"Yeah, right," she said.

After they'd hung up she thought about what to do next. How could she prove that Mike had planted the evidence? There had to be a way. She had to concentrate. Should she call a meeting of her staff, brainstorm it with them, turn them loose on this? But was that the responsible thing to do? Take them off their various assignments and put all her manpower into watching Mike, digging up stuff, trying to incriminate him because her lover was Jack Fincham, who was being framed for these murders? Definitely not responsible. She'd have to pursue this alone. And she didn't have the damnedest notion of where to begin.

Fincham sat across the steel prison table from his son. Kim hadn't come and he doubted she would.

"They treating you okay, Dad?"

"I'm fine. But how about you and Kim?"

"We're okay. And Dad, we don't need a babysitter."

"Alice isn't a babysitter, Jack. She's there if you need anything."

"But, Dad, I'm almost eighteen. If we need anything I can phone her."

Jack thought about it. "Think you can handle Kim?"

"Reckon I can. I mean, it's not like she's some out-of-control freak, you know."

"She have a boyfriend, Jack?" Fincham could see his son didn't want to answer, but he waited him out.

"Dad, what difference does that make to anything?"

"Look, Jack, she's grieving for the loss of her mother; and her father, who she hates at the moment, is in jail. She might need some . . . some kind of comfort and maybe she'll choose the wrong kind."

"You mean have sex with a boyfriend?"

It was hard for Fincham to actually picture his fourteen-year-old daughter having sex, but he nodded.

"Hell, Dad. And what if she does? What am I suppose to do about it?"

"Then she *does* have a boyfriend. Who is he?"

"If Kim wanted you to know that, she'd tell you, Dad."

"Jack, these are hard times. I wouldn't ask you to betray your sister if everything wasn't so fucked up." He'd never used that word in front of his son before and he felt a light jolt of guilt.

Jack Jr. weighed the situation and finally said, "Okay, under these circumstances I'll make an exception. Yeah, she has a boyfriend and he's a real nice guy."

"You know him?"

"Yeah. I do. He's in my class."

Oh, Christ. An older boy. "Tell me about him."

"His name's Pete Cross. He's a guard on the football team."

In his mind Fincham imagined a guy about six-foot-six, two hundred fifty pounds, a real brute. Some bruiser with his little Kimmy.

"So what makes you think this Cross isn't going to take advantage of her, the situation?"

"Ah, Dad, can we drop this?"

Fincham saw his son was blushing and he suddenly knew his daughter and Cross were already sleeping together.

"Jack, how long has she been seeing this guy and why didn't she tell us?"

"About six months and I think she did tell Mom."

"She told your mother, but not me? What the hell is that?" He pushed away from the table, knocking over his chair, and paced around like a lion.

"I guess," Jack Jr. said sheepishly, "because she was afraid you'd act like this."

"Like what? I'm just mad nobody told me."

"C'mon, Dad. We all knew you'd go ballistic if you found out Kim was dating a senior."

He stopped in his tracks. It was true. He never would have permitted it. "I thought kids didn't date these days. Thought they went around in groups."

"Yeah, sometimes. Sometimes they sort of pair off. It's not like dating in the olden days."

Olden days. Fincham knew his son meant in his time. He picked up his chair and sat down again. "Okay. I get the picture. So she's been sleeping with this guy for six months, huh?"

"I didn't say that." Now his son was flushed with anger.

"You didn't have to. Thing is, she has to take precautions. Did B.J. tell her about that?"

"Dad, we all know about that stuff. Don't worry. I gotta go now. Anything I can bring you?"

Fincham slowed his breathing, stood up. He was okay for now. "I hope I'll be out of here by tomorrow. I have a good lawyer."

"So you'll be home tomorrow night?"

"Sooner. Morning probably . . . maybe afternoon."

Jack, Jr. stuck out his hand for a shake and Fincham took it, then reeled him in like a fish and put his arms around the boy, holding him tight, patting his back.

"You're a good kid," Fincham said.

"And you're a good Dad."

When he was gone and Fincham was back in his cell he tried not to think about his daughter and this Cross guy, but it was tough not to. He needed to get the hell out of here and back to running his house. He wouldn't stop Kim from seeing Cross because he knew the disaster that could bring. But he had to be home, take charge, be a father.

Chapter Thirty-One

Judge Emile Breuer was presiding, which made Dove anxious. He was known to be tough, and should have been off the bench long ago. Breuer was a small man with pinched features and that strange, dyed maroon-colored hair.

Larry Wagner came over and they exchanged greetings.

"Too bad we got Breuer," he said.

"I know. What kind of bail are you going for?"

"I'm hoping for something in the low six figures. Bail will have to be set because it's a homicide."

"I know that, Larry."

"Course you do. Sorry. Thing is, since he's a police officer it could be in his favor."

"Or could go the other way?"

He nodded.

"Breuer has a vendetta against the police, doesn't he?"

"Sure doesn't like them."

"Oh, God. So what do you think?"

"Let's hope for the best. See you later, Sheriff."

As she watched him walk away, she realized that the door to the courtroom behind the bench had opened and Breuer was coming out. He reminded her of a lawn ornament.

The bailiff began his chant and Dove stood with the rest of the people. When Breuer was seated at the bench, the spectators sat.

Jack's case was the fourth item on the docket. When he appeared, he was in the orange jumpsuit and Dove could have cried seeing him that way, looking tired and worn.

Larry joined Fincham and the process began. By its end, Jack was being held on half a million bail. She was stunned as Fincham was led from the courtroom. He hadn't looked at her, but she understood that.

Larry Wagner and Dove talked in the corridor.

"What do you want to do?" he asked.

"Do?"

"Can you raise the money for the bondsman?"

It meant raising fifty thousand. "How would it look, Larry, even if I could?"

"I think it would look like you believed in one of your officers."

"I'm not sure I can get the money. Have to do some number crunching."

He nodded and gave her a hug. "Call me later."

"Will do."

Back in her office Dove worked with her calculator. There were three ways: borrowing cash on four credit cards, taking a second mortgage, borrowing from friends. The last was unthinkable; the second would take too long. That left the first.

Credit cards would be fastest and easiest. It would also leave her in horrible debt, which she'd never been in. Even owing on a mortgage made her uncomfortable, though she knew it was the only sensible thing to do. Her father had drummed into her head that you didn't buy what you couldn't pay for.

But Roy Dove was dead and this was a hundred years later. What was important here? She loved Jack and she couldn't bear the thought of him languishing in jail for what could be months. No, it wasn't acceptable. She had to find a way. Was there was anything she hadn't considered?

There was a knock at her door. It was Bethany.

"Sheriff?"

"Yes, Bethany."

"Could I talk to you about Lieutenant Fincham?"

"Sit down." Dove felt panicky. Did Bethany know something incriminating about Jack?

Bethany refused the chair. "We all heard about the bail? And we want to help? Everybody likes the lieutenant and we just can't see him hanging out in jail?"

"That's so nice, Bethany. But I don't know what you can do."

"Well, we've managed to pledge thirty-two thousand, Sheriff?"

"Sweet Jesus, girl. Are you serious?"

"Yes. Completely?"

Dove couldn't believe it. That meant all she'd have to come up with was eighteen and she could get that within a day. "How soon could everyone have it?"

"By tomorrow?"

"I could kiss you."

Bethany blushed. "Well, it wasn't just me? I think Lieutenant Hutt and Sergeant Jenkins came up with it? The idea, I mean?"

"Tell me the truth, Bethany. Is this going to be a hardship to anyone?"

"I don't think so, Sheriff? Everybody said they could do it real easy?"

"We'll need it in cash. You'll organize this? Collect the money?"

Bethany agreed that it would be cash and she'd be the bank. Dove thanked her again and told her to express thanks to everyone and she'd do the same when she had time. Then she left for her bank.

★ ★ ★ ★ ★

Three days later Jack was home. He and Dove sat in his living room.

"I don't know how I can ever thank them all. And you too."

"Don't worry about that, Jack. Just don't jump bail." She smiled and he took her hand.

He said, "So you think McQuigg might have planted that evidence?"

"It's the only thing that makes sense, even though it doesn't make sense, if you know what I mean."

"Yeah, I do. You think he hates you that much?"

"And by extension hates you. Yes."

She told Jack how he came to hate her because she'd had Clare and wouldn't have a child with McQuigg.

"But you said he helped with the search for her."

"He did. And I never understood that. Unless he wanted to find her dead, so he could gloat over my not being a good mother. I don't know."

They were both quiet, thinking. Then Dove said, "My friend Kay called him a maniac the other day. There *is* something wrong with him," she added as though she was far away.

"What? What is it?"

"And then Larry joked and said maybe he's the real killer."

"What the hell are you saying?"

"I don't know, Jack. I don't know what I'm saying." She felt cold and sweaty at the same time.

"It sounds like you agree with them."

"No. I don't agree. But it's a thought."

"Wait a minute," Jack said. "You know Mike McQuigg is not a favorite of mine, but do you realize you're talking about the man as a serial killer?"

"I know, I know. It's crazy. Forget I ever said it."

But Jack went on. "So it started with Clare . . . when he saw how much that hurt you, he then would've . . . oh, what the hell am I thinking? All those murders in other counties, other states."

"So?"

Fincham said, "You're saying McQuigg is a flat-out serial killer?"

She shrugged. "Do I remember correctly that the first recorded murder with the MO of our homicides happened after Clare died?"

"What was the date of her death?"

She told him.

"Yeah. The first one we know about was about a year later."

"Maybe he got a taste for it, dealing with other serial crimes, other killers," she said.

"Guess that could happen."

Dove closed her eyes, took a sharp intake of breath.

"What?"

"I had a terrible thought."

"Tell me."

"Maybe Mike *killed* Clare. Maybe she didn't *fall* down the well, maybe that sucker threw her down there."

"Ah, Arizona," he said.

"I know how impossible that sounds, but you have no way of knowing what a terrible man he is."

"We're talking about evil here."

She looked straight into his eyes. "Yes, Jack, we are."

"Thought you didn't believe in evil."

"I thought I didn't either."

"But you think McQuigg is evil?"

"I'm not discounting sick. But, if he did that to my daughter, it was to get at me. That's evil."

"Okay, let's say he's evil and he did that. Why would he kill all the others?" Jack took a pack of cigarettes from his shirt pocket, indicated that he'd like to smoke.

"It's your house," she said.

He nodded thanks. "So why would he do the others?"

"I don't know the answer, Jack."

"Arizona," he said.

"Why are you looking at me that way?"

He put down the cigarette, cupped her face in his hands. "I think you're going on fantasy here. And I think you want to help me and need a killer."

"Hey," she said. "I do want to help you. And I admit to grasping at something, but I also have a gut feeling about this."

"Which is that McQuigg is our serial killer?"

She removed his hands and stood up. "Yes. I think he is and I can't say why. And I certainly can't prove it."

Jack took a puff of his cigarette and looked at her.

"You think I don't know this is crazy?"

He shrugged.

"Well, I do. But we have to find a way to prove it."

"I'll do whatever I can to help. But it'll have to be unofficial."

"That might even turn out to be better. I have to think about this. Find a place to start. Why don't you come over tonight?"

"Okay. We'll talk more about it then."

She smiled. "We will?"

After they'd made love, she'd fed them an omelet in bed. Now they lay back, fulfilled.

"You want to talk about it?" Jack said.

"McQuigg?"

He nodded.

"I don't know anything more than I did this afternoon."

"You have a plan of action?"

"I don't know how to begin. How the hell do you investigate an FBI agent?"

"Seems to me you go about it same way you would anybody else."

"But, Jack, what do I tell the staff?"

"Same. Tell them you want to know everything about him over the last ten years. Where he was, what he ate, who he saw, where he went. Hell, Arizona, you know the drill."

"They all know I was married to the guy."

"So what?"

"I don't have one piece of evidence to go on."

"But they don't need to know that."

"You mean, just give them their assignments without explanation?"

"Say you have reason to believe and you can't divulge that right now. And they've got to keep it under wraps, too."

"Thin ice," she said.

"There's that."

"Think they'll go for it?"

"They have a choice?"

"No. I'm the sheriff."

"Right," he said.

"You know he will have covered his tracks, don't you?"

"Probably. But what the hell. We don't have any other leads or suspects, so this is worth a try."

"You don't think it's my personal feelings about McQuigg?"

"I honestly don't know. But so what?"

"I love you," she said.

"Me, too. You."

He took her in his arms and they kissed, long and delicious. But neither wanted to go further now and when they pulled away she said, "I can't talk about it anymore. Want to watch a movie?"

"Sure."

Dove got out of bed, went to the TV and VCR. "You know I haven't turned the damn thing on since this started. Just fallen into bed when I came home." She bent down to the VCR. "I was running a movie the night I got the first call."

"What is it?"

"Oh, an old forties thing. You wouldn't want to see it."

"Yeah, I would. I want to see some of these things you're always touting."

"This is a Dane Clark movie. You probably don't even know who he is."

"Do, too. *God Is My Co-Pilot*."

"Hey, that's good. I have to rewind." She clicked the back arrow and the tape made a whirring sound.

"I like war movies, hope you don't mind."

"Not if they're oldies, I don't."

"Tried to get Jack Jr. to watch it with me one night."

"But it wasn't in color, right?"

"How'd you know?"

"I know how these kids are," she said.

"So which Dane Clark is this?"

Dove didn't answer. She stared through him, as if he wasn't there or she didn't see him at all.

"Arizona?" He leaned forward as though he could reach her.

"Sweet Jesus," she said.

"What?"

"Remember I told you the only thing McQuigg and I had in common was old movies?"

"Yeah? So?"

"It just came to me, Jack. Dane Clark's real name was Bernard Zanville."

Chapter Thirty-Two

The shock the night before of finally identifying Bernard Zanville had Dove still stunned. It didn't *have* to be a name that McQuigg had taken, but it fit so perfectly.

When they'd been dating, one of their things was to research the real names of actors and test each other. Back then there was no Internet Movie Database, which made it tougher. But they'd managed. She couldn't remember them all, but Zanville/Clark had been one. The amazing thing was that she hadn't figured it out sooner.

She wasn't naïve enough to think no one else would use that name, or even be born with it, although they'd only found two, but McQuigg was the number one guy on her personal list. The terrible thing was it proved nothing at all. Nothing to anyone else. But Dove was positive.

McQuigg wanted to get at Jack so he could get at her. Still, he had to have started his pursuit of B.J. before Dove and Jack had become lovers. So had he planned to murder B.J. all along, simply to put one of her officers in a bad light? Or did he somehow intuit that she and Jack were going to get together?

Dove didn't know every detail, but without a doubt she knew that Zanville was McQuigg. She'd convinced Jack too. As soon as the FBI records of McQuigg's schedule, his whereabouts, was obtained, Jack would be going over it at home.

After calling her primary staff together that morning,

Dove had given the lieutenants and sergeants assignments on McQuigg. There'd been a lot of questions, but she'd kept her real reason cloaked, saying only that this was top secret and would be on a need-to-know basis for now. Then Dove asked Dale Jenkins to stay behind.

"So what did I do?" she asked, taking a seat.

"Nothing." She knew Dale felt this way because she was the only other woman on the force, and she expected to be monitored more closely than the others. Dove hoped Jenkins didn't think *she* was evaluating her every move. "Dale, you're one of my best people."

She smiled. "Thanks, Sheriff."

"That's one of the reasons I'm going to tell you something I haven't told the others." She explained all about McQuigg to her.

"Good God, Sheriff," Jenkins said. "I mean, he's a government official. Sure, I know. It happens. Still, much as I've never taken to the guy, I can hardly believe this."

"I know it's hard."

"I don't mean I don't believe you."

"I didn't think that."

"So what do you want me to do?"

"What I'd like you to do is to get to McQuigg's wife, any way you wish, except for saying you're from this office."

"Officially or not?"

"Well, that's up to you. I mean, if you think officially would be best, go for it. If not, try another method. I want to know what her life with him is like."

"Want me to start now?"

"Yes."

"You got it," Jenkins said. "Anything else?"

Dove told her that was it. After Jenkins had gone she

picked up the phone and called Ernie Cahill, the Culpepper Sheriff.

"Ernie," she said. "I have a question."

"Just one, Lucia?"

She didn't laugh with him but went right on. "Your case, the nineteen-year-old we talked about?"

"Yeah. What about her?"

"I'd like the names and addresses of the girls she was with when it happened and the same on the parents."

"Parents lived in California or some such. My girl—"

"What was her name?"

"Barbara . . . Barbara . . . Jesus Christ. Thought I'd never forget her name."

"Want me to call you back?"

"No, just gimme a second . . . senior moment, I guess. Oh, yeah, I got it. Barbara Ostrander. Yeah. That's it."

"So fax me the names and addresses of those girls she was with."

"Sure thing, Sheriff. But that was awhile back. Doubt if they'll be living in the same place. Have the same last names for that matter. Married."

"Send them anyway. I'll deal with it."

"You gettin' anywhere with this thing, Lucia?"

"I think so, but can't talk about it now."

"What about Fincham?"

"He didn't kill anybody."

"Yeah, that's what I thought. D.A. pushin' for a close, huh?"

"Something like that."

They said goodbye and then she called Sheriff Dabney and went through the same thing with his old case. Now she had to wait until she got the faxes.

★ ★ ★ ★ ★

Dale Jenkins thought the sheriff must be a little desperate to pin these murders on someone else other than Fincham for her own reasons. Still, everything she'd told her added up.

Jenkins thought Fincham was adorable and she couldn't blame Dove for getting it on with him. And she was pleased that the sheriff trusted her with this assignment. She wished she could tell John, her husband. He wouldn't repeat any of it to anyone, but Dove had asked her to tell no one, and she'd sworn. So she wouldn't tell him because that was just who she was.

Jenkins had decided to visit the second Mrs. McQuigg in street clothes. Less intimidating. She wore a yellow sleeveless blouse, because of the unusually hot, sticky weather, and a denim skirt.

When Eleanor McQuigg opened the door, Jenkins was taken aback. Dove had told her that McQuigg called her Betty Grable because he thought she looked like the old movie star (one that Jenkins had never heard of) so Jenkins thought she'd at least be glamorous. She was not. In fact, she appeared worn and haggard.

Jenkins flashed her shield and said she was from Culpepper County.

"What's it about?" Eleanor asked.

"I'm not at liberty to disclose that right now," she said. "And if you don't want to talk to me, you don't have to." Jenkins knew this last statement was risky, but she was betting on her hunch that the woman was lonely.

Eleanor McQuigg hesitated for only a second and then invited Jenkins in. There was the usual offer of coffee and Jenkins, who didn't want any, knew it would be more friendly if she accepted. So now they sat with their cups at the kitchen table.

They chatted about everyday things until Jenkins thought Eleanor was comfortable with her. Then she said, "Mr. McQuigg is with the FBI, is that right?"

"Yes," she said. "He's pretty important there."

Jenkins smiled. "So I guess you're proud of him then?"

"Oh, of course," she said without any feeling.

Jenkins pretended she didn't notice, said, "So you have a happy marriage?"

She didn't answer, looked into her coffee as though one might appear there.

After waiting quite a long time, Jenkins said, "Mrs. McQuigg? Are you all right?"

"I'm fine," she said, looking up with a false smile.

"Really?"

Eleanor bit her upper lip.

"I know you think you can't trust me, but you can." She hated herself for saying this and had to hit the reminder button that she was simply doing her job.

Eleanor McQuigg burst into tears that eventually turned to sobs.

Jenkins put her hand on one of McQuigg's and waited it out.

Finally McQuigg stopped crying, got up suddenly and went into a room off the kitchen. She returned almost immediately with a wad of Kleenex and sat down again.

Things were popping for the sheriff. She'd received the faxes from Cahill and Dabney and now had two of her men tracing the people down. When they found any of them, she would take over for the questioning.

And Jenkins had scored, too. Eleanor McQuigg hadn't revealed anything, but when Jenkins had asked her about her marriage, she'd collapsed in a squall of tears. Jenkins had left after trumping up a reason for being there in the first place.

Eleanor McQuigg's response to Jenkins's question had been enough to convince Dove that things were not wonderful there. Jenkins hadn't seen any marks or bruises on the woman, but she was wearing a long-sleeved blouse. And it was a hot, muggy day, with no air conditioning in McQuigg's house. Typical of him not to have any. He'd always been cheap.

Dove wished she could do something active, but she had to wait. She wanted to be *out there* and she'd pretty much decided that when her term was up she'd have to move, get a detective's job somewhere else.

But that was before Jack, she realized. When they got McQuigg, the charges against Jack would be dropped and he'd want to remain here. He wouldn't want to take Kim out of school and—

McQuigg burst through the door with Bethany right behind him.

"I'm sorry, Sheriff," she said.

"It's all right. Don't worry about it."

She left, closing the door behind her.

McQuigg stood there, his face red, veins in his neck bulging. "Don't say a fucking word," he yelled. "What the hell right do you have sending some shithead woman cop to my house to question my wife?"

"Finished with your Linda Blair-*Exorcist* impersonation?"

He didn't answer, but glared at her.

"I'm always afraid when you sound that way, you'll swivel your head three-hundred-sixty degrees."

"Fuck you," he said.

"What do you want, McQuigg?"

"I want to know what the fuck you're up to?"

"I have no idea what you're talking about." She prayed Jenkins wouldn't appear.

"You sent someone to interrogate my wife about me?"

"You have to be joking. Why would I do that?"

"That's what I want to know."

"You're barking up the wrong tree."

He moved to her desk and put his hands on it, arms straight. "You didn't send anyone to my house?"

"As I said, why would I do that?"

"That's not an answer and you know it."

Dove took a deep breath. "McQuigg, I didn't send anyone to your house, okay?"

"You're a liar."

"Thank you very much."

"I know you did it, but I can't understand why."

"Anything else?"

He stood up straight. "Don't fuck with me, Lucia. I'm watching you."

"Scary," she said.

He gave her a look, turned and slammed out the door.

He was guilty, she knew it. And he knew she knew it. Would he try to kill her? No. Too smart for that. He knew that if she knew, so did others. But most of all, he knew that so far she didn't have any proof.

And as suddenly as a wind coming up on the ocean, she was positive he'd killed Clare.

How could she have married such a person? What was wrong with her? No, she wasn't going to do this to herself. How to catch McQuigg was what she had to concentrate on.

It all made sense now. The fact that there'd been no trace evidence in any of the murders. Of course the killer was a professional and McQuigg was counting on that to pin Jack. Eventually it would point to someone in law enforcement, and certainly the murder of B.J. was perfect. Get Jack for that and then try to pin the other murders on him. Even if McQuigg couldn't do that much, he could get rid of Fincham, once again hurting her.

And the other murders that had nothing to do with her? She felt sick. They were McQuigg's sideline. Or maybe the main show. Well, at least he wouldn't be dumb enough to kill anyone else while Jack was under suspicion. Would he?

Chapter Thirty-Three

Jenkins had traced one of Barbara Ostrander's friends, Ernie Cahill's vic. She hadn't married and hadn't moved away. The best news was that she lived in Jefferson County, so that Dove didn't have to include Cahill in her visit to Jennie Marriott.

Dove and Fincham pulled up in front of Marriott's small house.

Jack said, "You're sure about this?"

"What?"

"Me going in."

"We've been all through this, Jack. This woman isn't going to know anything about you."

"Assuming she never reads a paper."

"The picture of you was lousy. Let's go."

The house was more like a bungalow. It was white with blue trim, and vines crept over the porch railing. The sheriff had called ahead so Marriott knew they were coming and that Dove wanted to talk about Barbara. The woman had been reluctant, but finally agreed.

The upper part of the door was glass and Dove tapped on it with her ring. In a few moments a large woman, wearing a formless dress, appeared. She looked frightened and Dove held up her shield.

"Oh, yes," the woman said, opened the door.

"Hi, Ms. Marriott. This is Lieutenant Fincham."

She limply shook Dove's hand, and eyed Jack suspiciously.

307

They both wondered if she recognized him; then when she offered her hand, but didn't really look at him, Dove knew it was shyness with a man.

Marriott led them down a short hallway and into a living room that was filled with overstuffed furniture so that it was cramped and dark.

When they were seated, Dove took a good look at Marriott. She was overweight, had lank brown hair and wore no makeup or jewelry. Her eyes were set close together and lacked any sign of life. It was hard to believe she was only twenty-four or five.

"I know how hard this is for you, Ms. Marriott, but we believe the man who kidnapped your friend, Barbara, is still on the loose."

"You can call me Jennie," she said in response.

"Fine. Do you remember if Barbara had a boyfriend at the time?"

"Oh, yes, but the police questioned him and there was no connection."

"And that was Bart Richards, I believe." She recalled this from what Cahill had told her.

"That's right."

"I know this may sound strange, but did she have any other boyfriend? A secret one, maybe?"

"No, I don't remember any."

"And she wasn't meeting anyone that day at the mall?"

"No. Definitely not."

Fincham said, "Did she ever talk about any other male besides Richards?"

"Let me think." She closed her eyes.

Dove didn't look Jack's way, although she wanted to, but was afraid Marriott might open her eyes.

"Yes, there was another name, but she never told us

about him, even though we tried to get her to."

"Was this a secret admirer or someone she had a crush on?"

"She never said. Just sometimes she would mention his name . . . it was kind of playful, sort of teasing us. But when we asked anything she'd say, 'That's for me to know and you to find out.' Like that."

"And the name was what, Jennie?" Fincham said.

"I'm trying to remember," she whined.

Dove said, "Okay. Sorry. Take your time."

"I don't go out, you know," Jennie said.

They were both taken aback by this declaration.

"Why not?"

"Since it happened. Barbara, I mean. Since she disappeared. I didn't even finish school. I tried, but I couldn't. I'd get to the front door and I couldn't cross over. It was a terrible thing. Terrible thing. What happened. Then when they found her body . . ." she started to cry.

Dove leaned forward and put a hand on Jennie's, which lay in her lap like a slab of lard. She thought the woman was crying more because of her self-imposed imprisonment than for Barbara's death. And it was perfectly understandable.

"What if I went out and it happened to me? Maybe it was somebody after all of us, ya know?"

"I can understand your feelings," the sheriff said.

"Can you?"

"Yes. I think I can." Dove felt that Jennie had to have been unstable before the abduction, and if she had, this could be a natural outcome. She didn't know what had happened to the other two, and asked Jennie if she did.

"They didn't feel the same, if that's what you mean. Finished school, went to college. I don't know after that. We lost touch." She looked away for a moment, then turned back, a smile on her face. "Bernie," she said proudly.

Fincham and Dove looked at each other. Fincham said, "Bernie?"

"That was his name. The one Barbara teased us with. I'm sure of it now. Bernie. Sometimes she'd say Bernard."

In the cruiser, Dove said, "It's McQuigg."

"We don't know that for sure."

"*I* know it. I know it here." She pointed to her gut.

"We haven't any evidence, Arizona. We can't go after a man because you and he once played some damn game."

"I know that, Jack. We have to find a way to get him."

"Meaning?"

"I don't know. He's so damn smart. I bet if he took souvenirs, like other serials, he hid them. He'd never have them in his house or on his property."

"And there wouldn't be any other evidence either."

"None," she said.

"Look. If it's McQuigg, he knows exactly what he's doing. No trace evidence, nothing to get DNA from, no mistakes. Short of getting him to confess, I don't know how we can get him."

"So what the hell are we saying, Jack? It's a wash and you're going to go on trial for B.J.'s murder?"

"You said yourself either the charges would be dropped or I'd win."

"Yes. That's true."

"So one thing has nothing to do with the other."

"Except this. If the charges are dropped, he'll kill again."

"Christ. I never thought of that. We can't have someone watching him for the rest of his life."

Dove looked at him, said nothing.

"What?"

"Have you ever heard of Ken McElroy?"

"Sounds familiar. Can't place it."

"He was the guy who terrorized Skidmore, Missouri, for years. Great big slob. He robbed, raped, maimed and shot townspeople. They were petrified of him, until they finally had enough. Then, while forty-five people watched, McElroy was shot and killed, but the police couldn't find any witnesses."

"Arizona, am I hearing what I think I'm hearing?"

She shrugged. "I don't know, because I don't know what I'm saying. And I *do* know what I'm saying."

"The thing is you can't be *totally* sure, no matter what you feel."

"I know."

She started the car. "I have to find a way to be *totally* sure. Maybe if I got him to admit it . . . let's say I accused him and he knew I wasn't wearing a wire, he'd confess."

"Maybe he would. And then what?"

"And then we'd see."

They looked at each other and, wordlessly, they both knew what she had in mind.

A week went by, and all the sheriff's people turned in reports on McQuigg that added up to nothing. This came as no surprise to Dove. He wasn't about to do anything as long as Jack was charged with the murder of his wife. They'd have to wait it out. She'd been in touch with Fincham's attorney and he was sure the grand jury would recommend that the charges be dropped. It was meeting in ten days. There was almost nothing left to do until that happened. Then she'd approach McQuigg and tell him what she thought. She was sure he'd be unable to resist the delight he'd have in telling her he'd killed Clare and all the rest. And once she heard it from him, then she'd consider a type of McElroy solution.

Kim, Jack Jr. and Fincham sat around the kitchen table eating a meal that Kim had prepared.

"It's good," Fincham said. She was her mother's daughter. A lousy cook.

"It sucks," she said.

Jack Jr. said, "Don't put yourself down, Kimmy. It's fine."

Fincham marveled at what a terrific kid his son was.

Then the terrific kid said, "What is it?"

"Bite me," she answered and looked into her food, pushing it around on the plate.

"C'mon guys," Fincham said.

Kim looked up at her father. "Do you know what it is?"

"Sure."

"What?"

"Beef stew."

Kim smiled, grateful.

Jack Jr. said, "I was only kidding."

"Yeah, right."

There was a temporary silence and only the scraping of fork against plate was heard.

"Kim," Fincham said. "Could you pass me the butter."

She did. Then said, "Are you going to marry the sheriff, Dad?"

The subject of his relationship with Arizona hadn't been broached since the first few days after B.J.'s murder, so Fincham felt nonplussed for a moment. He *did* notice that the question didn't seem to be hostile.

"I guess that would depend on a few things."

"Like what?"

Both kids were staring at him now. "Whether the grand jury decides whether there really is evidence against me or not. And you."

"Me?" she asked.

"Both of you."

"Here's the thing," Kim said. "We don't believe you killed Mom."

"I thought you did."

Jack said, "Maybe at first. It was a crazy time then."

"So what changed your mind, Kim?" He knew that Jack Jr. had never believed he'd done it.

"I finally put everything together and I know you'd never do something like that. Plus, there wasn't time. Not really. Dad, we know she was an alcoholic and we know she was . . . well, seeing someone."

It felt as though his heart had stopped. "Seeing someone?" Maybe now he'd get a definitive answer.

"Don't sweat it, okay, Dad?"

"Kim heard her on the phone."

"I was going to go into the bedroom to talk to her one night and just as I was about to knock I heard her laugh in a strange way. So I stood there and then I realized she was talking on the phone. I could tell she was high, not falling-down drunk like some times, but not sober either." She looked down at her plate, played with food again.

"Then what?" Jack asked.

"I knew she was talking to a man. Dad, you're not going to get all bent out of shape are you?"

If only he could tell her this was good news. "No. Promise. How'd you know she was talking to a man?"

"Oh, Dad."

"Okay, go on."

"She was giggling and saying some things I couldn't hear
. . . guess she was whispering. Then she called him by
name."

"What was it?" He knew.

"Bernie."

McQuigg, Fincham thought. That fucker had killed his
wife, no doubt about it. He couldn't wait to tell Dove.

"Anything else?"

"Do you think I was terrible to listen?"

"No," he said. "I would've done the same."

"See, Kim, I told you."

"Anything else?" Fincham asked again.

"If you mean did I ever see them together, I never did. I
saw her get in and out of a strange car a few times, but I
never saw who was driving."

"Can you describe the car, Kim?"

"It was a light color, but it was in the dark."

"And you wouldn't know the make, would you, honey?"

"If she'd called me in to look at it, I would've known,
Dad."

Fincham smiled at his son, nodded and turned back to
Kim. "It's okay if you don't know. But tell me this. If I do
have to go to trial, would you testify to that in court?"

Kim made a face. "Do I *have* to, Dad?"

Fincham knew that her reluctance had to do with embarrassment. As much as kids wanted attention, this was
not the kind they desired. This meant everybody looking at
them as themselves. Naked. He also knew that testimony
from his daughter wouldn't count for much, but it wouldn't
hurt either.

"It could help me," he said. "But I don't think I'll be
going to trial."

"Okay," she said. "If you really need me."

"I always need you, honey."

She smiled in an open and genuine way and Fincham realized that maybe he hadn't been showing his children enough love lately. He'd have to be sure to do that.

"So you didn't answer whether you're going to marry Sheriff Dove?"

"I said it depended on you. How would you feel about it?"

Kim said, "I guess she'd live here, huh?"

Fincham checked laughter. "Probably. Well, she'd live with us, maybe not here. Maybe we'd buy a new house."

"Same school district, though?"

He nodded.

"I guess then it'd be all right."

He wanted to tell them how wonderful Arizona was, how they'd both love her once they knew her, but held back. That was going too far.

"Good," he said. "Now, I guess it's up to the grand jury and Sheriff Dove."

"You mean you haven't asked her?"

"No."

"Oh, Dad. You're hopeless."

The two kids laughed and Jack joined in. He hadn't felt so good in a long time.

Chapter Thirty-Four

The grand jury found insufficient evidence to bring Fincham to trial. All charges were dropped. Now, in addition to finding the murderer of the missing girls, the Jefferson Police had the Bonnie Jo Fincham case to work.

Sheriff Dove assigned two deputies to this. Both she and Jack were now sure that McQuigg had killed B.J., but they couldn't prove that either. Still, the Sheriff's Office had to continue to investigate.

"What's next, Arizona?"

The two of them were in her office.

"I want to confront McQuigg."

"That scares me."

"Scared he's going to kill me?"

Fincham shrugged.

"Not a chance. Once he sees I'm not wired, he hasn't got anything to fear. And he'd want me to live with it, him murdering Clare, especially."

"You going to let him know we don't have any proof?"

"Yeah. Don't you think that would be best? Let him believe only I know. Not even you."

"Guess it would be. When you going to do this?"

"Soon as I can get a date with the sonuvabitch."

Dove got the date two days later. They met in a parking place at the edge of the woods. She went from her car to his.

"What's all the cloak and dagger stuff?" he asked.

"I want to talk to you about the murders."

"So why here? Why not on the phone, or in your office?"

"First thing I want you to do is pat me down for a wire, Mike."

He looked at her expressionless. "Why?"

"So you can be sure I'm not wearing one."

"Why would you wear a wire, Lucia?"

"I'm not. But when I ask you some questions, you may *think* I am."

"What the fuck is this about?"

"It's about you, Bernie."

She had to hand it to him. He didn't show the slightest reaction. He sat perfectly still and looked directly into her eyes. It was then that she had to remind herself that he was a psychopath. They could hide anything, everything, because they weren't, in her mind, humans, just fakes made up to look that way.

"Bernie? Why are you calling me Bernie?"

"You prefer Bernard? Or maybe Mr. Zanville."

"Get out of the car. I don't have time for games."

"I think you'd better listen and I think you'd better make sure I'm not wearing a wire."

He smiled and it gave her the creeps. She'd never liked his smile, but she'd never felt quite like this, either.

"Lucia, if you tell me you're not wearing a wire I can only deduce two things. Either you're not, or you've got it in a place I can't feel. So unless you're prepared for me to look into some orifices, then we can call it a day."

"Look anywhere you want." She'd been ready for this, thought he might suggest it; even so, it made her queasy.

"You mean that?"

"I certainly do."

McQuigg laughed. "You think I wouldn't do it, don't you?"

"I *know* you would."

"Get out of the car and let's go into the woods."

As they walked, he behind her, she felt a deep loathing. This bastard was going feel inside her and would enjoy her discomfort and embarrassment.

Leaves crunched under their feet, the only noise they heard, except for a low whistle from a slight breeze through the trees. Dove thought the weather was beginning to change at last. For a second she wondered if she'd ever see winter. Of course she would. Would it be cold? Would snow pile up? She almost laughed out loud realizing she was thinking about weather when she was about to go through an excruciating experience, then knowing that *that* was the reason her mind was elsewhere, so she didn't have to think about it.

"This looks okay," McQuigg said.

She glanced around. They were in a small clearing circled by trees.

"Take off your clothes."

The idea of stripping before him was repellent. It didn't matter that he'd seen her naked before. The sheer act of removing her clothes, piece by piece, seemed crude, as if she were a hooker. Should she face him?

"Quit stalling. You think you're Rita Hayworth or somebody?"

Dove couldn't help noticing his use of a forties movie star. He was definitely still in the game. Anyone else would have said Ashley Judd or Julia Roberts.

"Do you mind not watching while I take off my clothes?"

He laughed. "Lucia, I've seen it before."

"Yes, I know that, McQuigg. I just don't like disrobing this way, you staring at me. I'll tell you when you can look."

"Oh, goody."

"You're not going to turn around?"

"Nope."

Naturally he wasn't. Why did she think for a moment that he would? She would do this in as practical a way as she could. The less sexy, the better. First she took off her jacket, folded it and placed it on the ground. Then pulled the turtleneck over her head and next her brassiere. She sat on the ground, undid her sneakers, plucked off the socks and then came her slacks. She drew them down to her ankles and over her feet, folded them and placed them on top of her jacket. Next she removed her underpants as quickly as possible. She was naked and wasn't about to get up slowly, so she leaned forward onto her feet and jumped up. She was cold.

"Oh, boy, Lucia. You've gotten old."

Dove said nothing.

"Hey, you excited? You're shaking."

"I'm cold. Can we get on with this?"

"You think I relish putting my fingers up your cunt? Your asshole?"

She didn't respond.

He stepped closer and said, "Spread your legs."

She did.

McQuigg roughly shoved his fingers up inside her.

Although it hurt, she didn't cry out.

He pulled out his fingers. "Well guess there's nothing up there. Turn around and bend over."

Dove couldn't remember when she'd felt so humiliated. Maybe never. She did what he asked and almost immediately felt a searing pain. Again, she pressed her lips together to stifle any sound she might make. Then he withdrew.

"Can I get dressed now?"

"Yeah, yeah."

She sat on the ground putting on her clothes. Completely clothed, she said, "Are you satisfied I'm not wired?"

He gave her an annoyed look and started out of the clearing toward their cars. She followed.

When they were reseated in his car, he said, "I knew you weren't wearing one, you know."

She could have killed him on the spot, but said nothing.

"So ask me what you want."

"Oh, I'm not asking anything, Bernie."

"Stop calling me that."

"I'm telling you," she added. "I know you killed Clare. I know you killed the Scott and Boyer girls as well as one in Culpepper and one in Queen George. Not to mention the others around the country. And I know you killed Bonnie Jo Fincham."

"Is that right? And how do you *know*, Sheriff?"

"Oh, I have all kinds of ways of knowing about you, Mr. Zanville."

He stared at her for a moment. "Why do you keep calling me by Dane Clark's real name?"

She smiled. "Because that's the name you used to court Mrs. Fincham, and with some of the others."

"Beautiful, huh?"

Dove felt a thump in her chest as if to mark the beginning of what was going to be his admission.

"That was for you. All of it was for you in a way."

"All of what?"

"The murders. After I got a taste with Clare, I don't know. It felt good and I wanted to give you something to do. Not at first, not the ones in the other counties and states. I thought if you ever heard the Zanville name, you might make a connection."

Dove tried to quiet her racing pulse. Anger surged up in her. She stopped it before it spilled out and over this monster.

"I want to know why you killed my child?"

"That's the beauty part. Because she *was* your child."

"You're insane, McQuigg. I can't arrest you now. But I'll never stop trying to get you."

"Good luck, honey. Don't forget I'm a pro."

"So am I," she said and got out of the car.

Shaken and sick, she drove to Fincham's house. He could see her condition right away, and wrapped her in his arms. Dove began to cry. He didn't say anything, simply held her, stroked her hair. When the tears began to subside, he led her to the couch where he continued to hold her. "Oh, Jack," she said. "It was awful."

"I'm so sorry, love. So very, very sorry."

This made her cry again and Jack waited it out, holding and rocking her gently.

When Dove stopped she said, "He confessed."

"Jesus. Tell me all of it. If you can. I need to know and I think you need to talk."

"Yes. I do."

When she'd finished, she felt marginally better.

"You realize," Fincham said. "Aside from all the rest of it, those poor girls, he killed somebody connected to each of us."

"I realize."

"Why the shaving of the pubic hair on the others?"

"I think it was because of Clare. He made all the others look like little girls, but it's only a guess."

"Sounds as good as any other theory. I'm so sorry about Clare," Jack said.

She nodded.

"You think he'll do it again?"

"I'm worried he will, and soon."

"So what do we do?"

She wiped away her tears, sat straight up and looked him in the eyes. "Please try to understand this, Jack."

"Okay."

"We know now for sure that he's the killer. I mean, there's not the slightest doubt."

"Right."

"And we have no proof. There's not a goddamn thing we can pin on him."

"Yeah, I know."

"So we have to make a try for a McElroy solution."

"But how?"

"We have to tell all the victims' relatives and cross our fingers."

Chapter Thirty-Five

Dove and Fincham chose to speak to Emmitt and Mary Lee Boyer first. They sat in their family room as they'd done months ago, but it was different now. For one thing, the Boyers had aged. Dove knew how the death of a child could do that. And for another they were there to tell, not ask.

"Thank you for seeing us."

Emmitt said, "You got some news of the bastard who killed her?"

"Yes," Dove said.

"You got him?"

"We know who did it, but we can't prove it."

The Boyers looked at each other, then back at the sheriff, their faces showing confusion.

"We want you to know about this because it's your right. And we want you to understand that we can't charge him."

"Well, that just doesn't make sense, Sheriff," Mary Lee said.

"I know how you feel. But unless we have concrete evidence, then there's nothing to do. No grand jury would indict him."

"Well, if there's no evidence," Emmitt said, "then how do you know who done it?"

Mary Lee chimed in. "Circumstantial?"

"In a way."

"It's very circumstantial, not enough to make a case," Fincham said.

"So then, if it's circumstantial . . . and not even that much, how can you know this bum did it?"

Dove said, "Because he confessed to me."

The Boyers looked stunned.

"We were alone and I couldn't tape him. It would be my word against his. And I'd lose. He's my ex-husband and an FBI agent."

"What?"

"Agent McQuigg."

"Why, he talked to us," Mary Lee said.

"That's right. He was assigned to these cases."

Boyer stood up, went around the couch in a senseless march, flapping his arms and hands against his sides like a heron trying and failing to lift off. He walked to one end of the room and back to the other while all of them watched. Finally, he turned to Dove and Fincham.

"This is like some craziness. You're telling us that this . . . this goddamn guy killed those girls? This FBI agent? Why should we believe this?"

"Why would I lie to you, Mr. Boyer?"

"Maybe cause you want to get elected again?"

"I have no intention of running for office again."

"Then it's cause you can't solve this thing and you got to look good to us. Like you been tryin' and such."

"I can understand why you'd think that. I'd probably think the same thing if I were you. This FBI agent killed my daughter as well."

Mary Lee slapped her hand across her mouth, muffled a painful cry.

He said, "You had a child was murdered?"

"Yes. So you see, I understand how you feel."

"And this fella, this McQuigg, killed his own daughter?"

Mary Lee said softly, "Happens."

"Clare, my daughter, wasn't his child."

"Why? Why'd he kill her?"

"Mr. Boyer, the only thing I can tell you is that this man is insane. I believe my daughter was the first child he murdered. That was to hurt me." She saw no reason to explain to them the shaving of pubic hair on their daughter. But if he asked, she'd have to.

"And the others? He didn't even know he was hurtin' us. Didn't know us."

How could she put this? "By then, by then he liked killing. There were many other girls before Julie. Somehow he picked her. I'm sure there was no rhyme or reason to it, and we'll never know why she went with him, or even if she went willingly. All I know for sure is that he did kill her."

"And Iris and Rose? He killed the Scott girls, too?" Boyer looked like a man who'd found himself on an alien spaceship.

"Yes."

"But why? It don't make sense."

"You're not listening, Emmitt. Didn't you hear? The man is crazy. There's no sense to be made out of it."

He gave her a withering look, said nothing.

"Mrs. Boyer's right," Fincham said. "If we could make sense out of these tragedies, if we could indict him, or anything else, we'd do it."

Boyer sat down heavily. "I'll kill him myself," he said.

"Em-*mitt*."

"Then you'll go to jail," Dove said.

Boyer didn't reply.

"Please understand this. You'd be killing an FBI agent and you'd go to jail for the rest of your life." She felt totally hypocritical when what she'd hoped for was exactly this response.

"Maybe, maybe like him, I wouldn't get caught."

"And maybe you would," Dove said.

"Maybe I don't care."

"I can't listen to any more of this talk," Mary Lee said. She got up and left the room.

This was fine with the sheriff. Now it would be easier.

"You have to care," Dove said. "You've lost one child, and your wife and your other daughter need you more than ever."

"There has to be a way," he said.

Fincham and Dove looked at each other. They knew they couldn't suggest it, say anything leading. It was frustrating as hell when Dove knew she could give him a blueprint.

"You tell Scott yet?"

"No. We came to you first. When we leave here we're going to see the Scotts and tell them the same as you."

"Here's the thing, Sheriff. All my life when I had to do a thing . . . I done it. You have a problem, you figure it out, then fix it. My Daddy told me that when I was a boy. And that's the way I been doin' all my grown life."

"I understand," Dove said and left it at that.

"He kill other people around here we don't know about?"

"Not in Jefferson County." She told him about the other girls by name.

He nodded but didn't say anything.

"Another thing you have to be careful about is slander," Fincham said.

"Slander?"

"You can't tell people about this. If it gets back to McQuigg, he could sue you. Ruin your life."

"It's already ruined." The words thundered in the room.

Dove understood what he meant and she wanted to tell him that it didn't have to be that way; you could recover, go on, find a piece of happiness. But she said nothing.

"Maybe I'll just tell everybody. Stand up in church and tell."

"Don't do that, Mr. Boyer."

"You gonna arrest me, if I do?"

"No. Of course not. It's just that that isn't the way."

"What is the way?"

Oh, how she longed to tell him. "There isn't one."

"Gotta be. I know there's a way and I'm gonna find it. You tell Dennis Scott to call me when you're done with him and Abby."

Neither of them asked why, as they normally would, and agreed to Boyer's request.

Boyer said, "I think I need to be alone now, unless you got something else to say, something important."

Dove and Fincham stood up. "Nothing else," she said.

"Thank you for telling me, I guess."

Back in the car Fincham said, "You sure we're doing the right thing, Arizona?"

"No. But it's all I know to do. We can't let McQuigg kill anyone else."

"But what if Boyer *does* kill him? Or Scott, or any of the other people we're planning to tell?"

"Listen, Jack, we *do* have to tell these people and . . ."

"Why?"

"Because they have a right to know."

"Isn't true."

"Okay. *I* want them to know. Let me tell you something. If I'd thought all this time Clare had been murdered, I'd want to know."

"Then what would you do about it?"

"The truth? I don't know. But what these people do with the information is none of my business."

"Seems unethical," he said.

"Fuck ethics. There are times when ethics don't matter. When you've been so hurt, so destroyed, that nothing matters except to do what you can to make it . . . make it better. Or something. I don't care a fig about ethics right now."

"But you're not going to pull the trigger."

"Oh, Jack. I'm trying my damnedest to pull that trigger. That's *exactly* what I'm doing." She started the car.

They rode to the Scott house in silence. What she didn't tell Fincham was that she intended to send each survivor of McQuigg's killings a copy of a newspaper clipping on the Ken McElroy murder and a tape of Agatha Christie's *Murder On The Orient Express*. Not only did she feel fine about doing this, she believed it might help.

When they pulled up in front, and she'd turned off the ignition, Fincham reached out and touched her arm.

"Arizona? You think us taking this action is going to hurt us? I mean if something happens to McQuigg, will we be guilty?"

"I won't. Will you?"

"Maybe for five minutes. But I'm worried it might come between us."

"I can't speak for you, but I don't believe it will."

He leaned over and kissed her. Unlike a sexual kiss, it was as though they were sealing a bond. When he drew back, he said, "I think we should get married soon."

Dove smiled. "How about tomorrow?" she asked.

"Sounds good to me."

They got out of the car and walked to the house where they'd tell the truth to the second of the eight people they had on their list.

Epilogue

The Jefferson Standard, November 30th

An FBI agent was killed earlier this week in Crawford Park in what police are calling "bizarre" circumstances, a department spokesman said yesterday.

The victim, Michael McQuigg, was apparently driving on Wilson Street Monday night when his car was run off the road near the intersection with Hollar Avenue. Police said evidence at the scene indicated that Agent McQuigg was then forced from his vehicle and taken into the park, where he was killed.

There was no sign of robbery as the victim was left with over a hundred dollars in his wallet and was wearing a Rolex watch. The preliminary ballistics report indicates that the victim was shot numerous times by five different guns.

No suspects have been found.

About the Author

Sandra Scoppettone is the author of eleven crime novels for adults and five novels for young adults. Three of the adult novels were originally published under the pseudonym Jack Early but later republished under her own name. She has been nominated for an Edgar twice and has won the Shamus. Two of her books were made into television movies. One, *Donato & Daughter*, starred Charles Bronson, and the other, *The Late Great Me*, won an Emmy. All of her books have been published in many languages. She is also the author of *Suzuki Beane*, a cult classic. After living in New York City for many years, she moved in 1997 to the North Fork of Long Island, N.Y., where she lives happily even though she's still trying to find the take-out food places.